W0018935

Crossing Forces

CHANCE COLLISION

C.A. SZAREK

Chance Collision
ISBN # 978-1-78184-725-1
©Copyright C.A. Szarek 2014
Cover Art by Posh Gosh ©Copyright January 2014
Interior text design by Claire Siemaszkiewicz
Totally Bound Publishing

Published in 2014 by Totally Bound Publishing, Newland House, The Point, Weaver Road, Lincoln, LN6 3QN, United Kingdom.

Totally Bound Publishing is an imprint of Total-E-Ntwined Limited.

CHANCE
COLLISION

Dedication

The fact that this book came to fruition amazes me. The further I go to chase my dream, the more surreal it seems!

Thanks to my husband Shane for your support and input on 'the cop stuff'. Yes, I added a dispatcher just for you!

Thanks again to my former FBI agent friend Holly for mentally walking through crime scenes. Thank you to my detective buddy Matt for answering my incessant emails. The same goes for cops Jason and Mario and all the texts with random questions! Y'all are awesome for all you do, both for a living and sharing your expertise with me.

Thank you to my critique partners, Gina, Michelle, Clover and Jen. You ladies have made my stories stronger.

Thanks to Susie, too, who plays equal part critique partner and cheerleader! You're a fantastic writer and a valuable friend.

Amee, thank you for being my muse and my sounding board, and for holding my hand when I most certainly needed it.

To my two Jo's: Y'all are AWESOME, from Canada to Texas! Love you guys!

To Alanna, Toni, Kerry and Michelle: Thanks for always being there for me. Love you guys!

Chapter One

The paper airplane sailed down the long hallway, heading toward Chief's office. Pete cringed as the click of high heels registered at the same time as the feminine yelp.

Ethan dashed around the corner, and Pete hurried to follow.

"Hey, squirt, slow down," Pete called, but his partner's son was already out of sight.

Nikki, his boss's administrative assistant, bent down toward the little boy. Ethan's copper curls were several shades lighter than the young woman's, but Nikki's hair was as natural as the kid's. Usually neatly coiffed at the back of her neck, today her locks were loose and flowing. *Appealing.*

"What do you have there?" she was asking Ethan when he reached them.

"I'm sorry," Pete said. As she straightened, Nikki had a smile on her face. *Thank God.* "Didn't realize I'd get that kinda air."

Ethan retrieved the paper creation and slid a small hand into one of Pete's, looking up at both of them.

"It's no problem, just startled me. Not like a paper plane collision can do much damage." She smiled at the little boy, then met Pete's eyes.

"Yeah, except for maybe a paper cut?" Pete shrugged.

Nikki's smile slid into a grin and he got swept into the deep pools of her big brown eyes. She shoved her hair over a shoulder and Pete swallowed hard. The soft, wavy sea of red begged for a touch. A light floral scent tickled his nose with her pleasant perfume. It made her more intriguing.

Gorgeous. How had he never noticed before?

"Somehow I think I'll live." She laughed. The sound was sweet and he found himself grinning back. Like a besotted idiot.

"Unca' Pete. Did you see? It went faaaaaaar," Ethan piped up, tugging on his hand and jumping up and down. He veered the plane back and forth with his free hand.

"I did, squirt."

Ethan grinned, his blue eyes wide and bright. "What's your name?" the four-year-old asked Nikki.

Her white billowy skirt moved as she bent down and offered her hand. The fabric stopped at her knees. Damn, she had killer legs.

Pete averted his gaze from her asset-hugging lilac top and the cleavage peeking out as she moved to the child's level.

"I'm Nikki. Ethan, you're getting big! I know your mommy. Andi's my friend."

"And my daddy is Cole!" Ethan tugged his hand out of Pete's and shook Nikki's outstretched one.

A smile played at Pete's lips as he watched them.

"I know him, too. We all work together."

Ethan eyed her up and down. "Where's your gun?"

"Oh. I work for Chief Martin. I don't have a gun. I'm not a detective like your parents and Detective Crane," Nikki explained.

"C'mere, squirt," Pete said, hauling his partner's son onto a hip. "Hungry?" His shoulder didn't even twitch. *Good.* Never could tell when his year-old bullet wound would bother him. How much of *that* was in his head?

"Yeah," Ethan said, nodding.

"How'd you get little guy duty?" Nikki asked, brown eyes dancing. As she squared her shoulders, her lilac top hugged her breasts more.

Pete's stomach fluttered. He must be hungrier than he thought. He was too old for her, even if he didn't consider her off limits. Unlike his partner, he didn't date—or marry—at work. "Andi went into labor this morning."

"Ah, I hadn't heard."

Shifting his feet, he met her gaze. "Yeah, and Cole's with her, of course. Bella, his normal babysitter, is a camp counsellor for the rest of this summer down south in Livingston, and Andi's mom is on her way. She moved to Ohio a few years ago when she remarried. Cole's sister's even coming in from Seattle later today. But for now, I'm it. I don't mind, really. Me and Ethan are cool."

Nikki's eyes widened as she took in all the info he'd thrown at her.

Babbling? Really?

Come to think of it, that soliloquy was probably the most he'd ever said to her. He cleared his throat.

"My cousins are coming," Ethan announced.

"That's nice," Nikki said, an easy smile back in place.

Pete had never noticed the dimple in her chin before. He tried not to stare.

"My mama's having a baby," his partner's son continued.

Nikki ruffled Ethan's hair. "You're gonna be a big brother?"

Pete chuckled as the little boy nodded. He looked at Nikki's slender hands. She'd been close enough to touch his face. What would that feel like? Her skin against his—

Jesus, what is wrong with you? Lusting after a kid. What was she, twenty-five?

"I'm gonna be the bestest big broder ever!"

Her laugh jolted him. It was as tempting as she was.

"I bet you are," Nikki told Ethan, holding out her hand. The little boy slapped a loud high-five.

The buzz of Pete's phone offered him the excuse he needed to tear his attention away from the Chief's lovely administrative assistant. He offered a wave and turned away. He admonished Ethan to hush while he brought the phone to his ear.

"Crane," he said.

"How's Ethan?" Cole asked.

"Howdy to you, too, bud," Pete answered, hiking the little boy up higher on his hip. Kid was getting heavy.

Cole's sigh was all the answer he got.

"Everything okay?" he asked his partner's husband.

"Yeah, I guess."

"Isn't your wife, I don't know, having a baby or something?"

"Not yet. I just wanted to call and check in," Cole said.

Pete's bullshit meter lit up like a Christmas tree. He set Ethan down on his desk in the Criminal

Investigations Division room—where all the detectives officed—as they reached it, handing his partner's son the foam apple he kept around to squeeze when he was stressed.

Ethan made motor sounds as he steered the paper airplane around, then rammed the apple into it, making explosion noises.

He grinned at the child. "What happened?"

"What do you mean?" Cole asked.

Pete might have only known the guy for about a year, but it was obvious his buddy was trying to come off as innocent. It might've worked on someone else. "How's my partner?"

"She's...fine."

"Okay, quit hedging. You're starting to worry me. Is something wrong?"

"Sorry." Cole's tone was dejected. "Everything's fine. Really."

"What'd you do?"

"Andi's...in a mood."

"Well, hell, she *is* having a baby."

"She...asked me to leave the room." His fellow detective's voice dropped to a whisper.

Pete couldn't hold the laugh back. He shook his head, though his friend couldn't see him, ignoring Cole's growl. "Do you want me to come up there?"

"I can handle my wife," Cole shot back.

He held back another laugh. Damn good thing Andi couldn't hear her husband's declaration. "Want to talk to your kid?"

"Sure."

"Ethan, your dad's on the phone," Pete said.

The little boy's face lit up even before he handed over his cell phone. "Daddy!"

It was odd considering someone other than Iain as Andi's son's father. Pete's partner's first husband had never gotten the chance to be a father to Ethan, but Cole was a great dad. The former FBI agent was equal parts fantastic husband and hell of a cop, too. Stubborn, like his partner, but they were made for each other.

Iain would have liked the guy, as odd as that was to contemplate. A fellow cop and good friend of Pete's, Iain had been killed in the line of duty over four years ago, leaving a six-week-old baby and a devastated wife to cope without him.

Pete had been out of commission when Cole had come to town after a human trafficker. The slimy bastard had put two bullets in Pete, actually.

The FBI agent had turned Andi's life upside down. But they'd solved their case and fallen for each other. It was satisfying to see his partner happy again. She'd always meant the world to him. Cole was a good guy.

He heard the steady hum of Cole's voice as he spoke to Ethan. Pete smiled as the kid babbled away about the paper airplane and Nikki. Her carefree laugh bounced around into his mind and he sat straighter in the chair. *Get her out of your head, dude. You've bigger things to worry about than a chick you can't have.*

Pete snapped back to attention when Ethan handed his cell over.

"Pete?" Cole's voice was far away as Pete's fumbling fingers brought the iPhone back to his ear.

"I'm here."

"Well, I'm not. I need to go. Nurse's hollering."

"Showtime?"

"Maybe." Cole's voice kicked up a notch.

Pete smiled. "It'll be okay. Go have a baby. Keep us posted."

"You got it. Cass is gonna grab E-man later."

"Good deal."

Cole disconnected the call, and Pete glanced at the little boy sitting on the edge of his desk. Ethan was still making motor noises, flying the pliable fake fruit and his paper airplane around in circles.

God, he was growing up. Not a tiny baby anymore. Hell, not a baby at all. Pete had held him and changed his diapers, fed him so many times in the middle of the night he'd lost count. Almost like Ethan was his kid.

Andi had needed that from him. He loved her like a sister. It wasn't a chore to be more than her partner at work. She'd needed him.

But not now. She had a new love, a new life. And Pete was happy for her. But he'd been...displaced. They'd been partners for years. More than that, they'd been best friends. *Still best friends, dammit.* Now that she had Cole in her life, they saw less and less of each other outside of work.

Pete needed to get a life.

And isn't that pathetic?

His text alert went off and he glanced at his cell.

We need to talk. Do you have time for me tonight?

Liz.

Shit.

Sucking in a breath, Pete looked at Ethan and pocketed his phone. He didn't have time for the lovely blonde attorney.

"C'mon, squirt. Let's go to Dixie's and get some grub."

"Yeah!"

Pete grinned at the kid's enthusiasm and swung Ethan into his arms.

Liz would wait.

Chapter Two

Nikki tried to tear her eyes away from Detective Pete Crane as the tall lean form moved down the corridor with the child on his hip. Probably headed to his cubicle in CID, as most of the PD called it.

She'd always thought he was good-looking, but she'd never noticed just how green his eyes were before today. He'd stared at her, hadn't he?

He hadn't talked to her often, but he had a quick wit. Pete was always making someone laugh about something. He gave off the constant impression of being carefree and easy-going.

It wasn't odd to see him with his partner's son. Before Andi had remarried, Pete and Andi had seemed forever attached at the hip. Half the PD had assumed they were more than just partners.

Nikki was a friend of Andi, so she knew better, but she'd always been curious as to why Pete wasn't married. Or ever even hinted at being in a relationship. Of course, there was nothing wrong with being a private person, but Nikki had never heard Andi talk about Pete dating anyone, and he'd never brought a woman other than his mother to police department functions like the annual Christmas party or family picnic held every spring.

A man who looked like Detective Pete Crane, with those gorgeous eyes, high cheekbones and sculpted body, could likely have any woman he wanted.

So what was *wrong* with him?

Shaking herself, she sucked in a breath and headed back to her desk in the smaller front room of Chief Martin's executive suite. Nikki needed to check on Gram. She hadn't talked to her since early that morning, and the woman who'd raised her hadn't had much positive to say about the rehab center — or its staff. Gram's doctor was making her stay at Health Solutions for another few weeks.

Then Nikki would have to broach the *'You can't live by yourself anymore'* subject that she just plain dreaded. No one told Molly Jenkins what to do, least of all the *woman* she most certainly still saw as a child.

Worry roiled in Nikki's gut as she moved her chair and reached for the phone. In a matter of moments she'd memorized the number to her grandmother's private room at Antioch's one and only rehabilitation center. It'd only been open for a few years, and was close. Good thing Gram wasn't far from home.

The phone rang twice. "Hi, Gram."

"Nikki, baby." Nikki heard the familiar gravelly voice of the only family she had.

"Yes, ma'am, it's me. How're you?"

"I want to go home."

She swallowed back a sigh and sat straighter. "I know. But you need to listen to Dr Bishop this time."

"I am fully capable of —"

But Gram wasn't. Not anymore. "These things take time."

"Pish-tosh. Now you sound like *them,* child."

Of course, all medical staff was looped equally into *evil.* "Because I love you, Gram. Always."

"I can't get any sleep. They wake me at all hours to poke and prod me."

Nikki released a breath, cocking her head to one side. "They're doing what they need to do to make you better."

"Nothing's wrong with me."

She wouldn't contradict her grandmother with the truth. Nikki wanted her calm, not riled. This conversation wasn't going as planned. "I'm gonna come have dinner with you. I want to see you."

"Good. I want to see you, too."

"What'd you want to eat?" Her voice caught. The lump in her throat was sudden and unwelcome. She closed her eyes against the image of her grandmother on the kitchen floor the morning of the stroke.

Nikki's world had narrowed. Panic had surged and threatened to overtake her. She'd thought she was dead. That she'd lost Gram.

"Whatever you bring, baby. You cookin'?"

She cleared her throat. "I can. Or I can just grab a plate from Dixie's. Grilled chicken and the potatoes you like. Marge will make it special if I ask."

"Sounds good. I really do like Marge's red potatoes." Gram's voice deepened, her words slowing.

Terror jumped up from Nikki's stomach. "Gram?"

"Yes?" The word was accompanied with a yawn and Nikki screamed at herself to calm down. Her heart thumped.

Gram's fine. She's tired. It's not another stroke.

"I'll just call Marge if it's okay with you." Forcing her words to remain even, she fidgeted in her chair, biting back a curse when her knee rammed into her keyboard tray.

"It's fine."

"Good. I'll see you before six, then."

"Okay, darlin'." The familiar endearment rolled off her grandmother's tongue like normal.

Nikki smiled. Gram was going to be fine. "I love you."

"I love you, too, baby."

"Nikki?"

Her gaze darted to her boss poking his dark head around the doorframe from his office as she laid the phone in its cradle. "Yes, Chief?"

"I have a conference call until two. Can you order in lunch?"

"Sure. What do you want?"

Chief Martin smiled, making his greying mustache twitch. "Just the daily special at Dixie's. Order something for yourself, too."

"Gotcha, boss."

"Thanks." His voice faded as he disappeared back into his room.

"Two birds with one stone," Nikki murmured as she picked up the phone again.

* * * *

Berto jumped as he made a grab for the cell phone vibrating across the coffee table. *Unknown* flashed on the screen.

One of his daughters giggled, and he glanced in the direction of the two little girls. He slid his thumb across the touch screen to answer the call, strolling to the other end of the living room. As far away from the twins as he could get.

Calm the fuck down.

"Mata," Berto said.

Heavy breathing greeted his ear before the raspy voice. "Always hiding out in the open, 'eh?"

Shit. Caselli himself. Berto's heart dropped to his stomach and he turned his body away from the children, swallowing hard. "Go to hell," he croaked.

His old boss laughed, a cackle really that one would expect from a much older man — or a wart-nosed witch. Then Caselli inhaled, as if he was taking a drag on something. Probably a cigar. The crime boss liked his Cubans. "What did I tell you four years ago?"

Berto said nothing, but closed his eyes.

"You will always be mine, Alberto Carbone."

"Mateo Mata."

"Call yourself whatever you want. You. Are. Mine."

"Fuck off, Caselli."

There was another laugh that made Berto's spine tingle. Sweat broke out on his forehead.

The call wasn't a shocker. The three threats — promises — had arrived consecutively, starting over a week ago. Caselli's calling card of a dozen roses — first red, then white, finally black — and a *Thinking About You* greeting card always preceded a death.

Last warning — phone call.

Over the years, Berto had arranged so many of the same, as well as delivered the final blow, he'd lost count.

If he was smart, he would've packed his wife and the girls up and got out of Dodge. But he wasn't running. He'd been done with Caselli for more than four years — too bad the feeling wasn't mutual.

"You really fucked me over this time. Talking to the Feds? I always knew you had brass balls."

"What the hell are you talking about?"

No way was Caselli referring to the Carlo Maldonado situation almost a year ago. Berto wouldn't have had this long of a shelf life.

His old boss had even appeared to have given up on turncoat former FBI agent Cole Lucas. It wasn't a secret where the man had settled and taken a job in local law enforcement. Yet Caselli had let him live.

"Let's not be foolish. We both know it was you."

Nope. Berto had no idea what the bastard was referring to. How to answer? Denial didn't matter, even if it was the truth. Weakness would be perceived quickly. He shouldn't be concerned anyway. Caselli always went for the jugular.

"Whatever I did must have seriously pissed you off, since you're calling me yourself. Or have you failed to replace Bruno after, what, almost a year?"

Caselli laughed long and hard. "Want your old job back?"

"Fuck no."

The growl told Berto he was getting to the man after all. "You'd best get your affairs in order."

"I'm not afraid of you, Caselli." *Liar.* But Berto was more frightened for his family than he ever could be of his former employer. Sucking in a breath, he glanced over his shoulder.

His daughters shuffled dolls back and forth. Laughing, playing, bickering like sisters did. Innocence surrounded him. Berto didn't deserve a happy family after all he'd done in his life.

If Caselli was going to kill him, so be it. But what about Maria and the girls? They'd been through hell, but he'd gotten all of them out of the life. He loved her. She loved him. Understood him. Accepted him, despite his past before she'd stumbled into his sorry existence.

Shit. What the fuck am I going to do?

"*Mi amor*—" Maria took one look at him and froze in the doorway.

"Ah. Your lovely little whore," Caselli drawled in Berto's ear.

"Shut your mouth. You. Do. *Not*. Talk. About. Her."

His former boss cackled again.

Berto shot into the hallway, but his wife followed, grabbing his forearm. Close enough to hear Caselli's every word—Maria ignored his gesture urging her to join their twins in the living room.

"She's not involved in this. It's about me and you. *Only* me and you," Berto barked.

"Oh, but she's always been involved, my friend. From the moment you stole her from me."

Maria choked back a sob, her beautiful dark eyes going wide. Her nails sank into his wrist.

She was dressed for work in bright pink scrubs. Maria was scheduled for the late shift at Health Solutions. Probably had been on the way to kiss him and the girls goodbye before the forty-five minute drive into Antioch.

"Caselli, I'm warning you—"

At the use of the man's name, Maria's tears welled and spilled. She started shaking.

Berto drew her into his chest, squeezing his free arm around her.

"You are in no position to warn me." The voice was deadly calm—Caselli at his most dangerous.

Cursing under his breath, Berto threw his cell to the floor and stomped on it.

Maria met his eyes, trembling from head to toe. Her Venezuelan olive skin was pale. He'd never seen her so scared, even before they'd fled the life.

"Baby, it'll be—"

"How long, Berto?" Her accent deepened. In a moment, she'd revert to Spanish and scream at him.

"How long what?"

"Han llegado las flores?"

Berto closed his eyes. *Shit.* She knew him—and Caselli's ways—too well. He didn't want this. Thought they were done with this. "*Si.* But—"

"Colores?"

"All three." The words came out on a croak. "Three dozen roses."

Maria cursed in Spanish, but every word shook even more. "We need to leave." She sucked in a breath, then another, her ample breasts heaving.

"I won't run."

Shoving against his chest, she yanked away and glared, hands on hips. *"Loco.* What about your daughters? What about me?"

"He's after me. He's blaming me for something I didn't do. I have guns. I *will* fight." Berto rested his hands on her shoulders and shook her gently. "Go to work. It'll be okay. I promise you."

"You *dead* will never be okay." Her voice rose and fell as she fought more tears.

Maria swallowed and he wanted to kiss her throat, pull her into his arms and hold her.

Lying to the love of his life didn't sit well. But if Caselli killed him, Maria and the girls would be left alone.

He'd paid for her—more money than anyone would ever pay for a girl—and Caselli had promised they were out. Done. Square. She'd been pregnant with their twins already. Berto had cleaned out his stash to save their lives.

But *promises* from his former boss were always liquid. Contact from his ex-colleagues over the years had proved that if nothing else.

"Maria. *Maria.* Look at me."

Deep pools of midnight locked onto his face. She worried her lip.

"*Te amo,*" Berto whispered. "Forever. And it *will* be okay. I refuse to stop fighting him now." *Even though he'll kill me.*

His wife nodded, a solitary tear running down her cheek. She shook from head to foot under his grip. "Am I supposed to leave you like everything is okay?" Her whisper was more heavily accented than normal. Her long, wavy dark hair was pulled into a ponytail, making her look younger. Innocent.

Berto cupped her face and kissed her long and hard, as if he was tasting her for the last time.

There was only one thing he could do.

Chapter Three

Nikki smiled as she pulled into Dixie's tiny parking lot. The place was packed, like always. Two patrol cars were parked around back, which meant some of the APD officers were having dinner, too.

Lively conversation sucked her in as much as the cozy, familiar atmosphere. Photos of residents and public events from over the years decorated the walls, as well as antique road signs and ads.

Dixie's was an institution in Antioch. Marge and her husband Jimmy had opened the place before Nikki had been born. They spent more time in their restaurant than they did at home. Ran a light staff, too. It was a family affair, made up of their daughters, their husbands and now teen granddaughters. Once in a while they added a few kids during the busier times of year.

Maneuvering between stuffed booths and full tables as she wound her way to the counter, Nikki wished she'd lost the heels after work. It'd be just like her to fall on her ass in front of half the city.

Three cops sat at the corner booth in the back. Officer Shannon Crowley winked and waved when he caught Nikki's eye. Shannon's partner, Mark Rodriguez, nodded hello and the last, Officer Nina Ricketts, smiled.

Nikki returned their gestures and set her purse on the counter by the register. Marge was already hollering to the kitchen for her order. The round short-order rack above her head was full of old-school carbon copy receipt slips. Jimmy or one of his assistants would spin it and grab the next in line before they threw plates on the counter. It was an organized rush, but fascinating to watch.

"How's your gram, hon? I miss seeing you two every Sunday morning." Marge's gray hair was piled on top of her head in tight curls. Her white apron was pristine, but it didn't fool Nikki. The woman was the hardest worker in the place.

"She's getting better. But the doc is being cautious." Nikki offered a smile.

Marge regarded her seriously, reaching to squeeze her hand. "I know it's been difficult on you both. We're praying hard over here."

"Thank you, ma'am. Gram will appreciate that."

"Order up!" The shout from the back accompanied the ding of a bell. Jimmy's voice was as familiar as the rest of the place.

The older woman smiled as she stacked two white Styrofoam takeout containers in a plastic bag. "Here ya go."

"Thanks." Nikki paid and threw her purse over her shoulder.

"Give Gram our love," Marge said.

"You bet."

Nikki sucked in a breath after she settled back in her car. It was hard seeing her grandmother at the rehab center. Despite her age, she hadn't considered Gram fragile until she'd seen her huddled in a hospital bed.

"It's gonna be okay," she whispered, starting her Chevy Impala and inching out of the parking lot.

Before she'd even made it to the four-way stop at Main Street and Stewart Avenue, a giant black Hummer came out of nowhere from around the corner and cut Nikki off, pulling out of Marty's, the local mom-and-pop grocery store.

"*Crap!*" Nikki yanked the wheel and grabbed the bag from Dixie's to keep her and Gram's dinner from flying into the windshield.

The Hummer sped up without remorse as she slammed on the brakes. Nikki looked around as the black beast turned onto Main Street without so much as a turn signal. "Jerk," she muttered.

A flash of shiny black caught her eye on the way into Health Solutions. The oversized SUV that'd cut her off sat parked on the street across from the rehab center. The windows were too dark to see inside, but as often as she'd come to see Gram, she'd never seen the Hummer before. *Odd.* Antioch wasn't that big. Maybe someone had bought a new car.

"They sure as hell need a driving lesson," Nikki said as the automatic double doors parted on a *whoosh*. She waved to the nurse at the front desk before hanging a right toward Gram's room.

"Nikki." Gram's smile lit her face.

"Hi, Gram!"

Her grandmother sat higher in the bed. She lifted a frail hand and pointed a remote at the TV mounted on the wall above the bed. The volume faded, but the *clack-clack* of the *Wheel of Fortune* wheel still whirled.

Nikki set down their dinner on the table next to Gram's bed. The room was light and airy, welcoming, with the evening sun peeking in the window. Her car would be visible in the lot if she glanced to the left.

Gram reached for her hand, and Nikki tried to ignore the IV. She pressed a kiss to her grandmother's wrinkled cheek, straightening her nightgown as it slipped off one thin shoulder. It was pale pink with a floral print, one of her favorites from home. Gram had fussed until Nikki had brought her clothing to the center, but she didn't blame her. Sleeping away from home was bad enough.

"How was your day, darlin'?" Gram asked as Nikki slid a chair to the side of the bed.

"Good, but long." She reclined, sighing as she slipped her stilettos off.

"Tell me all about it while we eat."

Nikki grinned and reached for the plastic bag.

By the time they were through with dinner, she felt better about her grandmother's health. The conversation they'd shared was the most normal so far. Gram didn't slur her words—she stayed engaged and didn't doze off like she had in the days following the stroke. The next few weeks would go fast then Gram would be back home. *Good.*

Nikki would have to give up her apartment and move back into the house she'd grown up in. Unless she hired an in-home caregiver. Part-time or full-time, her grandmother would *hate* that. She chided herself not to think about it right now. *One day at a time.*

"Missus Molly, I have your medicine." Maria appeared in the doorway with a small tray. Her accent made the word sound like *meesus,* and Nikki smiled.

She liked the petite Venezuelan nurse very much. Even Gram couldn't hold the scowl when Maria spoke with them. She was sweet, often talking about her husband and four-year-old twin girls.

Gram said hello with a grumble about her pill and the nurse entered the room. Maria's shoulders were stiff, her back as straight as a board. She walked quickly, as if she was in a hurry, not with the leisure and care she usually demonstrated. The woman's hands shook as she put the tray down on Gram's bedside table.

"Maria, is something wrong?" Nikki asked.

"No, no, *señorita*." But the smile was forced. Maria shook her head, making her long dark ponytail swish around her shoulders.

Nikki frowned. She couldn't call the nurse a liar, but she was concerned. "Are you—?"

Two men burst into Gram's room. A flash of light accompanied a loud boom, then another. It took her a moment to process what she was seeing. *Guns.*

They were shooting guns.

At her grandmother's nurse.

Gram screamed. Maria didn't get a chance to. She collapsed at the foot of the bed, a starburst of red blooming on her side through her pink scrubs.

Nikki threw herself over her grandmother on the bed as the window shattered and gunshots continued.

The men said nothing as they trotted across the room and jumped over Maria's body. One by one, they leaped out of the window and sprinted across the parking lot.

Nikki stared, shaking all over as she tried to memorize as much about them as she could. Her mind raced and she ordered herself to retain what she was seeing.

Tall. Dressed in dark clothing. One with short dark hair, the other dark and loose, shaggy above his shoulders. Both wore sunglasses.

The Hummer inched forward as they wrenched the back doors open and scrambled inside. Without pausing, it sped off. The vehicle had been waiting for them. *Someone else is driving.* The windows prevented her from seeing if there were more than three of them, though.

"Maria!" Gram shouted.

Raised voices and running feet sounded in the corridor as Nikki hit her knees beside the nurse. Blood pooled under Maria's slight form. She was hit twice that Nikki could see, her right shoulder and left side.

"Call nine-one-one!" Gram shouted as the room filled with people.

Nikki pressed her index finger into Maria's throat. "She's alive." She looked up, locking eyes with a young doctor she didn't recognize.

He knelt beside her, pushing her hand out of the way to feel for the nurse's heartbeat himself. "There is a pulse, but it's thready. Nora, Josh, get over here and help me. We're not equipped for gunshot wounds! Call an ambulance!"

After scrambling to her feet, Nikki dashed for her iPhone as the two nurses joined the doctor, hovering over Maria.

Please be okay.

Chapter Four

Pete dragged his hand down his face.

"I'm sorry, Pete." Liz even *looked* remorseful as she stared up at him on his doorstep. Her body was stiff, and something in her eyes made him want to avoid her gaze.

Damn good thing Cole's sister Cass had already picked Ethan up. He wouldn't want witnesses for this.

The front doorknob bit into his hand and he ordered his fingers to loosen their grip. "Sorry?" he croaked.

"I didn't mean to—ambush you at home."

He'd never brought Liz to his house, for good reason. Home was private. His sanctuary. He brought *no one* there. *Looks like you don't have to be a cop to find out where someone lives.* "Well, come on in, I guess." He stepped back and gestured.

She pursed her lips, but entered the foyer. He guided her to the living room, but Liz didn't take the seat he offered.

"I'll make this quick." She squared her shoulders and wrung her hands in front of her, but then wrenched them apart and planted tight fists at her sides when she met his eyes.

Pete's gaze traveled up and down her attractive form. Liz was dressed as he'd most often seen her, in a dark gray skirt suit that accentuated her killer legs and screamed defense attorney—which she was. Her wavy, fair locks were pinned up but wisps had escaped after the long day. Her hazel eyes held mixed emotions he'd rather avoid.

She was beautiful, as always, even if her intentional impression was *aloofness*. That happened to be what Pete liked about her most. The only reason he'd started sleeping with her a few months before. *No risk.*

Liz was after the same thing he was—sex. *Only* sex. Or so she'd said.

But the look on her face, the feelings in her eyes, changed the game. Made her off limits.

All the times her gorgeous naked body had moved beneath his flashed through his mind. Full breasts, arched back, she always screamed when she came—

"What's on your mind?" Pete prompted.

Liz made a show of trying not to be obvious as she looked around his place. She'd never seen it before, and after all, his giant big-screen *was* impressive. "You ignored my messages all day."

"I was busy."

The look she flashed him was more sad than hurt.

Guilt crept up from the pit of his stomach. He'd been honest with her from the start, but he didn't want to hurt her.

"I see," Liz whispered. She averted her face, staring at the TV he hadn't bothered to turn off.

"Well, what was so urgent?"

"I met someone."

Oh.

Pete's text message alert sounded and rescued him from answering his lover. *Former* lover.

It's a BOY!!!!!

The screen shouted with Cole's message.

Micah Benjamin Lucas, born at 7:17pm. 8lbs, 5 oz, 21 inches long. He's perfect! Andi says he looks just like me. And believe it or not, I'm sitting here crying like a wimp. Pictures to follow.

When Pete met Liz's eyes, his smile didn't even get a chance to come to life.

Irritation flashed across her face. "I just thought you should know." Her voice dropped.

"It's okay. Liz—"

"I could have loved you, you know."

Pete swallowed back a curse, but she kept talking before he got a chance to open his mouth.

"I know that's not what *this* was between us." She wiped her face and shook her head. "I *know* it. But..."

"Liz—"

"It's fine, really. I did meet someone, and he's great. So I'm gonna go for it. Like I said, I thought you should know."

Sighing, Pete closed his eyes and forced a nod. It wasn't okay, *she* wasn't okay. And he was at fault. He'd been selfish with her. A total ass. He sincerely hoped there really was a new guy and she wasn't lying to cover unwelcome feelings. That would only make things worse.

His phone dinged twice—probably pictures of his partner's new baby.

Nothing like a royal dumping to ruin the occasion.

How can your fuck buddy dump your ass? You. Are. Pathetic, Peter Crane.

"I hope you'll be happy, Pete. And find what you're looking for."

Then she was gone, before he could assure Liz he wasn't *looking* for anything.

The front door closed at the same time as the phone rang. Pete cursed and jumped, expecting to see Cole's number flash on the screen. But it was work.

Shit. He'd almost forgotten he was on call.

He cleared his throat. "Crane."

"Detective, this is Sean from dispatch."

* * * *

The body crumpled just as easily as the little nurse's.
'Cept this one has more holes.

But it leaked more. The pool of deep red spread slowly from beneath the guy. Luca stepped back before the blood reached the tip of his shiny black loafers.

He scowled and holstered his Beretta, only to curse as the leather rubbed the deep cut on his thumb. *Fucking windowsill.* His whole hand throbbed.

They'd taken too much time at the rehab center, so he couldn't tell Caselli with a certainty that Berto's little whore was dead.

Oh well, it wasn't the first lie he'd told in his life. Wouldn't be the last, either.

"Let's go." The urgent bark made him scowl.

Who did Caselli's nephew think he was? Mickey's balls were getting too big for his diapers. Luca was running this show. Even the orders from the top confirmed it. The little bastard might be the boss's blood, but he wasn't supposed to question Luca.

"We go when *I* say."

Mickey frowned and glanced at the dead man, saying nothing.

"Did you take care of the Hummer?"

"Yeah. Parked it behind the warehouse and took the plates off. Wiped it clean, except jackass's prints" — Mickey gestured to their former driver before looking back at Luca—"are all over it. Did you get the ten grand back?"

"Yes." Taking a breath, he cautioned himself to calm. Mickey wasn't interrogating him, it was a just a question.

"How're we gonna get outta here?"

"We'll lift something." Luca looked around the old trailer. How long would it take for their *friend* to be found? He smirked.

Mickey muttered something that sounded like, "That's what I just said," but Luca ignored him.

Turning away, he surveyed the decrepit place. The wallpaper was peeling, rolling over on itself down every wall, the printed pattern barely discernible. The kitchen counter was no longer whole, with great chunks missing from the linoleum. Cupboard doors hung on hinges or were missing entirely. There were no sinks and the carpet in what passed for the living room looked like it'd had a bad experience with a lawnmower.

"Luca..."

"What?"

"The redheaded chick and the old woman saw us."

"And?" Luca snapped. "What did they see? We were in and out."

"What if —"

"Shut the fuck up. There is no *what if*. I have it handled."

Mickey frowned again and scratched his head. His shaggy dark hair fell into his eyes but he shoved it back. Opened his mouth, then closed it.

Smart. Because it was either pound him or shoot him. Luca's boss wouldn't appreciate either. And he had to prove himself to Caselli.

He hadn't spent the last ten years working his ass off for nothing. This—the whole Texas mission—was his chance to prove to the boss that he could handle more responsibility. Luca *could* run the show. Like Bruno had, and Berto before him. Only he wouldn't get sent up river like a dumbass and he sure as hell wouldn't be a traitor for a little pussy, either.

"Should have burned the Hummer," Mickey said.

Luca whirled on his boss's nephew. "You're a fucking stupid shit, do you know that? Fire brings *attention.* We're trying to avoid cops."

"I would have made it look like the dead asshole had a mishap with his meth," Mickey said.

"Yeah? How? When he's here playing Swiss cheese?"

Mickey shifted on his feet, grumbling something Luca didn't catch. Which was just as well. His restraint was waning. He was likely to do something he'd regret—but only after Caselli had found out.

Maybe he could off his boss's nephew and blame it on the cops. A shootout with the locals wouldn't be so bad if he could come out the sole survivor. But then again, he wouldn't want to trifle with *Uncle Tony's* temper until *after* Luca was considered his right hand. "Let's go get a decent ride and find a place to crash."

Mickey nodded and headed for the door of the crappy trailer without another word.

Dead guy didn't have a car, so they were shit out of luck there. They'd have to figure something out.

Luca had a call to make and a ranch to get to.
One down, one to go.

Chapter Five

Police cruisers covered the parking lot. The Chevy Tahoe that patrol supervisors always drove blocked the front doors of Health Solutions as Pete pulled in.

His stomach roiled. Something about knowing Nikki was inside bothered him more than it should. She was fine. It'd been confirmed by Sergeant Stein, the officer in charge of the scene. But still—she'd been *in* the damn room.

Calm down.

The scene was secure. One vic, shot twice, probably already on her way to the hospital. This was clean up, canvass and find out what happened. *Investigate.*

He'd done it a million times.

Pete slammed the car door shut and plastered on his game face, meeting Cole's partner, Detective Jared Manning, in the parking lot. The guy had an evidence kit slung over his shoulder.

"Don't think you'll need that. CSI's already on scene." Pete thumbed the white van with *Crime Scene Unit* displayed on the side.

The younger man shrugged. "Thought it might come in handy."

Pete nodded and they fell into step, heading into the long L-shaped one-story building. "Thanks for showing up since Andi's out."

"No problem. Cole's out, too, after all. It's a boy, did you hear?" Jared asked.

"Yeah. Cole sent me a text."

"Too bad the kid's arrival is overshadowed by this crap." Jared gestured to the chaos inside the rehab center.

Jared's expression was grim as they arrived at the room where the shooting had gone down. He yanked blue booties on over his shoes and nodded to the two crime scene techs already processing the scene.

Glancing from the doorway, Pete saw a pool of blood on the floor, glass everywhere.

Damn, would the woman even stand a chance with all that blood?

Marion was snapping away with her high-tech digi cam, her navy Crime Scene Unit windbreaker rustling with her movements. The yellow lettering caught his eye, distorting as she paused to push up the long sleeves. It was a warm evening.

Cole's partner went inside, appearing to do a visual sweep. He had a keen eye, so Pete let him do his thing. They both needed to note what they could, in addition to getting the lead tech's take on everything.

Doctors, nurses and other gawkers swarmed the hallway outside, talking over each other. They'd need to clear everyone out, weed through who'd seen what.

Nikki stood close to Sergeant Chloe Stein. Their heads were bent together as they spoke, Nikki leaning into the shorter woman when Chloe put her arm around her. Nikki's back was to an elderly woman on a gurney against the wall just down from the room. Two nurses were hovering at her bedside, their expressions concerned, voices low and urgent.

"I will not." The slight woman crossed her arms over her thin chest and glared hard enough to make Pete twitch.

"But, Mrs Jenkins, please—"

"I *will not* leave my granddaughter." Mrs Jenkins scowled.

Pete's feet carried him closer of their own accord, just as Nikki pulled away from the sergeant.

"Gram, I'm fine. Please let Rebecca take you to a new room." She spared him a glance, but nothing more. Her fear was glued to her grandmother.

Rebecca, the taller of the two nurses, sighed, her shoulders relaxing. She was a curvy, attractive black woman with short hair. When she glanced at Pete, she flashed a smile.

"I'll go with you," Nikki said to Mrs Jenkins. "Be right back," she told Chloe, but her gaze finally raked Pete.

He inclined his head as the sergeant told her to take her time. Pete let Nikki handle getting her grandmother resettled without protest. He'd speak to her when she was back. She probably needed the breather anyway.

"Detective."

Pete swung his head around, meeting Sergeant Stein's blue eyes. "Chloe."

She squared her shoulders. "The staff took Nikki and her grandmother out of the room before I made scene with Ricketts, or I would've told them to hold tight. Gram's and Nikki's clothing appeared clean, but you might want Neil to do a thorough check. Blood spatter on the bed sheets—I told the nurses not to touch anything. Nikki recounted what she could, and I've had dispatch put a BOLO out for the car. The vic was rushed to the hospital, stable, but I told the docs you'll likely head there and to not give you a hard time."

"Thanks. Good job." Pete nodded. He could only pray that the *Be On The Lookout* would yield something.

They *would* have to hightail it to the hospital. But he wanted to talk to Nikki first. "What's your take?" He studied his longtime colleague. She'd been a cop longer than Pete, and knew her stuff. Had anyone else been on duty, he would've asked for a lieutenant to run the scene, but Sergeant Stein was more than capable.

"It was quick. They were in and out."

"Like a hit?"

Chloe nodded, her light brown ponytail bobbing. "They were definitely after her. No one else was hurt."

"She gonna make it?"

"The doctor here got her stable, but I don't know. He said she lost a lot of blood." Chloe's eyebrows drew tight.

"Pete." Jared leaned out of the room. "C'mere."

Pete trotted back to the room, pulling elastic blue foot covers from his back pocket and tugging them over his cowboy boots. "Whatcha got?"

Neil glanced over his shoulder from the windowsill. "Some blood over here. Looks like someone got cut on the way out the window. Maybe we'll get a DNA match."

"Good deal," Jared said, before looking back at Pete. "Two different guns. A forty and a nine." Squatting down, he gestured to numerous shell casings on the floor. "Looks like about fifteen shots."

Marion hovered over the bed behind him, snapping pictures of various spots of blood. They were on the sheets as well as the bedframe.

She threw a wink at Pete. Tall for an Asian chick, she was a stunner, her dark hair in a librarian bun at the back of her head. Her ever-present camera bag slung across her body was almost as big as she was.

Looking around the room, Pete mentally cataloged everything. Blood on the floor, glass scattered everywhere. Smeared bloody shoeprints on the way to the window, but no full print.

"Neil, is there a flower bed outside? Below the window?" Pete asked.

The older, balding man nodded. "Yup. Got nice prints. I'll get out there to take an imprint ASAP. I see one complete boot outline and maybe another partial from here. Hope I get something from them both."

"Great," Pete said.

"No prints on the sill, though," Neil said, shaking his head.

"Damn," Jared muttered, straightening to his full six-foot-plus height. Cole's partner scooted around the photographer and she glared at him.

Pete arched a brow as Jared averted his gaze from her dark, almond-shaped eyes.

Jared cleared his throat and grabbed a notebook from his back jeans pocket, looking a little too conveniently busy as he jotted down some notes.

Pete bit back a snort. *Case in point.* Dipping your pen in company ink never resulted in anything good. But why would the sweet photographer mess with Cole's partner? Everyone at the PD knew Jared was a flavor-of-the-week kind of guy. Marion had always given off the impression of innocence.

"Neil, I'm done in here," Marion said, purposefully looking away from the dark-haired detective.

Shaking his head, Pete glanced at Neil. "Sarge said there didn't appear to be blood spatter on Nikki or Mrs Jenkins, but you might want to do a once-over."

"Already on it. There was nothing to collect, but the bedframe and spatter on the sheets clearly show direction of the fire." Neil turned his body toward the door and gestured away from the window.

Marion shoved her camera in the bag and hefted an evidence case. "I'll do the boot imprints and get some pics outside."

"Where's Chuck?" Pete asked, speaking of the third — absent — member of their team.

"At the lab. He was in the middle of something, so I told him to stay there," Neil said.

"I'll help out any way I can," Jared said.

The pretty photographer harrumphed on her way out of the room.

Pete smirked and Jared winced, but Neil didn't seem to notice.

"I'm gonna talk to Nikki and her grandmother, then we need to hit the hospital."

Jared nodded. "Sounds good."

Sergeant Stein was talking to Nikki when Pete returned to the hallway. Chloe made eye contact with him before he reached the two women.

"I'm going to see who saw what," she said. "Let you know what I find out."

"Thanks," Pete said.

Nikki offered a wobbly smile when their gazes met.

"Relax," he said. "Just talk to me like you'd tell your best friend what happened."

"I hate to sound like a cliché, but it happened so fast." She shook her head, scrunching up her nose.

He wanted to reach out to her, reassure her, but he made himself stand still, prove his attentive police professionalism. Andi always had him talk to witnesses first. She said he was better at it. Calmer. She considered herself too insistent.

"What do you remember?" Pete asked gently.

"Dark clothes. Two handguns. I don't know what kind, I'm sorry. They were loud. And big."

"It's okay. I wouldn't expect you to recognize the guns."

She made a face, looking away. "I work in a police department, you'd think something woulda stuck."

Pete grabbed her hand and squeezed, smiling slightly.

Nikki's brown eyes widened, but she didn't pull away.

Good. After the small touch, he wanted to hold onto her. "It's fine. Just tell me as much as you can, all right?"

She sucked in a breath. Her full breasts rose and fell and it took all he was made of to *not* stare there. "Oh, no," she whispered.

"What is it?"

"You're using that tone..." Nikki closed her eyes.

He frowned. "What tone?"

"That *'You're-a-witness-and-I-can't-see-into-your-head'* tone. Coaxing, candy-from-a-baby stuff."

Pete laughed, he couldn't help it. He wanted to kiss her hand or hug her. "Well, darlin', you are a witness."

Nikki's eyes locked onto his face and she paled. "Oh. God. *I am.*"

She wavered on her feet and he caught her, wrapping an arm around her shoulders and pinning her to his side. "Jared! A chair. Quick."

Jared dashed to grab a seat from down the hall, but not before Pete felt Nikki's side against his ribs, the curve of her perfect ass against his thigh. She was warm and supple. He wanted to turn her in his arms, pull her close and take her mouth.

Knock it off. She works for your boss. More than that, she's a witness in your new case.

Pete rested his hands on her shoulders after he pressed her into the chair. He couldn't pull away just yet. Not until he knew she was all right.

She stared up at him, expression lost. Nikki trembled beneath his grip.

"I'll get her some water," Jared said, disappearing toward the nurses' station.

"Take a breath. You're okay," Pete said.

Nikki nodded. Her tongue darted out to moisten her full bottom lip and his mouth went dry.

Tearing his gaze away, he made himself meet her eyes—and keep his gaze there. *Your mind out of the gutter would be good, too.* "Better?" he asked, but it was more of a croak.

"I think so," she breathed.

Taking a step back, Pete forced his hands to his sides.

Jared arrived with a paper cup. He pressed it into Nikki's palm and she muttered thanks as she took a sip.

"I'm gonna wrap up with Neil," Jared said, thumbing toward the room. He didn't wait for Pete or Nikki to answer him.

"Let me know when you're ready to talk," Pete said. Experience had taught him the less pressure, the better. It made witnesses remember more, helped them open up.

Once again she nodded, but she wrapped both hands around the paper cup and held it for dear life. "I'm okay, really."

"Good. Slow and easy, just talk to me."

Nikki cleared her throat. "Gram and I were talking to Maria after she'd given Gram her evening meds. These men rushed in and there was a burst of light in the hallway — that's what caught my attention even before I heard the gunshot. Maria dropped like a sack of potatoes. Then they were gone. In a black Hummer."

"A Hummer? Did you catch a plate or see any distinguishing marks?"

"I didn't see a plate, but it was a full-sized one. Not the H2 or the smallest one. There were two guys in here and one in the car."

"Oh?"

"When they jumped out the window, they both got in the back. The car took off even before the doors were closed."

"Did you get a good look at either of them?"

Sorrow crossed her face and Pete's stomach fluttered.

"Not really. They were both tall, wore dark clothing. Olive complexions. Italian or Hispanic, I guess. One had short dark hair, the other dark and a little shaggy, longer. Both had sunglasses on."

"Did they say anything?"

"No. Not a word. Came in shooting." Nikki sighed.

Pete squeezed her shoulder. "You did good."

Her expression said she disagreed, but she didn't comment. "They must've sat outside for over an hour."

"How do you know that?"

"After I picked our dinner up from Dixie's, they cut me off on Stewart, tearing out of Marty's parking lot like a bat out of hell. Then I saw them sitting on the side of the road when I pulled in here. Had they not almost hit me, I probably wouldn't have noticed, big black Hummer or not."

"Hmmm…" He and Jared would have to stop by the store and see if there were surveillance cameras. Or see if anyone remembered the Hummer or one of its occupants — at least *three* assailants.

"I wish I'd seen something else…"

"You did great. Honestly. Better than most. You knew what to look for."

"Thanks. I feel useless."

"You're far from useless." Pete smiled, looking down into her gorgeous face. Damn, he wanted to kiss her. Locking his jaw, he bit back a curse.

What is wrong with you?

Shifting on his feet, he cleared his throat. "At any point, did they threaten you or your grandmother?"

Nikki frowned, shaking her head. "They didn't say anything. Stormed into the room, shot Maria, blew out the window and then they were gone. They didn't even look at me or Gram."

"Okay."

"Damn. It's like some mob hit, or something," she whispered.

A hit.

Sergeant Stein had said the same thing. Who would want to kill a rehab nurse? Why?

"Is she going to make it? She has two little girls. Oh… God…" Nikki rocked in the plastic chair, her eyes shiny.

Pete's heart dropped to his stomach and he squatted in front of her, taking both her hands in his just as her first tear coursed down her cheek. "Don't cry. Nikki, it'll be all right," he whispered.

Before he realized what he was doing, Pete straightened, pulling her to her feet and into his arms. Fitting her against him was natural—even if only for comfort.

Nikki wrapped her arms around him without hesitation and buried her face against his neck. She sniffled. Her warm breath tickled the skin above the collar of his button-down and a tremor shot down his spine.

He rubbed her back in large circles. Warning bells went off in his head, but he ignored them, even though he was holding her more like a lover than a witness. *Close. Inappropriate.*

She lifted her head and their gazes locked.

Pete promptly slipped into her wide brown eyes. *Liquid mocha.*

She swallowed and he wanted to kiss her throat.

His eyes slid to her mouth. *Plump. Inviting.*

Pete needed to taste her. *Right. Now.*

He bent his head down.

Nikki's lips parted, that pink tongue making another appearance. But she didn't pull away. If anything, she tilted her face up. Moved closer.

Pete's warning bells blared into full-blown tornado sirens, but when Nikki closed her eyes and brushed her mouth against his, he soundproofed his conscience and took her mouth.

Sweet. Damn, she was sweet. Ripe raspberries or something sugary. *More.*

Deepening the kiss, he pulled her even closer, aware of the tightening in his jeans and how his cock throbbed as her pelvis rubbed his. He rocked on his heels as Nikki wove her arms around his neck and kissed him harder. Their tongues dueled and danced, both of them pushing and pulling, giving and taking control. Sliding his hands down her back, he followed the curve of her shapely firm bottom, squeezing and kneading.

"Pete, we're pretty much wrapped up. Neil said you can expect his report—"

Jared's voice jolted him and Pete tore his mouth off Nikki's. He met the guy's dark eyes. The younger detective's brows were arched as high as they could go. He froze in the doorway, one hand on the frame as if he had to brace himself.

It took all Pete was made of not to shove her away from him. Like they'd been caught doing something wrong.

You kissed her, idiot. Very *wrong.*

He ignored the voice that piped in with how *she'd* actually closed the distance between their mouths. Nikki had answered his first move.

Doesn't matter. Still wrong. She's a witness. Not to mention a co-worker. Your boss's assistant.

Nikki slid from his arms and swiped at her damp cheeks. They were tinged pink, her lovely lips kiss-swollen, her loose red locks mussed. She averted her gaze, but she couldn't seem to look at Jared either.

She'd kissed him. Kissed him. Why hadn't she pulled away? Had she enjoyed it as much as he had?

Pete ignored his train of thought and cleared his throat. Banished her taste from his mind. Ignored how he could still feel her mouth against his. "Are you all right?" Forcing words out, he grabbed her hand and she glanced back at him. Touching her only made him want to drag her back into his arms and taste her again. Hold her. Then take her home. Keep her with him. For her own safety, of course.

She nodded. "I should go check on Gram."

"We need to get to the hospital," Jared said, taking his blue booties off.

"Yeah. We…need to go," Pete croaked.

Nikki nodded, her teeth sinking into that full bottom lip.

He bit back a groan and jerked his eyes away. *Unprofessional loser.*

"Did you get everything you needed?" Nikki asked. Her voice was steady. She'd pulled herself together admirably.

Which is more than you can say for yourself. Grow a pair, will ya?

Jared snorted, but Pete disregarded him.

No. "Yes. Take care of your grandma. If you need anything, you call me, okay?" Pete said, clearing his throat.

"I will. Have a good night," Nikki whispered.

After muttering an appropriate farewell, Pete couldn't unglue his eyes from her hips, swaying gently as she disappeared down the hallway.

Jared punched him in the arm.

Glaring, Pete jumped, but amusement flashed across the other detective's eyes.

"Did you get everything you needed?" Jared asked, smirking.

At least there was no judgment in the guy's expression. Damn good thing Jared didn't have the balls to mention what he'd witnessed. Hell, knowing Jared, he thought they were already screwing.

Pete wasn't about to confirm or deny.

"Shut up."

Chapter Six

Nikki traced her lips with her fingertip. "Talk about out of the blue," she whispered, rounding the corner toward Gram's new room.

Detective Pete Crane had kissed her. *Kissed her.*

She'd kissed him back. Fervently. Begging him with her mouth for more.

Crazy. Right? She could still taste him. Feel the pleasant brush of his stubble against her cheeks. Smell the woodsy scent of his cologne.

Over the two years she'd worked for Chief Martin at Antioch Police Department, Pete had only spoken to her a handful of times. Only the *'Hi-how-are-ya'* variety. Nothing more.

Why had Pete kissed her? Why had it been so natural to kiss him back? Nikki hadn't questioned it.

The shaking in her limbs had ceased the moment his strong arms had encircled her. Warm. Safe. She could have burrowed into him and stayed there all night.

Done more than just kiss him.

His body was lean muscle, hard in all the right places. Had made her feel wanted. Especially a certain part of him. He'd been aroused. After only one kiss. For her.

Her body had answered. Warmth had spread down her limbs, settling low in her belly. Even now she ached in places that had been awakened.

Sucking in a breath, Nikki forced herself to calm down, but her heart galloped. A man hadn't enflamed her with just a kiss like that...ever.

"He was trying to comfort you. That's all." *Bull.* She couldn't even convince herself. Comfort from a friend—a professional one—didn't come in the form of a toe-curling kiss.

Not that she regretted it. She didn't. She'd kiss Pete again. In less than a heartbeat.

A tremor that had nothing to do with the evening's trauma shot down her spine and Nikki swallowed hard.

What is wrong with you? You saw someone get shot.

"Nikki-baby, are you all right?" Gram's voice pulled her out of her head.

I don't know. "Me? It's *you* I'm worried about." Jolting, Nikki squared her shoulders. How had she not realized she'd walked all the way to her grandmother's room already?

Get it together, Nikki.

Gram shook her head, her pale blue eyes misty. "That poor girl."

Nikki took both of the elderly woman's hands in her own. She pressed kisses to her grandmother's gnarled knuckles. "She'll be okay."

"Thank God *you're* okay." Gram pulled her hands away and cupped Nikki's cheeks like she had so many times when she was a child. After Pulling her close, the woman who'd raised her covered her face in warm kisses.

Nikki's soft laugh took her by surprise, considering what had happened tonight. "I'm okay, Gram. Promise. Thank God you're okay, too."

Keys jangled and someone cleared their throat politely. Nikki glanced over her shoulder and offered a smile to Sergeant Chloe Stein.

Probably in her forties, the petite, attractive woman didn't pull any punches. She kept the younger— mostly male—officers on her shift in order. They respected the hell out of her, and so did Nikki. She was a good cop.

Sergeant Stein smiled back, coming into the room, small notebook in hand. "Detective Crane asked me to talk to your gram, Nikki."

By *talk to* she meant *interview,* but Nikki appreciated the kid gloves. Even though a part of her was disappointed Pete wasn't the cop in Gram's new room. Detective Jared Manning had said they needed to head to the hospital.

Maria. Please… God, let her live.

Nikki took a seat in the chair next to Gram's bed, reaching for one of her hands and entwining their fingers. Nikki sat taller as Chloe came closer and introduced herself.

"I know you, Chloe Stein. I know your father, your family," Gram said, one delicate white brow arched.

The sergeant's cheeks actually went pink and Nikki relaxed, biting back a smile. Who knew the tough cop blushed?

"Yes, ma'am."

"Just because I had a stroke doesn't mean I lost my marbles." Gram frowned and Nikki had to cover a half-laugh with a cough.

Blue eyes wide, Chloe shot her a look that shouted she didn't know how to take the elderly woman.

Nikki flashed an encouraging smile and shrugged, leaning back in the chair.

When the sergeant took a breath and flipped her notebook open, Gram fluffed her blankets.

"Well, let's get this over with," her grandmother said, giving a curt nod. Her pale eyes met Nikki's before she looked back at Chloe.

"Yes, ma'am," Sergeant Stein said. "Just tell me what you remember."

* * * *

Berto raced down the hallway, his heart thundering, hands wobbly. He'd had to leave the girls with his ranch foreman, Brody. There'd been no time to call someone else, and Brody lived on site. Good thing his daughters adored the foreman.

He'd kissed his sleeping twins and raced to the small hospital right outside of Antioch. The forty-five-minute drive had racked his every nerve, but the damn nurse wouldn't tell him what had happened. Only that he needed to get there *now.*

An officer will meet you.

It was a wonder he hadn't been pulled over for reckless driving.

His voice had shaken when he'd made it to the nurses' station and uttered his cover name. Numbly, he'd followed a nurse to the waiting room.

Maria was in surgery. The doctor would find him afterward.

Not one, but two of Antioch's finest had met him. Uniformed cops who had introduced themselves, but their names hadn't registered. Still, they hadn't said much. Asked a few questions.

Shot twice. Lost a lot of blood. Ongoing investigation. The detective on the case would be there shortly. Wait here. They wouldn't be far if he needed them. Although it was left unspoken, he was not permitted to leave.

Berto's ass hit the chair and he cradled his head, squeezing his eyes shut.

His fault. The *entire* fucking thing.

He'd been a fool to think Caselli wouldn't make a go for Maria. The man was a ruthless bastard. Trying to kill Berto's wife—almost succeeding—was a move right up his former boss's alley. Hit him where it counted. His heart. His life.

Trembling from head to foot despite the hard surface underneath his ass, Berto fought the pain in his chest along with the rising sob. He was about to lose it like a pussy. Bawl like a baby.

The old Berto would hunt down the bastards Caselli had sent to do the hit. Kill them. Beat the ever-loving shit out of them first. Shoot them in the arms and legs to watch them suffer before the final head shots.

Now… Those two little girls, with their mother's big brown eyes… They *needed* him. Maria, too. His wife would need him more than ever.

He couldn't risk prison.

Even if murder would be just. Could he stand going through legal channels? Would it be enough to see them locked up instead of bloodied, broken, dead?

I can't lose her. I just…can't.

I'm next.

Caselli's roses were a promise. Only a matter of time. Kill Maria. Come after him. Checkmate.

Leave the girls orphaned, if alive at all. Caselli had no scruples about killing the children of enemies.

"Son of a fucking bitch!" Berto shot to his feet, pacing the small room and thanking God he was the only one in it. He buried his hands in his hair, gripping the short dark length and tugging.

Helpless was putting it mildly.

The bastard had accused him of talking to the Feds. Berto hadn't. But... He was going to have to make one call in particular. The choice had been made after Caselli's final promise tonight.

He'd hedged on the idea from the moment he'd stomped his cell. Thought about it more on the frantic drive to town. Made up his mind when the automatic doors to the emergency room had opened, even before the hospital rent-a-cop had directed him upstairs.

Berto had never been a rat, even long after leaving New York. Not even when that female detective— MacLaren or something—had come with Cole Lucas to question him about Maldonado last year.

To save his family, he'd sing like a choir of birds.

Berto glanced up when the door to the waiting room opened. The guy offered a head-nod like you did to acknowledge a stranger, then did a double-take. Their eyes locked as the very tall T-shirt and jean-clad man froze.

No. Fucking. Way.

"Berto?"

"Are you here for my wife?" They spoke at the same time.

Cole Lucas had just walked into the waiting room. Like he'd answered the call Berto had yet to make.

The FBI agent-turned-local-police detective came closer, dark brow furrowed.

"Are you here...to talk to me...about my wife?" Berto croaked.

Lucas shook his head. "Your wife? No." The guy shrugged and thumbed the Coke machine in the back of the room. "Just looking for a soda. Damn near had to search the whole hospital." He looked like he was about to say something else, but didn't.

Coins jingling in hand, Lucas headed to the vending machines lined against the wall of the waiting room. Then there was the click of a depressed button followed by the *thunk* of the can falling. He bent to grab it.

Berto swallowed hard. Wanted to demand what the hell was going on, but words dissolved on his tongue.

The pop and hiss of Lucas opening the can took Berto's attention. He stared at the red and silver aluminum. As the man brought the Coke to his mouth, a glint of gold caught his eye. Left hand. Wedding ring?

"What's going on, Berto? You're jittery."

When he managed to look back at the former FBI agent's face, the guy actually appeared concerned.

What happened to the SOB who'd blackmailed him into cooperating when Carlo Maldonado had come to town?

Words fell from Berto's lips. Rushed. Shaky. "He ordered my wife killed. I'm next." He clenched his jaw until pain shot through his teeth.

Cole Lucas' gray eyes sharpened. He squared his broad shoulders. "Caselli." It wasn't a question.

The waiting room door opened again with a creak, stopping any answer Berto might've been planning. What the hell could he say, anyway? He needed Lucas' help. But he wasn't going to beg for it. Even if the guy was a cop.

He glanced to the doorway, gritting his teeth when he took in who'd joined them. Though both men were dressed casually, they carried themselves as only cops did. Detectives.

The shorter one—but only because the other guy had to be six-three—was fair-haired and wore a pale blue button-down tucked into his jeans. His demeanor screamed *cowboy*. All he needed was a Stetson and a buckle, because he already wore the cowboy boots.

Not unlike the way Berto often dressed in his *role* as Mateo Mata, owner-operator of the successful cattle ranch, the Circle Bar B.

"Cole." The detective's voice was deep, eyes wide as his gaze went from Lucas to Berto. Obviously he was surprised to see his colleague here, too.

The dark-haired man slid around, shaking Lucas' hand and muttering congratulations. Lucas nodded and flashed a grin, showing dimples. The former FBI agent's stance relaxed, but only for a second.

What's that about?

The third detective was younger than Lucas or the blond guy, baby-faced. But he looked hard in a way, regarding Berto with a sober expression after dropping his smile and squaring his shoulders. He stood next to Cole Lucas. Partners?

"Hey, Pete," Lucas said, inclining his head.

Shaking hands, the two exchanged low greetings, then three sets of eyes bored into Berto.

He squirmed but tried to stand taller, ignoring the fact that these three men towered over him. For once, these guys were here to help. Right? He wasn't being arrested or hauled to jail—yet. They always suspected the spouse first, after all. Though Berto would off himself before he hurt Maria. Then again, it was his fault she'd been shot.

Fuck.

"You caught his case?" Lucas thumbed toward him.

The blond detective nodded. "Are you Mateo Mata? Husband of Maria, a nurse at Health Solutions?"

Berto nodded and met a pair of very green eyes.

The man put his hand out for a shake. "Detective Pete Crane. This is Detective Jared Manning. You know Detective Lucas?"

"Yes." Berto shot a look at Lucas, shifting on his feet.

"Don't worry, Berto. Detective Crane will have your back. Tell him *everything*," Lucas said, his steel gaze intense.

"Berto?" Detective Manning asked.

"This is Alberto Carbone," Lucas said before he could speak. "You might remember his name in my Maldonado report last year. We managed to keep him out of the courtroom, but only because we had a hell of a prosecutor."

Detective Crane nodded.

The cop's last name triggered a memory of the prosecutor Lucas had just referred to. The Assistant District Attorney who had handled Carlo Maldonado's case in court. Nathan Crane. Berto had seen his name in the papers. Was he related to the detective who had apparently picked up his— Maria's—case?

He'd rather have Lucas.

"The shooting definitely wasn't random then," Detective Manning said, dark brow furrowed.

"No," Berto and Lucas said at the same time.

Detective Crane ran his hand through his short hair, suddenly looking as haggard as Berto felt. "Might as well start at the beginning."

Numbness spread over his limbs, but Berto managed a nod.

Then he opened his mouth.

Chapter Seven

"What are you doing here?" Pete asked, frowning as he strolled to his cubicle, steaming Styrofoam tall of fresh coffee in hand. Not that Starbucks crap, either. Good, old-fashioned, cheap grounds the city paid for were his fave. Good coffee was subjective.

He swallowed back a yawn. He hadn't been able to hit the sack until well after two. Five hours of sleep and only one cuppa Joe? Nowhere close to cutting the day he was in for. He needed a caffeine IV.

"I just stopped by to look at the initial report from Neil. Good thing he's so fast. It was here waiting for ya." Perched on the corner of Pete's desk, Cole sipped from a travel mug with Ethan's picture on it. The kid was dressed as a cowboy, an adorable grin on his face the size of Texas.

"When's my partner getting discharged?"

"I got some time, promise."

"You really need to look up the word *vacation*," Pete said, arching a brow.

"Damn, you're giving me a harder time than Andi did. I've only been here about five minutes. Besides, Cass is with her. My sister's helping out."

"*You* need to be there for her and that baby right now, Cole."

"No shit. Now, then and the rest of their lives." His partner's husband put the stapled bundle of papers down and met Pete's eyes.

He couldn't fault the guy for wanting to know CSI's take on things—see what actual evidence they had. Didn't doubt Cole's loyalty or work ethic. Nor did he *want* to say no to the assistance. Pete just didn't want Andi upset. His partner needed her husband right now. Wrangling a rambunctious four-year-old was bad enough without adding a new-born into the equation.

He sighed. "Sorry. Not tryin' to ride ya."

Cole cocked his head to one side and crossed his arms over his chest. "Just trying to help out. Believe me, I know where I need to be, and I *want* to be there. I'll go in a few."

After sliding into his chair, Pete set his coffee down, reaching for the report.

"How's Nikki?"

Gorgeous as ever. He cleared his throat, refusing to think about their kiss. "I talked to her a few minutes ago, she was fine. Good even. She's stubborn and strong. Insisted on coming to work today. Trying hard for normal. Sergeant Stein talked to the grandmother last night. I have her report already. BOLO's still out. So far, no sign of the Hummer."

"Dude, this is Caselli. Nikki and her grandmother *saw* Guido-squared," Cole said. "You need to get her to a safe house, and slap a cop on Mrs Jenkins twenty-four-seven."

"Shit," Pete breathed. He'd been foolish not to consider that. The asshole had gone after Alberto Carbone's woman, after all. He shoved his hand through his hair. *Gonna be a looooong day.* "I'll go talk to Chief. Gut tells me Nikki won't agree easily."

"I get that. But it's for the best. Hell, take her to your place."

Pete's stomach fluttered and he shifted in the chair. His cock could certainly get attached to that idea. *Off limits, remember?* "I'll see what Chief thinks."

Cole stared at him for a moment, one dark eyebrow up, but his buddy didn't ask any questions about his denial. "Good deal, but she's probably going to insist on staying nearby — easy access to her grandmother. Andi says they're really close, but Nikki has her own place. She can't go home."

"Agreed."

"Also, you're gonna wanna call Dawson. This is her case." Cole frowned.

Pete smirked. *Bet that hurt, even after almost a year.*

Cole had lived and breathed the Caselli case. It'd been *his* case for almost three years, as Pete understood it. As an FBI agent, he'd been undercover within the vast Caselli trafficking organization — both drugs and women — for fourteen months.

Before he'd come back to Antioch, Cole had been partnered with Special Agent Selena Dawson, or Lee, as most called her. She'd accompanied them — him, Andi, Cole and APD SWAT — on a raid of a local warehouse where Cole's bad guy, Carlo Maldonado, had been holding Andi's kidnapped babysitter.

Lee was a badass, as Cole always called her. Long dark hair the last time Pete saw her, big brown eyes and olive skin, she was petite and curvy in all the right places. Agent Dawson wasn't a chore to look at, for damn sure.

He wouldn't mind seeing her — working with her — again. "Makes sense. Maybe she knows what's behind all this. I mean, Caselli's known where this guy's been for years. What spurred an act of revenge now?"

"Good point. I'll give her a ring." Cole paused, taking a sip of coffee. "I mean, if you don't mind. This being your gig and all."

"I don't mind. But you better get your ass to the hospital to take Andi and Micah home. You have a family. And if I remember correctly, my partner can be...cranky after giving birth." Pete winked.

Cole grinned, flashing dimples that made him look about sixteen. "Nah, she's happy." His expression shouted just how happy he was, too.

He smiled back. For some reason, Nikki's face popped into his head. Shaking himself, Pete ignored the image of the redheaded beauty with flushed cheeks, looking thoroughly kissed. "Seen Manning this morning?" His voice cracked.

Cole threw him a '*What's-up-with-you?*' look and Pete fought the urge to squirm. "Nope. But I think he's back to the burglaries we've been working."

"Ah. So your partner's not on loan to me even though you've taken *mine* out of commission?" He chuckled.

"Hey, now, are ya saying you can't handle things on your own?"

"Nah. I can one-man-show it for a while. But I'm sure Dawson will get her shapely ass on a plane as soon as you get off the phone."

Cole laughed. "Hmmm, I thought work *affiliations* were off limits?"

"Hey, dude. I can look and dream."

"What I got at home is better than empty dreams. You should try it sometime."

Nikki's big brown eyes flashed into Pete's mind once again. And her mouth. Plump lips he'd tasted. He remembered every inch of her soft curves pressed against his body. Chiding himself, he stood, resisting the urge to readjust the crotch of his jeans.

I hope you'll be happy, Pete. And find what you're looking for. Liz's words reverberated as clearly as if she was standing in front of him again. Another memory he didn't want. He frowned.

"Something wrong?"

Meeting his buddy's gray eyes made him want to groan. *Since when is Cole so perceptive?*

"Nope. I'm fine," Pete said, forcing a smile.

"Goin' somewhere?"

"Gotta talk to Chief, Nikki, then head to Marty's."

"Marty's?" Cole asked.

"Nikki said the Hummer cut her off after pulling out of the grocery store lot. I'm hoping they have cameras."

"Ah. Call me with what you find out."

Pete shook his head. "V-A-C-A—"

Cole growled. "I know. But do *you* know what Caselli's men look like? Can *you* recognize them?"

Frowning, he crossed his arms over his chest. "Point taken."

"Don't worry about Andi. We're good. But just make sure you call me when you get the footage, all right?"

"I might not need you. Have Dawson call me if she heads in and needs a ride from the airport."

Cole mirrored his frown. "She doesn't know them like I do."

"Okay, okay, I'll call you. But I'm calling your wife."

Dimples made another appearance. "Please do. You've yet to see my kid."

Pete left the CID room shaking his head. But he couldn't help the smile that curved his lips.

* * * *

"Hell no." Nikki crossed her arms over her breasts, glaring at her boss and Pete. "Absolutely *not*. I'm leaving here today like normal, going to see my grandmother, and then *home*."

"No. You. Are. Not." Chief Paul Martin glared right back. His hazel eyes flashed and his greying brown mustache twitched, like it did only when he was *very* irritated.

Nikki didn't give a shit.

"Listen, Detective Lucas knows what he's talking about." Pete's hands were spread wide, imploring. The detective's green eyes were concerned, handsome face drawn, serious. The usual smile he wore was nowhere in sight.

At least Pete wasn't trying to order her around like her misguided boss. Who did Chief think he was, her father?

Pete sat on the edge of the chair, his gaze intense.

Nikki's stomach fluttered and she remembered his mouth on her own. Warm lips moving, his tongue twined with hers. Desire claiming, spreading...arousing them both.

What are you, a hormone? These men are ordering you around. Make choices for you. You have no say in what they want you to do.

No. She was independent. Grown. Strong like Gram had raised her to be. Capable of making her own

64

decisions. She knew what was best for her, and for her grandmother.

"I'll be fine at home. I have a gun. I know how to use it," Nikki said.

Chief frowned.

Pete shook his head and spoke before their boss could. "These guys aren't your average thugs. This is more serious than you think—"

"They didn't pay *any* attention to me or Gram."

"Doesn't matter," Chief barked.

"I agree." At least Pete had the decency to look as if he felt bad.

Dammit.

"What about Gram?"

"Rodriguez is already at the rehab center. Crowley will switch out with him at nineteen hundred hours, and Monroe at oh-seven. She'll have twenty-four-hour protection," Chief said.

Nikki's heart went into overdrive.

This is real. We're both in danger.

She swallowed hard. Tears were born and the two men blurred. She and Gram were witnesses. Pete and Chief were worried they'd be *victims*.

No. She refused to end up like her parents.

Pete grabbed her hand and squeezed. "I—Chief and I—need you safe."

"You're family," their boss said, his voice about as gentle as she'd ever heard it.

She blinked. *Do not cry in the chief's office.* "Where am I going to go?" Her voice wavered, and she allowed the detective to entwine their fingers instead of pulling away from him. Nikki fought the urge to leap forward and wrap her arms around Pete. She wanted to feel safe, and the last place she *had* was in his arms the night before. Trembling started, rattling her teeth and moving down her spine.

Stop this. Right now. Get yourself together, Nikki Harper.

"It's gonna be okay," Pete whispered, holding her hand even tighter, but he wasn't hurting her. His thumb started slow soothing circles along her knuckles and Nikki sucked in a breath, then another.

Her body stilled, her breathing evened. She wanted to thank him, because Pete — his touch — somehow grounded her, but her voice was nowhere to be found.

Chief exchanged a look with her detective then met her eyes. "The city owns a few houses in town. Unassuming places. You'll stay in one until this blows over. Crane will get this guy."

"Guys," Nikki corrected, but neither answered her. She wiped her face with her free hand. "I don't want to tell Gram. She'll just worry. It's bad enough she'll see a cop all hours of the day."

Pete nodded. "Whatever you want to do."

Nikki met his eyes and couldn't look away. The feel of his arms around her, his solid muscles against her, teased her mind. His woodsy cologne tickled her nose. She wanted to slip into him like she had last night. She wanted his lips against hers again. Wanted more than just his kiss. He wanted her. She'd felt it last night. Saw it in his gaze right now.

Attraction sizzled between them. Her body warmed. Nikki didn't need to talk to Pete, she needed to touch him, caress his face, kiss him —

Chief cleared his throat and Nikki jumped. But so did Pete.

"Can I go home to get some clothes?" Her voice cracked and she fought a cringe, pulling her hand out of the detective's.

What happened?

More than just the memory of a little kiss. Not that she'd ever describe it as *little*. The kiss in the hallway of the rehab center had been the kind to curl toes and suck a girl into oblivion. Detective Pete Crane knew what he was doing.

"I don't see why not, if you make it quick," Chief said.

What? Oh...yeah, home. Her apartment. Pack a bag. She made herself meet her boss's hazel eyes. Forced a smile and nodded thanks.

"I'll take her." Pete was still looking at her.

"Good," their boss said, but his voice was lost as Nikki tried not to stare at Pete.

"Nikki, I need a moment with Crane."

Pete's head shot around to Chief. "Boss?"

The chief's gaze was glued to her detective. His jaw was locked and he looked less than pleased. Was something wrong? His tone was hard. Irritated. Shouldn't he have calmed? She'd pretty much agreed to go to a safe house.

Nikki took her time standing, pressing her knees together to keep them from wobbling. Chief Martin appraised her and she almost shifted on her feet. What'd she missed?

"Out," Chief barked. "Close the door."

Chapter Eight

Pete fought the urge to squirm in the chair under the weight of his boss's gaze. What was up with Chief Martin? They'd always been cool.

"You are the *last* person I ever thought I'd have to say this to."

"Say what?" Pete sat taller, pressing his back into the plush padding of the chair and feeling like he was a high-schooler in the principal's office.

"Keep your damn hands to yourself."

"Excuse me?"

Chief arched a salt and pepper eyebrow, and steepled his hands on top of his desk. "I'm not stupid."

Guilt, hard and fast, hit Pete in the chest.

"I didn't miss your little moment with Nikki." Chief's voice was even, but his hazel gaze shrewd.

Little moment was right, but damned if Pete would ever admit it out loud. It'd taken all he was made of not to grab her and kiss the living daylights out of her.

Nikki's tears, however slight, had just about killed him. Worse than last night. All he could think about was taking away her fears. Holding her. Comforting her.

"She's my witness." *And a kid. I have no interest in her except what relates to the case.*

Right?

Liar. Voicing it to his boss wouldn't make the lie true.

"Exactly."

Pete tapped his cowboy boot on the floor, screaming at himself to sit still. "You got nothing to worry about, boss."

The Chief stared in a stretched moment of silence, then his chest heaved as if he'd sucked in breath. He ran his hand through his greying hair. "She...means something to me. A damn lot to me, actually."

Pete frowned, leaning closer to the edge of his boss's oversized desk. More than an employer-employee relationship. His boss wasn't...infatuated with Nikki, was he? That would lend itself to awkwardness if Chief ever found out they'd kissed. Or it could get Pete's ass kicked—literally.

Chief used to be a boxer. Of the prize-winning variety. His office was plastered with framed photos and a championship belt was proudly displayed on the wall behind his head.

"Her father and I were partners."

"Nikki's dad was a cop?"

The older man nodded, looked away then cleared his throat. "We grew up together. High school, the Army, the academy, patrol partners and even made detective together." His boss's hazel eyes were misty when he finally met Pete's gaze.

Shock rolled over him and he squared his shoulders. He'd never heard that particular tone come out of Chief's mouth before.

Face drawn tight, his boss was saturated in sorrow. "I blame myself for what happened to him. And his wife, Nikki's mom."

"What happened?" Pete whispered.

"A case gone wrong. Bad guy took revenge on Jim and Meg." Chief shook his head, jaw clenched. He made a fist and glared, but not at Pete. "I got the bastard, but not until after he'd left Nikki an orphan at age five."

"Ah. Her grandmother raised her."

"Yes, and has no love for me," Chief said. "Protect Nikki, Pete. Don't let her out of your sight. I mean it."

A thousand questions raced through his mind, but he didn't push his boss. If Pete wanted to find out what'd happened, he could look in the archives. The subject change meant Chief didn't want to talk about it.

"I'll protect her. And get Caselli's men." A vow to his boss's soft, but firm order.

"Call the FBI. If this case does involve Caselli, Special Agent Barnes will want to inform her unit. They're still working to get him."

Pete nodded. "Lucas is going to call Dawson. She took over for him last year."

"Good. Cooperate with her if she comes to town."

"You know it, boss. Lucas will help out, too."

Chief snorted. "He wouldn't stay home if I fired him." But there was no malice in his tone, just pride. Not that Cole's ego needed a boost, but their boss often bragged about his former FBI agent detective.

"Probably not." Pete laughed.

"Call the county and see if you can get someone from the Sheriff's Office to sit on the Circle Bar B. These guys are going to make a move on the husband.

Whether he wants the help or not, we're gonna keep him alive."

"I know a chief deputy over there, I'll see what I can do. Also, I can see if either Dawson or Lucas knows anyone in the Marshal's Service. Maybe we can talk about WitSec."

Shaking his head, the chief took another breath. "I don't think he'd agree to witness protection even if the wife dies. But it's not a bad idea. I'll talk to Barnes if she graces me with a call."

Pete nodded. He wouldn't doubt it if Cole's former supervisor gave their boss a call. She still ran the Human Trafficking Unit that was after Alberto Carbone's ex-boss.

According to the news, they'd been making some headway over the last few months. Enough to make national headlines anyway. Was that the clincher that'd made Caselli move against the gangster-turned-rancher after all this time?

Comparing notes with Dawson wasn't going to be a bad idea, for sure.

Knowing Lee, the FBI agent would fly in, rent a car at the airport and pop into the station without so much as a phone call. *Well, hope she's quick about it, then.*

"Take Nikki to the house on Montgomery. It's the biggest and nicest of what we've got. Check on Mrs Jenkins, too."

"Ten-four." He stood, nodding and making a mental checklist of what he needed to get done. Things were about to get complicated now that Nikki would have to be a tag-along.

"Seriously, Crane."

Pete paused, one hand on the doorknob.

"If you touch her inappropriately, or one hair on her head is harmed by anyone or *anything*, your ass — your badge — is mine."

He threw a smile over his shoulder, but his gut tightened at the warning in Chief's tone. A hard promise, the likes of which Pete had never heard from the man before. "You worry too much, boss."

Besides, he agreed. *Nikki's not for you.*

The reinforcement should help. No — *would* help. He'd keep his hands to himself and his cock in his pants.

After slipping out of the office, he closed the door silently.

When Pete turned around, he met a pair of very brown eyes.

* * * *

Luca cursed and wrenched the wheel of the piece-of-shit Ford to the right, avoiding the parked car by mere inches as he scanned the parking lot. Where the *fuck* was Mickey?

Caselli's idiot nephew had taken off on his own when Luca had been stupid enough to give in to fatigue and get a few hours of shut-eye. He'd awoken in the crappy motel room alone — and pissed off.

"Fuck."

Shaking his head, Luca clutched the butt of his Beretta with his free hand. His knuckles smarted but he didn't loosen his grip. When he found the bastard, he *was* going to kill him. No matter what his fucking boss said.

Sometimes Caselli could be a pussy. Was he afraid of a little bloodshed? The boss had been hacked that Luca had disposed of the local meth head — the driver who'd gotten them away from the rehab center. Luca had saved the man ten thousand dollars. Couldn't Caselli be happy about that? His boss was a cheap-ass most of the time, after all.

The points Luca had hoped to score with a job well done had not only dissipated, but he'd had to endure a tongue-lashing that would have been a beating if he'd been in the same room as Caselli.

And the smirk on Mickey's puss when he'd overheard part of the conversation had sealed his fucking fate. The little bastard wasn't going to make a fool out of Luca.

"Fuck Mickey. Fuck Caselli," Luca muttered. "I know what I'm doing."

Doubt didn't even enter his mind. But he needed to head out to Berto's ranch and finish the job. Show his boss he *could* perform.

The news had reported that the nurse was alive—his boss was pissed about that, too.

Well, she could have a mishap in the hospital. Luca would deal with that as soon as he'd found his *co-worker*.

Could Mickey have gotten it into his head to go to the hospital and finish off Berto's whore? *No way.* Caselli's nephew wasn't that smart. Besides, Luca had kept that part of his boss's phone rant to himself.

If he couldn't find Mickey, he'd just handle things then deal with him later. And he *would* find him. *Would* deal with him. Until Mickey bled.

The fight they'd had the night before shot into his memory and Luca gritted his teeth. Mickey was convinced they needed to silence all witnesses.

"The old woman saw us. So did the redheaded chick."

"So what?" Luca had snapped.

"*Saw* us. As in will-tell-the-police what we look like." Mickey had crossed his arms at that point, shaking his head until his shaggy hair shifted on his shoulders.

What Luca hadn't admitted was that their boss had ordered them to leave the women alone as well. Agreeing—even a little bit—made his blood boil. They didn't want the exposure more bodies would bring. Not that he minded the killing. On the contrary, that was his favorite part. Seeing the life fade out of someone's eyes—that got his cock hard. It didn't matter. He'd do the Berto job and finish off the whore. Then hit the road. Go home to New York within a few days. Who the fuck cared who saw them? They wouldn't be in Texas long enough for it to signify. Like small-town cops crossed the country after guys they couldn't identify.

Luca should have known better to assume the argument was over. Mickey wouldn't just let things go. The bastard thought he could act behind Luca's back.

"That fucker," he muttered, glancing at the faded green numbers on the clock in the crappy Taurus. "I don't have time for this shit."

The Circle Bar B was at least forty-five minutes away. Luca needed to scope the place and make a plan to rid the world of Alberto Carbone. Maybe explosives would be fun. It'd been a long time since he'd blown something up.

By the time he'd hit the highway to head southwest, Luca was plotting all sorts of creative ways to dispose of Berto—and Mickey. Could he do it at the same time? A twofer? Perhaps he could wait to kill his boss's turncoat. He could find Mickey and bring him back out to the ranch. Tell the idiot he needed help with the job. Tie them together in the barn? Set it on fire?

Luca chuckled.

Whatever he decided, it'd be good. Hitting the road to go home alone wouldn't be so bad. He'd worry about how to explain being sans Mickey to Caselli later. Accidents happened, after all. *Oooops.* Luca grinned and patted his gun.

Then again, he hadn't told Mickey their two witnesses were off limits. Caselli didn't need to know that. Luca wouldn't be able to help killing Mickey if the guy disobeyed his uncle, could he?

When he turned down the county road toward the Circle Bar B, a pothole the size of Texas threatened to swallow the car he'd boosted.

Shit, he should have stolen a truck. The rough road jarred him until his teeth rattled. It was going to give him a damn backache. Not to mention, he was rather out of place in the low-to-the-ground sedan. The few vehicles he'd passed were all pickups of varying sizes.

Luca drove by the huge iron gate with the ranch's name and logo shaped in an arch over a paved driveway, then circled back around. His instincts flared and he hunkered down in the bucket seat. Following the speed limit was a must. He couldn't be conspicuous.

The house was sprawling and sat about half a mile back from the roadway. The property was edged by a combination of decorative iron fencing as well as the more practical stuff to keep horses and cattle contained.

"Why the hell does Berto want all this shit?" Luca frowned. Drugs and women were easy money. Fuck the hard work that came with the crap in front of him.

Scanning the roadway as well as the vast property, he inched the car closer. Could he get away with turning down the road? There was no one around.

Woods edged both sides of the roadway just beyond the fencing that belonged to the Circle Bar B. A small clearing marked a dirt road formed by large tire tracks. It seemed to curve around into Berto's land. There wasn't a gate he could see. Was it a back entrance or something? Was there a place for him to park and watch?

The glint of a shiny reflection had Luca swinging his head around. His gut clenched and a string of curses fell from his lips. The steering wheel bit into his palms, his knuckles smarting as the silver cruiser made a slow turn down the main entrance of Berto's ranch. He didn't catch the name of the county, but the car boasted *Sheriff's Office* under a star-shaped seal on the door.

"Fuck me."

More fucking cops?

From the rear view, Luca watched the Dodge Charger stop at the gate and hit what looked to be an intercom. He couldn't slow or stop without being noticed, so he hit the gas and exercised his vocabulary some more.

If Caselli didn't want him to kill witnesses, he certainly wouldn't want collateral damage in the form of dead cops. Even if it would be fun as hell.

"Son of a bitch."

Things just got complicated.

Chapter Nine

"What's wrong with him?" Nikki asked.

The damn door had prevented her from hearing anything but deep voices as her boss and Pete had talked.

Getting kicked out of Chief's office was new. If she was the subject of the conversation, she had a right to know everything.

Pete cleared his throat. "Nothing. He wants to make sure you're protected."

"Right." She narrowed her eyes, but suddenly her detective wouldn't look at her. Considering he hadn't been able to *stop* just moments before, Nikki didn't buy what he was trying to sell for a second.

"Let's go. I don't want to be gone long. Besides the safe house, the PD is about the best place for you to be. So let's get what you need and get back here. I don't like the idea of being unsecure."

Nikki frowned. "So I'm stuck with you, left to your every whim? I *am* an adult, you know."

That green gaze burned her. "You're stuck with me all right. But your safety's not exactly a whim, darlin'."

Trying to glare failed, and she couldn't help but melt a little. Pete's use of Gram's familiar endearment was like a caress. Not at all like when her grandmother said it. A tremor shot down her spine. She swallowed and took a step back when she really wanted to wrap her arms around him. "What about Gram?" Her voice shook and she cursed.

"She's gonna be fine. Like Chief said, she'll always have an officer with her."

"No. I mean, I need to see her. Every day."

Pete frowned and Nikki glared.

"It's non-negotiable, Detective. I see my grandmother daily."

"We'll see what we can do."

"No." Nikki shook her head. "No. Way. This is not going to mess with my life."

"Nikki—"

Cursing him to hell and back, she whirled away and stalked to her desk. "I'm not going to be a victim to this…situation."

Pete's sigh sounded in her ear. He was behind her, he'd followed closely, but she couldn't look at him. Ignored the feel of his body heat at her back.

Attraction or not, kiss or not, he wasn't going to get away with ordering her around.

"That's what I'm trying to avoid," he said.

"I'm being punished."

"Keeping you safe is not a punishment." The conviction in his voice made her glance at Pete, but she refused to get taken in by the concern in his expression.

"So, what, I'm supposed to follow you around until this is over?" Nikki snapped.

"No."

"No?"

"I'm supposed to follow *you* around." One corner of his inviting mouth lifted and she tried to glare again. She couldn't, but Nikki refused to let it go. He couldn't cover this up with humor.

"Aren't you, I dunno, supposed to *solve* the case?"

"I will." Pete cocked his head to one side. "Don't worry about me, I can multitask."

Nikki snorted. "So what am I supposed to do? Sit on my ass?"

Pete's eyes raked her frame and she ignored how her body warmed. "Or you can be my junior detective." He winked.

She bit her lip to keep from giving in to a smile. Damn Detective Pete Crane and his charm. "How about you do what you need to and *I* worry about me?"

He shook his head. "Not in the cards."

The ringing of a cell phone put the brakes on Nikki's retort.

"Crane," Pete said as soon as the iPhone was against his ear. He listened. "Shit." His eyes rested on her for only a moment before he turned his back, but Nikki wasn't having it.

She slipped around him, standing close enough to hear a male voice on the other end of the phone.

"...been dead no more than a day. Raleigh Carter's here. He found him. He's insisting on speaking to you. In person."

Jared Manning. Detective Cole Lucas' partner. Why was he calling Pete? And...dead? Who was dead?

Her heart sped up and she clenched her jaw, forcing her hands to remain at her sides and not on Pete. Touching him would have made her feel better.

"Yeah, yeah. He always pulls that crap. He won't even talk to Andi when he's got some info." Disgust dripped from Pete's voice. He threw a look in Nikki's direction but didn't gesture for her to move away. No doubt he knew she could hear his conversation.

"Can you come out here?" Jared's tone mirrored Pete's.

"Is he high?"

"Nope. He was supposed to meet Billy so they could party. Ended up finding him dead instead. That's about all he'll tell me. But he swears he'll open up to you."

"Son of a bitch." Pete dragged his hand through his fair hair.

"Tell me about it. Neil's on his way."

"Did you call the ME's office yet?"

"Yup. Max is headed this way."

"Good. Assistant to the Medical Examiner himself. We need someone who knows what they're doing." Pete frowned as Nikki heard the *click* of the call being ended. He shoved his phone into his jeans and met her eyes. "Change of plans."

"I need to go to my apartment." Nikki's voice was irritated, but her expression wasn't angry. Still gorgeous, of course.

Pete cleared his throat. "Yes. But I don't know how long this will take. I'm sorry. You could've stayed at the station. You're safe inside the building."

"And have you forget about me? No way. I want to go home, and I want to see Gram later today."

"I couldn't forget about you." *She has no idea, does she? That's for the better, bucko.* Pete studiously ignored her statement about seeing her grandmother. He didn't want to argue. It wasn't like he was going to try to keep her away from the woman who'd raised her, either. She had to realize it was different now.

She was belted in, but her arms were crossed over her ample breasts, shoulders tight. Nikki had no desire to be with him and a part of him was bothered by that. His gaze settled on her lips, but he made himself look away.

Nikki harrumphed, staring out of the window.

Pete sighed. Something about taking her to a murder scene roiled his stomach, but his CI, Raleigh Carter, was notoriously unreliable. And if Manning had tried to bring him to the PD instead of Pete going on scene, the part-time confidential informant/full-time pain in the ass would've done something stupid, like attempt suicide in the cruiser and end up in the psych ward.

"I'm sorry about all this, I really am."

She didn't answer, and his instinct was to make her feel better.

"When you live in a small city and you work at a police department, sometimes you get complacent. You forget that bad things can happen to anyone. Anywhere. To good people. It's —"

"I'm not complacent," she snapped, but at least she was looking his way again.

"Uh, I didn't mean anything by it." Pulling the car to a stop at a red light, Pete met beautiful dark eyes. He couldn't read her expression and his gut tightened for some reason. "I'm not going to complain about *you* getting stuck with *me*." He reached for her hand and squeezed.

Why the hell did you say that? The boss warned you. You agree with what he said, idiot. You never should've kissed her. Ever. You will not do it again. Stop thinking about it.

But when Nikki's expression softened, Pete almost changed his mind. She squeezed his hand right back.

"I'm sorry." Her voice was soft, emotional. "It's just... I never thought I'd be...a witness. You're worried they're going to come after us. There's only one thing worse than a witness. A victim."

Pete sucked in a breath. "Nothing is going to happen to you. Or your gram."

A horn blared and they both jumped.

"Light's green," Nikki said, one corner of her mouth up.

Biting back a cringe, he nodded and hit the gas as a small pickup whipped around them at top speed and offered a one-finger salute.

"Jerk," Pete and Nikki said at the same time. They exchanged a glance and a small laugh. The weight lifted off his chest.

"At least you can give them a ticket, if you want," she said, flashing a smile.

Pete chuckled. "I haven't written a ticket in years. I wouldn't know where to start."

"I'm just saying. It's handy and all."

Grinning, he nodded and wanted to touch her again. Anything to keep them connected in some way. But he straightened his spine and berated himself. He didn't need Chief's warning to keep his hands to himself. He wouldn't touch her, and he wouldn't kiss her. Pete wouldn't hold her. Wouldn't be tempted by her in any way, shape or form. He'd do what was right—what he always did. His job.

He *would* protect her and her grandmother and arrest Caselli's bastards.

"Where're we going, anyway?" Nikki's voice pulled him out of his head.

"The old trailer park."

"I haven't been by there in years."

"It's pretty empty. Only a few trailers left there. We chase meth-heads out of there all the time, but the guy who owns the property really wants to clean it up. Maybe even get some nicer trailers and modular homes and open the place back up."

A few months before, he and Andi had been on a case involving a meth lab in one of the old trailers. The owner of the grounds had reported it himself. After a few bankruptcies, he was still struggling. Pete felt for the guy, he really did. It would help the city if the man was able to open the trailer park back up. Legit residents would force the meth population to find a new stomping ground. Maybe outside of Antioch.

"The Antioch slums." Nikki's tone was amused.

Pete smiled. "If we had a definite slum, it'd be the old trailer park, for sure."

Their city of about fifty thousand had started out as what people in Texas liked to refer to as a 'bedroom community,' but they'd been expanding the last twenty years. Not very much in population, but they had a warehouse district, their own hospital. Even a movie theater scheduled to open in the fall.

There were two apartment complexes of several hundred units. Nikki lived in the newer of the two, the Enclave, which had only been around for a few years.

Places like Health Solutions, and many bigger chains of retail stores were starting to come closer to town, and in the last six months they even had a posh hotel open up—The Covington was advertising itself as a four-star stay. Antioch, which had always been rather affluent, was growing. Too bad the crime rate was, too.

Pete pulled down the road that led to the heart of the old trailer park. The small building where the office used to be wasn't visible from the main thoroughfare, a prime location for riffraff. The property was surrounded by woods, trees canopying the length of the street like an awning. Due to lack of maintenance, it was more *Texas Chainsaw Massacre* than *Pleasantville*.

"This place really is hidden," Nikki said, as if she'd read his mind. She looked around, making a face as she surveyed.

"Yeah, that's why it attracts crap."

"But if cops chase them out of here all the time, why do they always try again?"

"I dunno. If you figure that out, lemme know." Pete winked.

She flashed a smile. "Thinkin' out loud."

"You're fine. You're supposed to be my junior detective, remember?"

Nikki stared, one auburn eyebrow raised as if she was trying to solve the Pete puzzle.

Pete cleared his throat and shifted in his seat. He'd meant nothing more than a tease, but if he didn't concentrate on something else, he would slip into the depths of her eyes. "We're here," he said unnecessarily, pulling the powder blue Crown Vic next to the white one Jared always drove.

The Crime Scene van was next to a navy one with *Medical Examiner* written on the side in yellow lettering. Police cruisers littered the place.

The day shift sergeant, Jason Connell, was in front of the trailer, and one of his officers was marking a perimeter with yellow police-line tape.

"Wow," Nikki whispered, staring in the direction of the run-down double-wide.

"Maybe you should stay in the car," Pete said, switching the engine off and palming the key.

"Do I have to?"

Instinct flared. Keep her safe. Keep her from seeing a dead body. Keep her innocent of that shit. But she'd already seen a shooting, a friend injured. Chief's voice teased his mind. *Don't let her out of your sight. I mean it.* But his boss sure as hell hadn't meant drag her to a murder scene.

"What was that?"

He met her open, sincere gaze. He hadn't answered her question. "I don't mind if you come, but stay out of the way, and don't contaminate the crime scene."

"Okay..."

"Just stick with me and you'll be fine."

The smile she offered made his heart go into overdrive but Pete chided himself and squared his shoulders.

Chapter Ten

A murder scene. A victim. A dead victim.

It was real, not on TV.

Nikki swallowed hard and slid closer to Pete. She wished she could shut her eyes and block out the sights around her. Hell, she should just go back to the car, but she didn't want to be alone. Away from her detective.

Pete's back was straight and he kept shaking his head as he talked to a thin guy with stringy black hair and grungy clothing. Even if Nikki hadn't known he was a meth user from what she'd heard Jared Manning tell Pete, she would've seen it from one look at him.

He was twitchy. Like all over. His face was pocked and scarred and his jeans hung low, hip bones prominent. He was too thin, and his teeth were rotted.

Gross. Seriously, what's the appeal of something that makes you decay?

She schooled her expression when Mr Meth looked her way, but he didn't stare — thank God.

"Are you lying to me?" Pete asked.

"No. Jesus, man, I'm telling you the truth. He said he scored big! Said he did a job and got paid ten Gs."

"What kind of job?"

"I don't know, man. I swear."

"Where's the money, Raleigh?" Pete's voice was even, but Nikki could tell he was irritated.

"Do you think I'd be here if I found ten thousand dollars?"

"I guess I appreciate your honesty." His retort was dry.

Jared Manning snorted. He stood with his arms crossed over his chest. When his dark gaze met Nikki's, her detective winked.

He'd not asked one question when Pete had showed up with her in tow. Then again, she didn't want his two cents. It was bad enough he'd caught her kissing Pete at the rehab center.

A tremor shot down her spine and her body warmed.

Pete... Her attraction to him had come out of the blue, but it certainly wasn't unwelcome, despite the tragedy in her life.

She glanced back at Jared. He was hot, no doubt. Pretty much the epitome of tall, dark and handsome. Probably about six-three and built like a linebacker. But Detective Manning wasn't a temptation—even though he was closer to her age and had more than enough muscles to make a girl swoon. He leaned on his car, long frame appearing relaxed, belying his intent expression as he stared at Pete talking to the drug addict.

"When's the last time you talked to Billy?" Pete asked.

"Yesterday afternoon. He said he'd catch up with me last night. He never answered my calls. I was pissed 'cause I thought he took off with the dough. When he wasn't at his place, I thought he might be here. Looks like he didn't take off on me after all."

"That it?"

"Yeah, man. I swear."

"Where were you last night?"

"Home with my old lady. Promise. You can check."

"You know we will," Detective Manning said.

"Billy didn't say *anything* to you about what the job was about? Or who he was with?"

Mr Meth shook his head, his scraggly hair flying around his face.

Pete sighed. "Okay. You know the drill. Call me if you remember anything else, or if you *hear* anything. I mean it, Raleigh."

The guy nodded, his pale blue eyes widening. "I swear I will."

"You'd better."

"I can go now?" Mr Meth sounded like a little kid.

"Yeah. I'll have one of the guys take you home."

"No. No. I'll walk." He looked at Nikki, flashing a mostly toothless, rotted smile. It was all she could do to hold back her cringe. The guy left like his ass was on fire.

Jared Manning straightened and pushed off the white, unmarked police car. "Damn waste of time, if you ask me."

"Yeah, probably. But you never know. The thing is, he *will* call me if he hears anything," Pete said.

"We didn't let anything leak," the other detective said.

"Nope, but you know scum talks to scum. If he sees the Hummer or hears anything about Caselli's guys, he'll tell me. You know it doesn't take much to make him shake like a leaf."

"If you say so. Did you get what you needed inside?" Jared gestured to the dilapidated double-wide.

Pete hadn't been in the trailer for very long. For that, she was grateful. Nikki had felt naked standing in the yard watching the uniform cops. Cold, despite the warmth of the day.

"Yeah. Billy Madden was small time. He didn't deserve an end like that."

Nikki agreed, but she couldn't exactly say *poor guy* and move on. He was a criminal. He'd chosen his path and lost. What other outcome could he have expected? *Idiot.*

Drugs and crime had a way of leaving a person with an early expiration date. She remained silent, observing the two detectives talk.

"I'll tell Max they can move him then, if you're done," Jared said.

Pete nodded and Nikki watched Jared jog to the steps and disappear inside the trailer.

"You all right?" Pete asked.

Nikki met his eyes. "Sure. Thanks for asking."

His smile was small and tentative, but his green eyes were warm. She wanted to sink into him.

"What was it like inside?" Nikki asked.

"Worse than your gram's room at Health Solutions." His expression sobered. "Nothing you need to worry about, though."

If she closed her eyes she would *see* Maria's blood all over the white linoleum floor. She hadn't fallen asleep until well after three, calling herself every cowardly name in the book. Nikki kept replaying what had happened, like a horrible movie in her head. The end never changed. Maria was still covered in blood lying much too still. The shooters still got away.

"Hey, hey. It's okay." Pete's low voice grounded her — again.

"I know."

"Where'd you go? You disappeared on me."

"Health Solutions," Nikki admitted.

Pete gripped her face with gentle, calloused hands. "I promise I'll keep you safe."

She nodded as his thumb brushed her cheek. His touch felt so good, Nikki wanted to have his arms around her. *Safe* meant her detective's embrace. The hard wall of his chest.

The creak and *ka-thunk* of a gurney being lowered down stairs caught her attention, and his hands fell away from her.

Nikki shivered, suddenly cold. But the black bag strapped to the gurney was what sent a tremor down her spine.

"Did you know him well?"

"He's been one of my CIs for a few years," Pete said. "Not sure that qualifies as knowing him well, but it was something. He didn't deserve this."

"Shot five times, including in the head," Jared Manning had told Pete when they'd arrived.

"Hope he didn't suffer," Nikki managed. But how could he not have?

They stood silently as two guys in white coats loaded the gurney into the navy-blue van then shut the doors with a slam that jarred her.

Jared came out of the trailer with Neil, the CSI supervisor. Marion, the pretty Asian photographer, was next. How did she deal with what she saw at every crime scene? Nikki rubbed her arm.

The other detective jogged over to them. "I got this if you want to go. Thanks for talking to Raleigh Carter."

"No problem. Let me know if you need me."

Jared nodded, smiling in Nikki's direction. "See you both soon."

She let Pete answer for them and soon they were alone—sort of—again. There were still uniformed cops everywhere, but no one was really paying them any attention.

"Let's go get your stuff," Pete said. He put his hand low on her back and Nikki trembled for a different reason. He paused. "You cold?"

"N-n-no. It's gotta be like ninety out here."

Pete nodded and smiled, and she let him guide her back to the Crown Victoria.

* * * *

Rushing through her apartment was a blur. Pete had told her she didn't have to hurry, but something made her nervous. Made tingles shoot up and down her spine. Like someone was watching them. But she didn't mention it to her detective.

Stuffing pantyhose, a few bras, underwear and socks into her dad's green Army duffle, she looked over her shoulder. Had Pete seen? Not a big secret she wore undergarments, of course, but there was no reason for the detective to discover her pretty, frilly panty fetish. She loved them, collected them. The more satin and lace, the better.

Her favorite color was red, hands down. *Sexy* and *barely there* were the ones that made her feel the best. Desirable. Like a woman.

Pete was looking in the other direction, hand not far from the gun at his waist. His fingers twitched as if he wanted to draw the weapon. Did he feel that someone was watching them—like she had—after all?

Nikki ignored the tremor that threatened her whole body. Leaving the bag on her bed, she slipped into her walk-in closet and stared at her full hangers.

Gray pinstriped pants faded and she saw a pool of blood on white tile. Closing her eyes, she saw a black body bag. The sense of the surreal melted into reality and her head spun.

This was really happening.

Her hand on the soft fabric should have helped, grounded her in some way, but it only reminded her that she was pulling the clothes off the hanger to fold and put in her duffle.

Not to leave for a trip, but to run, hide. Like —

"Are you almost ready?"

Nikki whirled and ran into the wall of Pete's muscled chest.

"Whoa." Strong hands covered her shoulders and the warmth of his skin sank through the soft material of her short-sleeved, tan sweater.

Her body heated and her cheeks burned.

"I didn't mean to startle you. Are you okay?"

She was mesmerized by the green of his eyes. So much so that Nikki's gaze refused to move and words wouldn't form.

Nod your head, idiot. Something. Anything.

"Nikki? Did I hurt you?" His voice dropped. Softer, concerned. Somehow, that made her want him even more.

"N-n-n-no."

Desire unfurled low in her belly and she stared at Pete's lips. She wanted to feel them again. Wanted to taste him.

The sharp intake of breath told her Pete felt it, too. Again, like in Chief's office. His pecs heaved against her breasts, reminding her how close their bodies were.

Nikki leaned up and brushed her lips against his. But instead of accepting her invitation, dipping his head for a real kiss, Pete released her shoulders and took a step back.

He cleared his throat. "We should get to the safe house. Wrap up, get what you need. Chief said the place is already stocked with groceries."

Her heart skipped. His tone was so normal. Like he was unaffected...entirely. "What?" she croaked.

Pete's expression tightened. Was that a wince?

Her eyes smarted and Nikki screamed at herself. *Get it together.* She blinked and sucked in a breath. "Okay. I only need a few more things." She forced her voice even, proud of herself for containing her emotions.

With a nod, he turned his dark cowboy boots and left her closet.

Despite the warmth in her body for Pete, Nikki was left cold. Stung. He'd pulled away from her.

Never mind. It doesn't matter. Chiding herself, she gathered several mix-and-match outfits and took her time folding then rolling them to lie in the Army duffel. She wasn't ready to face Pete just yet, so the breather helped.

By the time she entered her living room, her spine was straight and her shoulders squared. She was going to be fine. Pulling away from a small kiss wasn't really a rejection, was it?

Pete was pacing along the length of the wall on the left. The one with no windows. Fair brows drawn, his expression suggested he was deep in thought, but Nikki wasn't naïve enough not to recognize he could spring to action at the drop of a hat. His posture screamed cop. On the prowl.

The detective was dangerous, in more than one way.

"I'm ready." Her statement made him freeze.

His emerald eyes burned when their gazes locked and her body flushed. The heat certainly didn't suggest rejection now. She refused to get swept away.

"Don't stand near the window." Pete's command was low and even.

Nikki still jumped. "Is something wrong?" Damn, she should have told him she'd felt like someone was watching them.

"No. Just a precaution."

Liar, her instinct shouted. She forced a nod and moved closer when he gestured for her to come to him.

He grabbed her upper arm, but didn't hurt her. Pete led them out, stopping to take her key and lock her door with nimble fingers. They moved downstairs from her second floor apartment quickly. Before they could reach the car, a petulant mew distracted Nikki and she paused.

"C'mon, we need to move. This is too open." Pete tugged her biceps, but she couldn't move without tripping—Daisy was already weaving in and out of her legs.

"I forgot."

One eyebrow arched, Pete looked down at the calico stray then met Nikki's eyes. "Forgot what?"

"I didn't feed Daisy today." She slipped from his grip, bending down to run a hand through the multi-colored fur of the cat that had adopted her. The feline revved her purr and bumped her hand for a scratch behind the ear.

"You have a cat?"

"Sorta. She's more like a complex cat."

"Someone else can feed it then." Pete pulled her up, resting his hand at the small of her back.

"Pete —"

"Now, Nikki." His tone brooked no argument and she shivered, despite the warmth of his touch.

There is something wrong.

"I don't want to leave her." The words tumbled out of her mouth. Silly, but true. One more way this situation was messing with her routine. Who would feed her cat?

Pete ignored her, ushering her to the unmarked police cruiser. He shoved her inside, then slammed the driver door

She didn't miss him staring out the rear-view mirror after he'd yanked his seatbelt on.

"Something *is* wrong," Nikki said.

"Nothing's wrong."

"I don't believe you."

Once again he ignored her as the engine roared to life. Irritation flared. "You make me hurry after you'd said to take my time. You pace in my living room, make me leave my cat. What the hell, Pete?" *You ignored my kiss, too.* "Tell me what's going on. What did you see?"

"Nothing to worry about." He was looking around, his eyes sweeping the parking lot, the buildings. All the parked cars.

Nikki's heart thundered and she clutched the Army duffle until her knuckles whitened.

Pete said nothing, even though his jaw was tight, his handsome face serious. The consummate detective.

She could grill him. It wouldn't matter — he'd still tell her she had nothing to worry about. Stubborn man. She wasn't a child who needed protecting — she could handle the truth.

Skin crawling, she shifted in the seat of the police car. Someone *was* watching them, following them. Nikki felt it in her bones.

"What about my grandmother?" she whispered.

"She's fine. I'll call Rodriguez and have dispatch send someone else over."

Her blood chilled. "There's someone watching us." She didn't bother making it a question.

"Maybe." Reluctant. Like he didn't want to tell her.

Nikki almost thanked him for being honest, but with his small confirmation, she froze, fear rolling over her waves.

"It's gonna be fine." Pete's voice was sure, but he didn't reach for her.

Chapter Eleven

The rest of the morning into the afternoon, he was jittery. Pete had brought her back to the station in lieu of the safe house. He'd felt eyes on them from the moment they'd hit the stairs to head up to Nikki's apartment. Who might be watching them wasn't a shocker. But *how* was the damn word that kept bouncing around in his head.

It didn't make sense they'd know who she was. He'd not been able to spot anyone following them and he'd done several loops around the city before pulling up to the secure area at the back of the PD. If they'd managed to stay with him, they knew where Nikki was now. He could only pray they wouldn't put it together she worked there.

At the station she was safe. It was a secure facility, and he didn't see Caselli's men walking up to the building in daylight.

More coffee wouldn't calm him after the rushed lunch. However, Pete rounded the corner and headed to the kitchen anyway. He'd left Nikki in her office with the Chief.

She'd insisted on working if she was going to be at the PD and he didn't blame her. Let her have normality while she could. Besides, it'd postpone the argument they were destined to have about her seeing her gram tonight. He had zero desire to risk taking her back to the rehab center. Nikki would be stubborn about it, no doubt. If he had to cave, maybe he could get Manning to back him. That way he could make sure everything was kosher at Health Solutions.

"Detective Pete Crane." The smoky female voice rolled over him like a caress.

Pete grinned as he turned around to see Special Agent Lee Dawson striding down the hall with Nikki.

Seeing them side by side jarred him. Both gorgeous, but Lee was shorter, at just a few inches past five feet. Even though they both had curves in all the right places, Nikki was the one who made his cock stir. Made his protective instincts flare. Made him want to hold her and keep her away from all the dangers in the world.

Lee could kick ass and protect herself. Like Andi.

Nikki was different. Innocent. Sorta. She did know how to kiss a man.

"How the hell are ya?" Pete put his hand out for a shake, but Lee stepped close and threw her arms around him.

Though he was surprised, the hug wasn't unwelcome. He squeezed her against him before releasing her. It was then that Lee reached for his hand for a hard shake.

"What? No trademark *howdy* for me?"

"Well, ya know, I have to change it up from time to time." Pete chuckled, then felt a hot glare in his direction — and not the good kind.

He looked over Lee's head and his gaze collided with Nikki's brown eyes for a split second. His boss's secretary wasn't glaring at him. She was staring at Lee, her auburn brows drawn, beautiful face sporting a look that could peel paint.

What the hell? Is she jealous? He was torn between pleasure and mortification.

The feel of her lips brushing his in the closet danced into his mind and he suppressed the unmanly shiver that threatened to shoot down his spine.

Nikki had to stop kissing him. Pete wouldn't be able to push her away much longer. God knew how he'd managed then. Her full breasts had been flat against his chest, her hips flush to his.

Damn. He wanted her. It was only getting worse. And he couldn't have her.

Off limits. She's off limits, not just because of what Chief said. Pin that to your brain, dude.

"You look good, Crane." Lee made a show of looking him up and down.

Nikki's glare became a scowl. If the FBI agent noticed, she didn't react.

"Thanks. Not so bad yourself." Pete threw a smile at Nikki. Unfortunately, her expression didn't soften.

Lee smiled, slow and sensual, one hand on a hip. Her dark hair swept up into a ponytail, she was dressed casually, in dark jeans and a tight navy and gray New York Yankees T-shirt. Her weapon was holstered at her waist. "Thanks, I try." She winked.

Sexy was the word that came to mind, but recognizing it didn't tamp his ardor for his little redhead.

"Looks like you're taking a page from Cole's uniform book," Pete said, gesturing to her casual outfit. The last time he'd seen her she'd been wearing what he considered work attire—khakis and a button-down. Cole, on the other hand, had never come to work in anything but jeans and a tee.

The FBI agent laughed. "I was in the field when he called. I hightailed it home to pack a bag and got my ass on a plane. You got something for me?"

"Yeah, unfortunately I do."

Lee glanced at Nikki. "Thanks for helping me find Detective Crane."

It was a dismissal, and his boss's assistant didn't like it. She nodded and squared her shoulders. Looked at him. "See you later?"

Pete smiled. "You know it, darlin'. Don't leave the station, though. I mean it, Nikki."

Her brown eyes narrowed, spearing through him.

He swallowed back a wince. Shouldn't have made his statement sound like an admonition in front of Lee—Pete wouldn't have liked if someone had done it to him.

Just when he opened his mouth to offer an apology, Nikki harrumphed and turned on her stiletto-clad heel, rounding the corner as fast as she could.

He watched her go, staring at the sway of her hips. Pete wanted to go after her.

Lee's laugh made him meet her dark eyes. "She's not a fan. What'd you do to her?"

Pete shook his head. "Nothing. She's my witness for the shooting so we're kinda...glued together right now. Caselli's scum saw her. Lucas thinks she could be a target. I've got to get her to a safe house in a bit. We were on the way, but my day got thrown a curveball."

Her gaze was keen, and she nodded. The brown of her eyes was a beautiful color, darker than Nikki's. He preferred Nikki's, but ignored that little revelation.

"Want some company?" Lee asked.

"Well, I'd say yes, but I got it. She's gonna be…temperamental when I tell her I'm not keen on taking her to see her grandmother at the place where the shooting occurred. It's a rehab center. Nikki's grandmother is recovering from a stroke."

"Lucas briefed me, but I'd like to see the site if it's all the same to you."

"Okay. Maybe it'll work out so Nikki can see her gram after all."

"I got your back, Detective." Lee patted her sidearm, and Pete smirked. "Lucas said something about a surveillance video?"

"Yeah. We need to see if we can get it. I don't think the grocery store will be uncooperative, but who knows."

"All right. Let's talk, then I'll go with."

"Sounds good." Pete resumed his original course of heading to the kitchen. "Coffee? I could use some caffeine."

"Yeah, couldn't hurt. Hey, where's my old partner anyway?"

"Hopefully checking *my* partner and their new baby out of the hospital. Today's the day."

"Ah. I forgot to say congrats." Lee's dark eyes flashed with what looked like pain, but she schooled her expression quickly and put a smile back on.

Hmmm…what's that about? She wasn't married, at least she didn't wear a ring. Pete wouldn't pry. "You can tell him later. He wants to review the footage."

Her smile slid into a genuine grin. "Of course he does." Lee laughed. "Cole Lucas couldn't let anyone else do *his* job."

"Nah, not at all. But he's helping me out, so I'm not complaining."

"Yeah, I've had to call him from time to time. He's done the same for me."

Pete poured coffee in an APD-logoed travel mug and started a new pot while he cream and sugared up.

Soon they settled into chairs at his cubicle in the CID room. "So how's NYC treating you?"

Lee smiled, taking a sip of her coffee. "Not so bad. Work's great. Me and Downs are taking them down one by one."

"Good deal. Like your partner?"

"Clint Downs isn't as pretty to look at as Cole Lucas, but he's all right. A little stuffy from time to time."

Laughing, Pete shook his head. Cole had told him Lee wasn't shy. His partner's husband always referred to Lee as *get-what-you-see*. She didn't have issue with saying how she really felt. Rather refreshing, actually. Working with her was going to be fun. "Does that translate to *he always follows the rules?*"

"To a tee. Not many gray areas, if you know what I mean. But what can I say, he's my partner." Lee shrugged. "We work well together. Kicking Caselli-ass and taking names."

"That's awesome." He and Andi were the same way. They'd been working together so long they always anticipated the other's moves, sometimes even thoughts. Andi and Pete made a true team.

He gestured to Lee's shirt. "I see you changed teams, traitor."

She arched an eyebrow. "Never was a Rangers fan, truth be told."

He gasped and clutched his chest. "How dare the native Texan say such a thing."

Lee laughed and Pete grinned. She was lighthearted and a part of him needed that. Maybe she'd even keep Nikki out of his inappropriate thoughts.

Nah... Not likely.

"So what's going on in Antioch? Tell me about this curveball to your day."

"Well," he sighed. "A body with holes in it."

* * * *

"He said *what?*" His partner's brows shot up.

"Keep your voice down, please," Pete said, gesturing with flat palms. He glanced over his shoulder, but no one entered the kitchen.

Andi frowned, rocking the tiny dark-haired baby in her arms when Micah whimpered. She didn't look away from Pete. "Seriously. I've seen him flustered. Frustrated. Yelling. Angry. Hell, even ornery. But to *threaten* you?"

"Chief didn't really threaten—"

Disbelief flashed across her blue eyes. Andi shook her head, chestnut ponytail dancing around her shoulders. "You said he used the word *badge.*"

"I didn't take it as a threat. He's just worried about her. Chief got a taste of Caselli last year, too. He wants her safe. Protected. She's as good as family to him." Pete wasn't going to go into what Chief Martin had said about Nikki's parents the other day in his office.

His partner's frown deepened. "I don't like how you're defending him."

Pete swallowed and shrugged, shoving his hands into his jeans pockets.

"What aren't you telling me?"

That I kissed her. Then I barely pushed her away when she kissed me. That it is a struggle to keep my hands to myself. "Nothing, partner. Just that I can't leave her alone. She's...stuck with me."

"Uh-huh..." Andi nodded slowly, still appraising him. Her pointed stare was a change. *He* was usually the more perceptive of the two of them. But she knew him well—too damn well.

Pete forced himself to stand still. "Hey, I didn't really get a good look at the little guy." He gestured to the infant in her arms. *Please buy the distraction.*

A brilliant smile lit his partner's beautiful face. "He's perfect," Andi whispered.

"Lemme hold him." Pete strode forward and gently took the sleeping baby from his mother.

Micah didn't stir as Pete nestled him closer to his chest. Andi grinned when he glanced at her. The baby was beautiful, like his parents. His hair curled at the ends, instead of all over like his older brother, and it was dark brown. Pete could see Andi in his little nose, but Cole's stamp was all over the kid. His mouth moved in his sleep and the hint of dimples was visible in both cheeks. "Damn, he does look like Cole."

Andi laughed. "Yup, he sure does. I hope his eyes settle into gray like Cole's, too. But Cole wants him to keep the baby blues." She pointed to her own eyes.

Pete's gaze swept her form and he had to smile. His partner radiated happiness. She glowed, gorgeous despite the fatigue under her eyes and the outfit of cotton pajama pants and matching pale blue tee with overlapping hearts on the front of it.

"Time will tell," Pete whispered, unable to tear his eyes away from Andi.

They'd been through too much to name together, but he was so glad she was happy again. Remarried to a great guy and the mother of two adorable little boys. Andi was made for Cole, as much as she was made to be a damn good cop. How she balanced everything was something to admire.

His partner had always fought for what she wanted. For her it was love… Family.

Nikki's smile flashed into his head and Pete frowned, making himself focus on the tiny bundle in his arms.

"Something wrong?" Andi asked, taking a step closer to them.

"Hmmm, no." Pete met her eyes. "He's beautiful and I'm so happy for you, partner."

She smiled, but still studied him. Like Andi didn't believe a word out of his mouth. "Thanks. I wouldn't trade him for the world."

Pete chuckled. "Not even for a full night's sleep?"

"I'm not desperate quite yet. He's only three days old. Catch me in a few weeks." Andi winked.

Laughing again, he shook his head. "No thanks. You make Cole help you this time." He didn't want to say more. Didn't want to wipe the teasing from her expression by mentioning Ethan's infancy or how many nights Pete had helped her after she'd lost her first husband.

"As if he has a choice." Andi raised her voice and giggled as Cole leaned in the kitchen doorway.

"Hey, I heard that," Cole said. He grinned, flashing dimples.

"Did I lie?"

"No, but you didn't admit you order me out of bed at gunpoint when it's my turn."

Pete chuckled. "I believe it."

Andi mock-glared, hands on her hips.

"I have the video set up if you want to check it out," Cole said. "Had an actual reason for coming in here. You know, didn't want to invade partner time." Amusement rippled across his expression.

Andi rolled her eyes as she gently retrieved their son.

Micah fussed as he awoke and she rocked him. "I'm gonna feed him in the bedroom before he starts wailing."

Pete nodded and kissed her cheek.

Cole caressed his son's little head and planted a kiss on his wife's mouth as she walked past him. He made like he was going to swat her ass, but she glared over her shoulder. Pete held back a laugh and Cole chuckled.

Nikki sat on the couch, her arms crossed over her breasts, and threw a dirty look at him when he followed Cole into the living room. Lee leaned against the wall and offered a nod as Cole grabbed the remote.

Great. Still irritated at you, dude. Pete assumed she was jealous over the way he'd interacted with Lee. From the first thing that morning, all she'd had was a tight expression for him. When he spoke, she answered curtly, in the fewest number of words possible.

What gives? The previous evening they'd shared had been pleasant. He and Lee had taken her to see her grandmother then they'd had dinner together—takeout from Dixie's—before Lee had headed back to The Covington.

Being alone with Nikki hadn't been so bad, though he'd had to glue his hands to his sides and scream at himself not to reach for her. He'd sat on the opposite end of the living room of the big house on Montgomery Street as they'd watched the late news and they'd parted ways at about eleven to get some sleep.

Separate bedrooms.

Close so he could protect her, of course, but not close enough.

Pete had imagined her naked beneath him before chiding himself and finally falling asleep. He'd had vivid dreams where he'd done a hell of a lot more than kiss her. Morning wood had been annoying, but he'd not given in to the urge for a quick release because Nikki was down the hall. Unfortunately, the condition had only worsened when he'd heard the shower in the master bedroom running.

Calling himself every name in the book, he'd managed to ignore his erection through his own shower in the guest bathroom, banishing the image of a bare Nikki with water sluicing down her supple form.

Put the brakes on that thought train. Right now. A tight crotch was never good...especially with an audience. *Think about the case, dammit.*

That morning, they'd met Lee at Marty's to get the surveillance DVD from the owner, so he hadn't taken Nikki to the station yet, despite the fact that she was dressed for work, in a pretty pink flowy skirt that stopped at her knees.

Her top matched, though it had a few different shades of pink all over it. The neckline dipped low enough to make him want to look harder. He kept making himself stare at her shoes. Even her stilettos matched.

Gorgeous didn't really cover it. The outfit gave her an air of innocence, though the way her brown eyes flashed irritation when their gazes met suggested otherwise.

Yesterday, Chief had had her spot-train one of the rookies to take her place until the case was over. Both Officer Tommy Nelson and Nikki had been less than pleased with the situation. But the PD day-to-day didn't stop because she'd witnessed a crime.

With jerky movements and abrupt statements, she'd shown the kid how to use the complicated phone system and told him where she kept everything.

Mysteriously, Chief had stayed in his office the whole time, without a word to say on the matter. Pete had perched himself in a chair to watch the interchange. Poor Nelson was going to be afraid to come to their boss's office when this was all over. Nikki's attitude fairly shouted *my territory* even though she wasn't actually rude to the young cop.

Pete would have preferred she remain at the station, safe inside when he had to be out working the case, but Chief really did want her with him.

Cole hit play and Lee came closer toward the sizable flat-screen hanging on the wall, her hands behind her back.

He took a seat beside Nikki, who stiffened and scooted away. He sighed. *No use pushing her.*

Looking at the screen, Pete shifted to the edge of the couch. The recording was clear, much more high-tech than he would have expected of a mom-and-pop grocery store that'd been in Antioch going on fifty years. It was even in color. Had to be HD.

Wow. Hopefully we'll get what we need.

Cole fast-forwarded the first images—the manager opening for the day, cashiers coming to work, the first customers of the day. He didn't stop until the time stamp in the right-hand corner said sixteen thirty. A half-hour before Nikki got off work.

People came and went, until Pete saw a familiar figure. "Stop. There's my dead guy. Billy Madden."

Cole rewound a few seconds then punched play with vigor.

They watched Pete's now dead CI walk into the store.

He wasn't alone.

Nikki gasped and inclined forward.

Less than two steps behind Billy Madden, two men entered Marty's like they owned the place. Both were dressed in dark clothing. Both wore sunglasses. Both had dark hair, one short, the other scraggly.

"That's them. It's really them," Nikki breathed.

Pete reached for her hand and squeezed. Instead of pulling away with a snide comment like she'd done all day, she let him stay close, entwining their fingers. He wanted to throw his arm around her shoulders and pull her to his side, but he didn't. Her hand would have to be enough. At least he could comfort her.

"What the hell?" Cole muttered, his gaze intent on the three men frozen on the screen.

"Billy's with Caselli's guys?" Pete mused.

"Guess now we know what his *big score* was," Lee said.

Cole got inventive with curse words, shaking his head.

Pete smirked, glancing at his buddy, then back at the giant TV. He didn't need to ask if Cole recognized the two thugs with his former CI.

"Luciano Marchetti. Goes by Luca. He's a nobody to Caselli. Lower than Maldonado was."

"Trying to make a name for himself?" Pete asked.

Cole dragged his hand down his face. "I guess. Maybe Caselli is giving him a shot to replace Bruno."

"Makes sense," Lee said. "With the guys we've taken out, plus new info, he hasn't replaced Bruno Gallo. Not really. He's tried a few guys out, but they haven't done it for him." She took a step closer, peering intently at Cole's TV. "The other guy... Isn't that Mickey Donati?"

Cole hit rewind. The three figures strolled forward again in slow-mo. He hit pause. "Yup. Caselli's freakin' nephew. Another shocker, as far as I'm concerned."

"Yeah," Pete said. "Sending his blood..."

"Oh, Caselli doesn't give a shit that they're related," Cole said, meeting his gaze.

"Then why?"

"He's a flippin' idiot. Dumb as a box of rocks, for real. And young. Probably not even twenty-five." Cole made a face.

Pete swallowed back a wince and forced his eyes on the TV, studiously *not* looking at Nikki. She wasn't twenty-five yet either. Her birthday was a month away, in August. Guess information about her was a perk of taking her statement and having to write a report. But it made wanting her even worse. *Letch.*

"We brought him in for a chat a few months ago. He didn't give us anything, but when we saw him about a week later, his arm was in a cast and he had a nice limp. Caselli didn't have him killed, but someone beat the shit out him. Probably at his order," Lee said.

"Guess the little blood tie kept him alive, though," Pete said.

"I'm just shocked he would entrust such an *important* job to these two. I mean, he wanted Berto and his woman dead, right?" Cole gestured to the TV. "Mickey's only in the organization at all 'cause he's Caselli's sister's kid. Now Luca, on the other hand, fancies himself as the world's biggest badass. Not surprised he took out your dude."

"He had to be the driver," Nikki said.

Cole and Lee swung their heads around.

Nikki squirmed next to him and he squeezed her hand again. She inched closer but he still didn't allow himself to put his arm around her.

"Good thinking," Pete said, giving her a smile. He almost teased her about being his junior detective after all, but with the mood she'd been in all day, he didn't bother. Probably wouldn't coax the smile he was dying to see.

"Makes sense. You said you saw these two leave Health Solutions?" Cole's tone was gentle as he addressed her.

Nikki sucked in a breath and nodded. Her lovely breasts rose and fell and Pete made himself look away.

He met Cole's steel eyes. "Is Marchetti smart?"

"He's pretty ruthless, but Caselli's never noticed him."

"Hmmm." Lee cocked her head to one side, her dark hair shifting around her shoulders. "His name doesn't signify. But we've been working our way through his guys. Maybe all he has left is bottom of the barrel."

"I didn't interact much with him when I was under, but I hung out with the main players once Caselli considered me made. He *was* one of the ones that came after me and Maldonado when I was trying to bring him in."

"So Luca here took out Billy Madden," Pete said.

"I'd bet money on it," Cole said. "More likely him than Caselli's nephew."

Lee sighed. "Makes sense. But how did he get mixed up with Luca and Mickey in the first place? And why?"

"I guess we'll just hafta find out," Pete said.

Chapter Twelve

Nikki scowled and slammed the dish in the sink. Then chided herself. What did she care if Pete needed to have a word with Lee? *Alone.*

Shaking her head, she sighed and ran the water until it was too hot. The bite and burn on her skin made her suck in a breath. But it was good — like a reality check.

"I don't care anyway. Let him talk to *her.*"

She grabbed a sponge and started scrubbing the frying pan she'd used to make dinner for the three of them. "It's not like I want to be alone with him anyway." *Yeah, like that gets you anywhere, stupid.*

Last night, he'd stayed as far away as he could manage while still being in the same room. Like she was diseased. He'd barely said goodnight when they'd parted ways and had left her to deal with trying to sleep in a strange place. The house was nice. Sprawling. But it wasn't her apartment. It wasn't *home.*

Nikki got the message. Despite the kiss at Health Solutions and the way he looked at her with heat in that green gaze, Pete didn't want her. He'd constantly moved away when she'd scooted closer. He'd pulled away from her kiss. And when the FBI agent had come into town, it'd gotten worse, more pronounced.

Maybe Pete was into Lee.

They'd been awfully friendly in the hallway at the PD. Every interaction, all day yesterday—not to mention today—was natural. Laughing, joking, even when talking about the case. Obviously they liked each other.

Her stomach clenched. *No.* But why did she care anyway? It was like she was...jealous...or something.

Nikki groaned. She *did* care. And *that* pissed her off.

She squirted dish soap onto the Teflon and scrubbed harder than necessary on the non-stick surface. Her fingertips smarted.

"Dammit," she whispered.

"The dishwasher works, you don't have to do that."

Nikki yelped and dropped the pan. It clanged in the stainless steel sink, making her ears ring. She turned around, wet hand clutching the fabric of her tee over her heart. Her pulse raced.

Pete stepped forward, running a hair through his thick blond locks, and winced. "Sorry. I always seem to make you jump."

She tried to convince her heartbeat to slow. Pete's expression softened and her face warmed. Swallowing back a gulp, Nikki forced words out of her mouth. "It's okay."

Their gazes locked and she was swept into him. Intensity and fire were in his eyes. A zing of awareness sparked between them and Nikki moved closer. Felt the heat coming off his body. But then Pete stepped back and squared his shoulders. Looked down at his dark cowboy boots. Shifted on his feet like a teenager caught doing something wrong.

What the hell?

He cleared his throat and finally met her eyes again. "Thanks for making dinner." His tone was natural. As if the moment they'd just shared didn't signify.

"What's wrong with you?" Nikki blurted.

Pete stared, shoving his hands in his jeans pockets. He bunched up his broad shoulders and opened his mouth then closed it.

"Well?" She dried her hands with a dish towel then tossed it on the counter behind her. Propped her hands on her hips and stared right back. Dared him to be honest with her.

"What are you talking about?" His voice cracked.

Nikki narrowed her eyes, irritation flaring. "You're hot and cold. Frankly, it's driving me crazy." There. She'd said it. Now what?

Her heart thundered in her ears as she waited for her detective to speak.

He didn't.

Pete took a step forward. She didn't move away.

Nikki looked up into his handsome face. His cheeks were ruddy and his eyes carried the same intensity he'd regarded her with only moments before.

A groan tore from his lips then she was against the hard wall of his chest. Her breath was forced out as her breasts flattened into his pecs and he wrapped his arms around her.

Her hip hit the edge of the sink as Pete's mouth came down on hers, but Nikki didn't care. He was kissing her again, and it was heaven. She snaked her arms around his neck and pushed closer, opening her mouth as he slanted his for a deeper kiss.

Proof that Pete wanted her—at least physically—pressed into her belly, so she rocked into him and kissed him harder.

In a tangle of lips and limbs, they stumbled into the living room without breaking the seal of their mouths. They landed on the couch.

Pete's weight on top of her stole her breath all over again, but she didn't care. She kept kissing him, winding her tongue around his as he cupped her breasts through her favorite printed T-shirt. Her nipples peaked and she arched into him, needing more. The warmth of his big hands seeped through the cotton material, but it wasn't enough.

Nikki wanted his hands on her bare flesh. Wanted his lips on her. Needed him to suck her into his hot mouth. Everywhere.

She moaned his name when finally he yanked the front of her shirt up and brushed her belly. Wiggling to help him free the rest of it from her jeans, her thigh rubbed the erection straining against his own denim.

Pete groaned. "Darlin'…"

Nikki closed her eyes and sighed. The endearment was a caress that slid across her skin. Making her as hot as his hands.

Her sex throbbed and he hadn't even touched her there yet.

"Touch me, Pete." The whisper sounded desperate to her ears, but her detective didn't make her wait.

Air hit her at all angles as he pushed her shirt up, exposing her bra and her hips when he tugged her zipper down and pushed the denim out of the way. Without preamble, he shoved his hand into her pants, pushing into her panties. But he leaned down at the same time, popping one breast out of the frilly pink lace cup. He fondled her hard nipple with nimble fingers before enclosing it with his hot mouth and teasing with his tongue.

She moaned and threw her head back, her body swallowed by multiple sensations. Pleasure rolled over her and she writhed.

His fingertips on her clit had her trembling and begging for more. Nikki lifted up, rocking into the sure movements that circled the sensitive bundle of nerves. Desire flooded her. She was wet and achy. For him.

Pete was relentless, rubbing until her sex pulsed from the inside out. She needed him lower, inside her.

He moved his tongue in tandem with his seeking fingers and she clenched her teeth to keep from crying out.

As if he'd read her mind, he slipped one finger lower, parting her slick folds and dipping inside her. The confines of her jeans didn't allow for deep thrusts, but the friction was enough to bring her close to the edge.

Nikki called his name and buried her hands in his hair.

He rocked forward, his erection hard and long against her hip through his jeans. It wasn't enough. She wanted to see him, touch him. Have him inside her.

Pete's teeth teased her nipple and she screamed. It was too much. She arched into him and gripped his thick shoulders with both hands, nails digging in.

As the orgasm roared over Nikki, the first gunshot shattered the living room window.

"You have *got* to be fucking kidding me," Luca spat. That fucking idiot had actually taken a shot at the house.

Mickey moved in after he'd shot out the bay window facing the street in soccer-mom-land, firing his forty several more times at the two-story brick monster of a house. Caselli's stupid nephew ran right up the porch steps and kicked in the front door.

"Fuck. Fuck. *Fuck!*" Luca slammed the driver side door of the pickup he'd jacked to follow his colleague around. It hadn't taken him long to find him today, but Mickey didn't know he was disobeying a direct order from the boss.

For the past few days, Mickey had been leaving on his own, following the redheaded chick, obviously. He'd found her without Luca's help. Small town or not, maybe he wasn't so stupid after all.

It'd taken Luca all damn day to find him after he'd gone out to the Circle Bar B.

Mickey wouldn't let the *kill-the-witnesses* thing drop. He hadn't been all that concerned that Luca had seen law enforcement on Berto's property. He'd just insisted they'd kill Berto as his uncle had commanded. In due time. 'Don't worry about it,' Mickey had said. Like *he* was running this show. That alone had pissed Luca off enough to stay close-lipped about Caselli's order to leave the witnesses alone.

"Fuck. That." Yanking his Beretta out of his waistband, Luca pulled back the slide to chamber a round, cursing in English and Italian.

He was really going to have to kill the boss's nephew.

There was no other choice. Good damn thing he had the balls to do it. Would even take pleasure in it. Mickey had always been a little shit.

Mickey yelled and several more gunshots went off.

Someone in the house was returning fire. Two windows shattered. Luca ducked and dodged as he jumped onto the porch and flattened himself against the house next to the open door.

A deep male voice shouted orders and Luca whipped into the house. Mickey was facing off with what had to be a cop. The blond guy commanded Caselli's nephew to lower his weapon, but of course his *friend* was non-compliant.

Luca did a quick visual sweep of the room. Glass everywhere. All four of the windows were either sporting holes or completely gone. The closest exit was the front door. Stairs to the right and a dark hallway to the left. There was probably a back door through the kitchen but he wouldn't chance the unknown.

The redheaded chick was lying flat on her back behind a large L-shaped brown sofa. Her legs were obscured, as if she'd been running for cover but hadn't quite made it. The cop was crouched in front of her, gun raised.

Her long red hair was spread out like a curtain on the carpet and her head was to one side, neck at an odd angle. There was a starburst of darker red spreading through the gray fabric of her tee but he couldn't tell where she was actually hit, side or shoulder. Arm?

Holy shit, her jeans were open, and her shirt was up. Too bad he was too far away to see her tits. Looked like Mickey had interrupted a hell of a good time.

She was too still. That stupid fucker had probably killed her.

"God damn it," Luca muttered, raising his Beretta.

The cop cursed savagely when he saw Luca, but didn't move his gun off Mickey. He didn't need to worry about lil' ol' Luca.

"I told you to stay away from this," Luca barked.

"What the fuck are you doing here?" Mickey growled, but didn't move his gun away from the cop, either. Barely even spared him a glance.

Good. Won't be hard to fix this.

The cop watched them like a tennis match.

Luca heard sirens and frowned. Mickey's dark eyes widened as Luca aimed, but he didn't speak or beg. Maybe he was too stupid to realize what Luca intended.

He pulled the trigger and dropped Mickey like the sack of shit he was. One shot to the head and Caselli's idiot nephew was dead.

"Gotta go," Luca said to the cop, raising his hands in submission, despite the Beretta in his right one. "Sorry about the mess."

The cop took a few shots at him, but Luca turned on his heel and beat feet to the door, slamming it behind him even though it wouldn't stop a bullet. He leaped down the three porch stairs then ran down the street. The truck he'd stolen was no good for round two.

Tires screeched to a halt and sirens blared as three police cars stopped outside the house. Luca ducked behind the side of the closest residence, peeking around in time to hear the pounding of boots up the porch steps and the shouts of "Police!"

He didn't stay to watch.

Chapter Thirteen

Panic surged like never before in his life as Pete hit his knees beside Nikki. His hands shook as he holstered his weapon, and it had taken a couple of tries. She was too still.

"No." The whisper was anguished even to his own ears. He pressed two fingers to her neck. Her pulse pushed back, thundering under his fingertips. "Thank God," he breathed.

Cops poured into the living room and Pete took a moment to yank Nikki's shirt down over her exposed breasts and zip her jeans.

This was all his fault. *Selfish bastard.*

"Crane, we've secured the perimeter. Suspect is nowhere in sight." Officer Eric Bartlett holstered his gun and came closer.

"Ambulance just pulled up. Are you hit?" Chloe asked as she strode into the room. She kneeled, joining him on the carpet.

"No. Just Nikki." His voice cracked and he had to clear his throat — twice.

"This one's dead," another cop called out.

He looked over his shoulder to see one of the guys squatted down next to Mickey Donati.

"Pete, she's gonna be okay. Breathing is great, heart rate is strong." The sergeant pushed Nikki's red locks out of her face after she checked vitals. "Looks like she has a bump on the head. Bullet hit her right arm, but it could have been worse. "

Two paramedics shouldered them out of the way and Pete stood. Numbness swallowed him whole as he forced himself to back up. His arms shook but he ignored them and locked his knees so his legs wouldn't wobble.

What the fuck happened? The question didn't go unanswered as his conscience fired back. *You were thinking with your dick. And she got hurt, asshole. Shot. She got shot.*

"Chief Martin and Agent Dawson are on their way. You'll have to give up your weapon. Ballistics will need it." Chloe's voice pulled him out of his head. "I'll help Manning or whoever takes over if he benches you 'cause of the shooting."

"I didn't kill him."

Her pale blue eyes widened, and she cocked her head to one side, shifting her light brown ponytail. "What?"

"Luciano Marchetti killed him."

"What the hell?" the sergeant muttered.

"That's what I said."

Nikki moaned as the two paramedics raised the gurney and Pete jolted forward, shoving the guy out of his way.

"Pete?" Her groggy voice made his heart leap.

He grabbed the hand of her uninjured arm and met her wide brown eyes. "I'm here. Right here. You're okay, darlin'." He wanted to kiss her but didn't.

Chided himself for the urge. Thoughts like that had gotten her hurt in the first place.

"Pounding headache. My arm hurts..." She moved her head back and forth on the cushion of the gurney.

"You got shot, darlin', but it's not bad. Promise."

"Detective, we need to take her."

Pete wanted to growl at the stupid medic, but he didn't. He backed up, reluctantly letting go of her hand.

"Pete, don't leave me." Her panicked tone made his stomach flutter.

He glared until the paramedic stopped the gurney again and moved out of his way. He caressed Nikki's cheek and smiled down at her. "You couldn't make me leave you, sweetness. I'm right here."

Her expression softened and she sighed, easing her gorgeous brown eyes shut. "Thank you, Detective."

Pete's heart went into overdrive as he stepped back and let the paramedics take her from the living room. He glanced at Chloe.

"Go with her. I got this. I'll talk to Chief and send your FBI agent your way. I already got my guys canvassing."

He nodded, because if he spoke he'd say something stupid.

* * * *

Pete watched her feet dangle off the bed in the emergency room as the doctor patched up her arm. It wasn't bad. A graze that had torn the skin of her right biceps. Some stitches should do it.

After he'd held her hand in the ambulance, she'd come around and calmed. Nikki had thanked him and kissed his knuckles. Making him feel like more of an ass.

He should feel better that she wasn't badly hurt, but guilt swallowed him whole.

Your fault. Your fault.

The two accusatory words reverberated in his brain, becoming a crappy mantra of blame he couldn't quash.

He'd lost control. Of himself. Of the situation. Sucked into her. And she'd been hurt. It could have been worse than her arm. She could be dead.

Pain constricted his chest that all the breaths in the world failed to fix.

Failed was a good word, too. He'd failed in his duties to protect her. He'd failed in his vow to himself not to touch her. Kiss her. Hold her.

All-around failure.

She smiled over the doctor's shoulder and Pete wanted to tell her not to bother. It sure as hell didn't fix the pain in his gut...in his heart.

The sweet curve of her lips reminded him how she'd tasted. The feel of her mouth under his. Her every supple curve against his body.

Seeing her climax, the flush on her cheeks, heavy-lidded eyes of chocolate, the heaving of her gorgeous naked breasts as she'd panted through it. The hard little buds of her nipples and the feel of her skin on his tongue.

He'd almost come in his damn jeans, and she hadn't even touched him. He wanted her to touch him, wanted her hands on his bare skin, pulling him close. He ached for her. And it was wrong. For so many reasons.

"Pete, I'm okay." Her voice was even and calm.

"I know it," he croaked.

"Then why do you look like your best friend died?"

"You're good as new, Miss Harper." The young doctor's statement prevented Pete from answering Nikki—*Thank God.*

The guy in green scrubs patted her uninjured shoulder and flashed a smile that could have only been considered flirty.

Pete bit back a growl. "Can we go then?"

"As soon as the nurse checks you out, Detective." The doctor appraised him with wide blue eyes.

Even Nikki was looking at him with an arched brow and an expression that said *What's your problem?*

Shit, shoulda dialed back the tone. Pete cleared his throat. "Thanks."

"Do you need any pain meds?" the doctor asked Nikki.

She shook her head. "If I need something, I'll get it from the drug store. High-powered stuff always makes me feel like crap. I'd rather deal."

He nodded and excused himself.

Pete couldn't help the glare he sent the doctor's way. He pushed off the wall he'd been holding up and went to her bedside.

"Hey, dude. He wasn't the one who shot me." Nikki's tone was amused. Her head was cocked to one side, as if she were trying to figure him out.

He shifted on his feet. Opened his mouth to answer, but his phone blared from his pocket. "Crane," he said without looking at the screen. He couldn't tear his eyes away from Nikki's brown ones.

"How's Nikki? And what the *hell* happened, Crane?" Chief Martin shouted in his ear without preamble.

Pete winced. He'd known this was coming. He preferred the conversation over the phone rather than have his boss scream in his face in person, for sure. "She's okay."

Nikki's gaze sharpened. No doubt she could hear Chief.

"What the hell happened?" The repeated question was at the same volume and Nikki echoed his wince.

"Caselli's guys burst in, boss."

"Where the hell were you?"

Seriously, Chief was going to lose his voice if he didn't stop screaming. Pete held the iPhone away from his head. "We were in the living room. Together."

Nikki averted her eyes. Pete sighed as their boss's rant continued. There wasn't much he could say. Chief couldn't beat the shit out of him — mentally anyway — more than he already was.

Then the tirade started in on Pete himself.

Nikki snatched his cell out of his hand. "Knock it off," she barked.

He reared back at her sharp tone and tight expression.

Damn, his little redhead was pissed.

"First of all, I am fine. Detective Crane has done everything possible to protect me. Taken me everywhere with him for three days. He's not psychic. Even you thought they'd make a go for me. This isn't Pete's fault. So knock it off, before he tells you to screw yourself and quits. Then who'll protect me?"

Silence on the other end of the phone.

No. Way.

Pete bit back a smile. He almost thanked her for the vote of confidence, but he kind of agreed with his boss. He *had* failed.

Dammit.

He sighed and dragged his hand through his hair for the hundredth time that night.

After a solid thirty seconds of silence, their boss cleared his throat. "I just want to make sure you're all right."

"I am." Nikki softened her voice and met Pete's eyes finally. "I have no doubt Pete will keep me safe."

"Can I talk to Crane—please." The *please* was definitely an after-thought.

"As long as you won't yell at him."

Chief said nothing.

"I'm here," Pete said.

"You didn't kill Donati?"

"No, sir. Marchetti did. Came right in and popped him."

"Shit."

"Yeah, pretty much what I said, except he kinda saved our asses. Close-quarters shootout is where I was at," Pete said, shaking his head.

"Dawson's on her way to the hospital. She's pretty puzzled, too. Get with Lucas in the a.m. and see what the hell he thinks. But tell him to stay home. I don't want to see him at the station. There are phones for a reason. And check on Alberto Carbone. I called Health Solutions and sent another officer over. Tell Nikki her grandmother is fine. I also doubled the guard on Maria Mata at the hospital."

"You working my case, boss?" The words were out of his mouth before he paused to think about them. He shouldn't have pushed the man when his girl had had to save his ass.

His girl?

Nope. She'd never be his girl. *Thought we'd decided to forget everything?* And since when had he started referring to himself as *we?* Pete was losing it.

"You saying no to my help?"

"No way, boss. Sorry."

Chief harrumphed. "Keep me posted."

"Will do."

"Take Nikki to your place tonight. Best we've got on short notice."

"My place?" Pete choked on his words.

Nikki narrowed her eyes, but said nothing.

"That an issue?" his boss asked.

"No, sir."

* * * *

"'I told you to stay away from this.' He said that?" Lee frowned, leaning forward on the edge of Pete's black leather ottoman.

He nodded.

Nikki yawned loudly from her seat beside him.

Pete glanced over his shoulder and met her misty eyes. "Why don't you go up to bed, darlin'? Take mine. I'll crash on the couch. Lee, you can have the guest room upstairs."

They'd agreed that the FBI agent would stay at his house, too. At least for the night. He sure appreciated the second gun. Maybe she should move in. He might be able to keep his hands—and other body parts—off Nikki if there was constant...supervision. Lee's presence hadn't dimmed his desire for the redhead, though.

"It's been a long night for us all," Lee said gently, looking at Nikki.

"I don't want to take your bed, Pete."

Yeah, he didn't want her in his bed, either. Not without him wrapped around her, anyway. "Go ahead. Get some sleep. My couch isn't so bad." He patted the black leather cushion between them. Oversized and comfortable, it could actually sleep two side by side. He shut out the picture of the two of them curled up on it together the moment his mind coughed it up.

Reluctantly, Nikki stood. She stretched and her ample breasts hitched higher. Her shirt exposed the soft skin of her belly.

Pete itched to touch her. Take her up to his room, lay her out in his bed and make love— *Knock. It. Off.*

"You win, I'm tired." She yawned a second time, and hid it behind her hand.

"Night, Nikki," Lee said. "Get some Zs, girl."

"Night, Agent Dawson. Night, Pete." Her brown gaze lingered his way and a tremor shot down his spine. He had to force his eyes away.

"Call me Lee, please." The FBI agent flashed a smile.

Nikki nodded, her delectable mouth curving up.

Watching their polite conversation helped a little. "Night, darlin'." Pete made his hands remain in his lap. He didn't *need* to touch her. Really.

He stared as she ascended the stairs, swallowing hard as her jeans hugged her ass with every step. Wished he could see more when she disappeared at the top.

Lee cleared her throat and when their eyes met, one corner of her mouth shot up. She said nothing as she studied him.

Pete shifted on the edge of his couch. "I didn't have the heart to call Cole tonight."

"Yeah, I didn't either. There's always the morning."

Score one for him. She'd bought his distraction. "There's so much we need to piece together." He sighed.

"Sorry I wasn't there for ya tonight." Lee's tone was full of regret.

Pete grabbed her hand. "Hell, no, don't you try to bring any of this on yourself. We were done for the night. It's cool."

"I should've stayed at the safe house with you."

Yes, she should have. Then again, if she *had*, he wouldn't have been able to taste Nikki. Hold her, kiss her like he'd been dying to all day.

Dumbass, she wouldn't have gotten hurt if Lee had been there. What's happening to me?

Sucking in a breath, he banished the internal monologue and ordered himself to get it together.

"Well, in your defense, I did chase you off. I knew he'd followed us when I took her to her apartment, but I wasn't able to spot him. I was a fool to think we were safe."

"Not a fool. But hey, now it's one down, one to go."

Pete managed a small laugh. "I know it. I guess I should thank the guy before we cuff him?"

"Yeah...about that..." Lee's eyebrows were knitted.

"What is it?"

"I called Downs to brief him when Lucas told us who we're up against."

"And?"

"My partner said pretty much the same thing as Lucas about our dude. Ruthless. But he also gleaned some info from the inside this morning. There's been some more movement. We were right about something."

"Vying for second in command?"

"Yup. I knew you were a bright one." Lee flashed a smile.

"I hear a *but*."

"Got me again, Detective." She nodded. "Luciano Marchetti won't come quietly. If he fails to kill Berto—like he failed with the guy's wife—he doesn't have much to go back to. Plus my gut tells me Caselli's gonna be pissed about Donati. Blood's thicker than water and all that."

"Right. So this is Marchetti's final chance, right?"

"That's what me and Downs think. I'm sure Lucas will agree when we conference in the morning."

"So we're looking at a shootout—at best."

"I don't see him offing himself, so yeah."

Pete sighed and reclined back. "We'll be careful. And bring a body bag."

"I like the way you think."

"Cole's always said you were a badass." He winked.

"I prefer the term *practical*." Lee laughed. "Besides, you said it, not me."

He smirked and Lee chuckled again.

Chapter Fourteen

Pete sighed and rolled over. He'd woken from the third naked-Nikki dream, hard and aching, unable to banish his memories. No matter he'd decided that was exactly what he needed to do.

The leather couch creaked as he shifted his weight, willing his cock to soften. *Nada.* Ignored all commands. Throbbed for attention. But not from *his* hand.

Releasing a breath, he lay flat on his back. His stupid blanket was tented. He stared at the vaulted ceiling of his living room. Better than the safe house?

Hell no. Nikki's in your bed. And you are not.

Trying to make himself think like a cop, he rewound the evening in his head. Unfortunately, the first thing that popped up was Nikki's soft bare skin. Her taste on his tongue. Her feel beneath his fingertips. She'd been so wet for him. Tight. Hot. She'd come hard, her sex squeezing his fingers like a glove.

His cock pulsed.

"Dammit." Pete punched the back of his couch. "Seriously, think of something else."

Be. A. Cop.

Closing his eyes, he put himself back in the house on Montgomery. Heard the gunshots, heard the window shatter. The door had exploded like a bomb. Instant sensory overload.

He'd jumped off the couch and pulled his forty-caliber SIG, ordering Nikki to cover. When she'd screamed, his heart had stopped. Pete had squeezed the trigger to return fire, only to find her unconscious halfway behind the couch.

Blood. All he'd seen was *her* blood.

When the bastard had shown himself, they'd entered stand-off territory. Pete had recognized Mickey Donati immediately. His first thought at seeing the guy alone was that Luciano Marchetti must be at the rehab center to finish off Gram. Thank God that hadn't been true.

Marchetti had been ballsy—killing Donati and not even taking one shot at Pete or Nikki.

I told you to stay away from this.

"What's your game, Luca?" The impression he'd gotten from Cole was that his partner's husband hadn't known the guy really well. Hopefully he'd still have an insight.

Sitting up and stretching, Pete swallowed back a yawn and pushed his shoulders into the cushions of the couch. The house made a settling noise and he looked around his living room. There was nothing, no danger, but as his eyes swept the large room, he couldn't help but feel an emptiness in his gut.

He'd had the big house built when he'd made detective at the age of twenty-four. Naïvely, he'd imagined it filled with a family—someday.

Then he'd broken up with the first serious girlfriend he'd had after college. Less than two months after he'd moved in. She'd never set foot in the door. Turned down his marriage proposal as well as his home.

That'd sealed the deal. Changed his mind about wanting *things* for himself. For his life...his future.

He hated to admit it, but even years later, her rejection smarted. How could he have read her so wrong? He'd been devastated. Cara had ripped his heart into a million pieces. Then she'd put it in a blender and handed it back. He hadn't had a relationship since then.

Pete didn't see the wife and kids in the distant picture anymore. Besides, Andi and Ethan had always seemed enough, filling the void, even though they didn't belong to him.

'Everything happens for a reason.' How many times had his brother, Nate, said that to him? Who was supposed to be the older brother, anyway? The guy sounded like their mother *way* too much.

The four-bedroom house was just a building filled with stuff he'd accumulated over the past ten years. Too big for one person, but it was his.

Shaking his head, Pete wandered into the kitchen. Sprawling and pristine, with stainless steel appliances, his kitchen was a cook's dream. He hardly ever used the place. Preparing meals for one was depressing.

The breakfast nook sat barren in the corner, but he ignored it and opened the refrigerator. When nothing food-wise appealed, he closed the icebox, encased in the darkness of the room. Not even light from the street lamp leaked inside. The clock on the microwave said it was just past three.

Great, the morning was going to suck.

His feet took him up the stairs without thought. Pete paused on the top step. The room Lee slept in was at the end of the hall on the right. Farthest away from the master suite. The door was closed.

His office was made up in the smallest of the bedrooms, and it was to his immediate left. The door was open and the nightlight on the wall illuminated his desk in the corner. Usually left neat and tidy, as he didn't spend much time there, preferring to use his laptop in the comfort of the recliner in the living room.

The silence could have swallowed him whole as he walked down the hall, staring at the door of his own bedroom.

Nikki's in there. Go back downstairs.

But his hand turned the doorknob anyway.

She slept on her side facing away from him, her beautiful red hair loose and spread out on his pillows. His masculine black and blue striped comforter covered her, but one arm rested on top of it, as if she was too warm.

Pete stared, frozen just inside the room.

Nikki belonged in his bed.

Shaking himself, he hastily shut—and locked—his bedroom door.

Seriously, get out of here.

Evidently his conscience was in the off position, because Pete went over to the bed.

She was in a deep sleep, her breathing even, the rise and fall of her gorgeous breasts barely visible beneath his blanket. But he knew what they looked like. Craved touching them, touching her. Tasting her.

After staring down at her for what seemed like hours, he chided himself and scooted around to the other side of the king-sized bed—oddly enough, the normal side he slept on. He sat as gingerly as he could as to not disturb her.

What are you doing?

Pete sucked in a breath and covered his face with both hands. What an apropos question. But his conscience should have inserted a *hell* in there somewhere.

Nikki made a sound in her sleep and he stilled on the edge of the bed.

The rustle of the comforter and sheets made him close his eyes.

Go downstairs. Now.

"Pete?" Her whisper was heavy with sleep.

He couldn't look at her.

More shifting of the bedding and Pete could feel the heat coming off her sleep-warmed body through his ribbed tank.

God, he wanted her. His cock jumped, making the crotch of his navy sweats move. The slight friction only made the ache in his balls worse.

"Is something wrong?"

Finally, he managed to shift his body and look at her. He propped his bent knee on the bed, sitting half on, half off. Hopefully she wouldn't notice his britches. "No," Pete croaked.

"Okay." Nikki yawned.

Innocent. Adorable. Beautiful.

From the glow of the nightlight on the wall as well as the dim illumination coming in from the window, he could see her sleep-tousled red locks resting in waves around her shoulders, teasing him as much as her creamy skin did. Her pajamas consisted of a skimpy pale green tank that didn't leave much to the imagination.

Not that you need imagination. You have a great memory.

His cock stood at attention all over again as he fantasized about what she had on below the blankets and how fast he could get it off her. "I should go. I'll see you in a few hours."

"What time is it?"

"After three."

"Oh. Late. Are you sure you're all right?" She sat up and the comforter slipped to her waist, exposing the curve of her braless breasts through soft cotton. He could see the dark outline of her nipples.

"Yup," Pete forced out, tearing his eyes away from what he shouldn't look at.

As he went to stand, Nikki's hand shot to his forearm. "Don't go."

"I need to."

"Why?" Her brown gaze was earnest.

It's the right thing to do. But he couldn't say the words when she looked at him like that.

He should open his mouth and apologize for what'd happened at the safe house—between them as well as the shooting. Needed to explain it couldn't happen again. No kissing. No touching. And most definitely no sex. Which was exactly what would've happened if Caselli's guys hadn't burst in.

Pete had let his guard down and she'd been shot. *His fault.*

Tell her all that. She deserves to know.

"It's late. I really should go."

"All the more reason to stay. It's your bed after all." She took a deep breath that had him gulping. Nikki lifted his comforter to invite him into his bed. "I don't want to be alone." The tremble in her voice made Pete snap to attention.

Honest vulnerability. Also his fault.

Nikki was scared, and he was the biggest jerk in the world.

Instead of pushing off the bed and leaving, Pete pulled his other leg up. He got under the covers beside her, his stomach fluttering at her smile.

"Pete…" His name on her lips was breathless as she moved closer to him.

His cock twitched.

"Y-y-yeah?" He cleared his throat. *Man up and keep your hands to yourself.*

"Can you hold me?"

Shit. Kill. Me. Now.

* * * *

A knock jolted him awake. But something solid and warm kept him from sitting up. Light streamed in from his bedroom window and Pete cursed not drawing the curtains the night before. How had he forgotten that?

The sleepy female moan stirred his cock again. Nikki had her head on his chest, her arm flung across his middle like she owned him. Somehow the notion appealed, but then reality swallowed him whole.

Nikki was in his bed.

Shit. Shit.

When the night came barreling back into his head, Pete blew out a breath. He hadn't had sex with her. That he would have remembered. But holding her…falling asleep with her in his arms…it was right.

Knock knock. This time it was more insistent.

Glancing at the clock on his nightstand, he winced at the offensive time of five after six and gently disengaged himself from Nikki.

She sighed in her sleep and burrowed into his pillow. Pete smiled a little and wandered to his bedroom door. Braced himself for Lee.

He looked down and cursed his hard-on, willing it to soften. No juice. His cock was saying good morning.

Maybe she won't notice. Yeah. Right. His sweats made it pretty obvious.

"Sorry." Lee looked him up and down, her gaze stopping for a split second below his waist.

Sonofa — Hiding half behind the door hadn't worked.

"I looked for you downstairs, but..." Her expression was chagrined, and her eyes darted everywhere but his face — and his crotch, of course.

Pete shifted on his feet anyway. Like his mom had caught him in bed with Nikki. "It's not what it looks like," he blurted.

"Uh. I needed a towel. About to take a shower, if that's all right with you. None in the bathroom." At least she looked at him, but Lee's dark eyes called him a liar.

"Shit. Of course. Sorry, I don't have any in there. Let me get you one from my bathroom." Leaving the door ajar, he sprinted into his bathroom and grabbed two gray towels.

"Thanks," Lee said.

"Welcome. Eggs in the fridge. I'll make us something to eat in a few."

She nodded, pausing as if she was going to say something.

"Really, it's not what it looks like," Pete said, swallowing back a wince at his defensive tone.

Lee gave a half-smile. "See you downstairs."

He groaned as he closed the door. *Fuck. Today's gonna be a blast.* Leaning on the cool wood, he shook his head. The hard door at his back bit into his shoulders. Instead of being an irritant, it felt good. Grounded him.

Should have never come into the room — even if Lee hadn't been down the hall.

Nikki yawned and stretched, arching her back so he saw her breasts first.

Great, like morning wood needs more help.

She sat up, rubbing sleep from her eyes. "Morning." Her sleepy smile had his stomach fluttering. Nikki looked warm and happy and all he wanted to do was crawl back into his bed and hold her some more.

Kiss her. Get her out of her skimpy sleep clothes — *Knock it off.*

Pete pushed off the door and forced himself to return her smile. "Morning."

"Sleep well?" she asked, her expression becoming shy.

Damn, could she get more endearing? He cleared his throat. "Yes, I did. Towels are in the bathroom, if you want to take a shower. I'm gonna head downstairs. Told Lee I'd make breakfast."

"Are you sure you don't want to shower first? It's your place and all." She stared, a slight smile on her face.

Was she going to ask him to join her?

Pete swallowed back a gulp. His cock stirred and he fought the urge to whirl away from her. The light of the morning bathing his room from the windows wouldn't help hide Mr Happy any more than his attire. "No, no, you go ahead." Words fell from his mouth and he backed toward the door. He needed to get out of his room. *Now.* Thank God he had clothes in his office.

His heel bumped into something soft. Then there was a clatter of something hard to the laminate floor.

He flailed his arms to keep from falling on his ass as his balance went sideways. His right leg shot into the air.

"I'm so sorry!" Nikki scrambled from his bed and grabbed the green Army duffle from behind him, but not before his gaze zoned in on what had fallen. A small round plastic container. Birth control.

She grabbed it and tossed it in the bag, yanking the drawstring tight before meeting his eyes.

Heat crept up his neck, but her expression was normal. She wasn't the embarrassed one. *Wow. What are you, fifteen?*

"Are you all right?" The concern in her voice made him jolt.

Answer her. He cleared his throat. Again. *Speak, idiot.* "Yes. Fine." *C'mon, be normal. Crack a joke like you would've if someone else had almost fallen on their ass.* Pete just looked at her.

"Pete?" She took a step closer. Her gaze searched his face.

Making himself flash a smile, he forced a nod. "Nothing like losing your balance before the ass crack of dawn."

Nikki grinned. "There's the Pete I know."

Their eyes locked and her hand settled over his wrist. Pete sank into her, shifting on his socked feet. He needed to kiss her.

But when her lovely face tilted up in invitation and she closed her eyes, he put himself in check. "I should go downstairs and let you get ready."

Those beautiful baby browns flew open and hurt crossed her expression. "Oh," she whispered.

His gut clenched and he cursed himself to hell and back. That particular look on her face was why he never should have touched her at the safe house. Why he wouldn't kiss her again. He would only hurt her. Nikki didn't deserve that. She deserved...better.

"I'll see you downstairs. You like egg and cheese omelets?"

She nodded, her eyes misty.

Pete fought the urge to close his eyes. Crying? He'd made her cry.

Could you be a bigger asshole?

He wanted to change his mind, pull her into his arms and wipe that look off her face.

Instead, he fled the room, closing the door soundlessly and keeping up the name-calling symphony in his head.

Chapter Fifteen

Luca froze, his eyes darting around the shitty motel room. Had he actually heard something? Damn, he was paranoid, and he wasn't even on coke. Grabbing his Beretta, he racked the slide. Aimed at the door and waited. The familiar sound grounded him.

"Fuck." Wiping the sweat from his brow, he refused to acknowledge the slight shake of his hands. Shit, maybe he *needed* some coke.

Caselli had called. It'd gone badly.

The boss did give a shit about his nephew.

Who fucking knew Caselli could find out about Mickey's death via the news? One little murder in a small nowhere city... Not national news as far as Luca was concerned.

Unless there was someone already watching.

Caselli's trust of him had always been tremulous at best—hell, the man really didn't trust anyone. Maybe he and Mickey had been followed the whole time. Maybe that was the real reason behind Mickey's stubbornness about the witnesses. Had someone been pulling his strings? Strings Luca had inadvertently severed? The boss's nephew never had been the brightest crayon in the box.

He'd been told to get his affairs in order.

"No. Fuck no."

Well, no matter how the info had reached New York, Luca suddenly had a target on his back. One he had to shake. He still had every intention of being important to Caselli. That didn't include *dead* important.

Luca could change Caselli's mind about killing him, he really could. If he finished the job he'd been sent to do, his boss had to forgive him for killing Mickey.

He wouldn't deviate from the plan. Kill Berto and his whore and get back into his employer's good graces.

If he followed every other Caselli rule, he'd be good to go. Safe to go home.

It'd been two days and no one had come for him.

Spending time lying low had been good. He'd been able to observe everything from under the radar and had only left the motel twice.

When his stomach had finally threatened to digest itself, he'd called a cab in lieu of stealing another car and grabbed some fast food. He'd seen Berto getting into a giant black pickup in the hospital parking lot. Naturally, Luca had told the cabby to follow.

His old friend hadn't gone far. The grocery store—didn't stay long, either—then back to the hospital. Interesting.

Driving back to the ranch and blowing something up there would be a waste if Berto was staying local for his little whore—how sweet.

But even more sweet if Luca could get a twofer.

And he sure as hell would.

Thank God the cab driver hadn't asked any questions. Guess even in a small city they knew better than that. Maybe it was in the manual or something.

Pacing his room wasn't going to do any good. He needed out—he needed a plan. He needed to go to the hospital. Definitely would have to boost a car. Cab ride wouldn't be a safe bet this time. Besides, he needed a getaway ride, too.

Too bad he'd had to lose the Hummer—he'd fucking loved that beast.

A door slammed and Luca jumped. He cursed thin walls as much as his nerves. He'd never been afraid of Caselli before. Scratch that—he'd never been afraid of anyone.

He respected the fuck out of his boss, to boot. Caselli had broken away from his father and built an empire.

Then again, the man had never wanted to kill his ass before.

Gun at his side, he peered out of the peephole of the door to his room.

Nada. He couldn't see a damn thing and the old paint against his nose smelled like shit.

What's the next step?

Luca surveyed the small room. It was so crappy he wouldn't even pay for sex here. Well, then again, it'd depend on how badly he needed to get laid.

Actually, a piece of sweet tail wasn't a bad idea at the moment. Antioch might be small, but there had to be a bar around the place. A working girl or two?

Maybe he wouldn't have to pay for pussy. He wasn't a bad-looking guy. After running his hand through his dark hair, he straightened his navy dress shirt. Women liked him.

He strode over to his black duffle and dug inside until he found some cologne, sprayed some on his neck and yanked his collar.

The mirror was cracked, but he could see enough to admire his reflection. "You look damn good, Luca."

If he could just stop talking to himself, maybe he'd get somewhere. Luca laughed, shaking his head. Caselli was after him and he'd just convinced himself to find some pussy instead of taking care of the problem. Maybe the Texas heat had gone to his head.

"Kill Berto and his whore. *Then* find a piece of ass." Nodding, he was satisfied with his compromise.

He grabbed the small nine-millimeter SIG he kept as a backup gun and strapped the ankle holster on. He donned a black blazer and secured his forty in the back of his waistband. Looking in the mirror one last time, Luca smiled.

The black bag and semi-formal outfit could have him passing for a pharmaceutical rep. Handy.

Now he just had to lift a ride to the hospital.

* * * *

Nikki's hand shook even before she answered her phone.

Something's wrong.

"Hello?"

"Nikki Harper, please." The familiar male voice was crisp, efficient.

"This is she."

"Nikki, Dr Bishop."

Shit. She'd recognized his voice, but a part of her hadn't wanted to admit it. Never good when the doctor himself made the call. "Y-y-yes?"

"This morning your grandmother's vitals weren't looking so good. So I had her transferred to the hospital for some tests."

"And you're just telling me now?" She clutched the cell to her ear so hard her hand smarted. The phone creaked.

It was almost seven. The whole day she'd been thinking about Gram, assuming she was safe at Health Solutions with two of APD's finest. Surely someone had called Pete if they'd had to move with her. Unless he just hadn't told her. Nikki's heart dropped to her stomach. What if the officers hadn't gone to the hospital with her grandmother?

"You know your gram. She didn't want to bother you unless there was something to worry about." Dr Bishop's voice gentled.

"So, there's something to worry about?"

"She'll be fine, but her heart's out of rhythm. I'm keeping her overnight for observation before releasing her back to the rehab center. Consulting with Dr Garrett, the best cardiologist I know."

Nikki squared her shoulders. "Heart problems?" That was new.

"Perhaps it's just the excitement of the past week, but she needs to rest."

"Okay. Can I see her?"

"I don't see a problem with that, but take it easy. Nothing exciting."

Like bad news. As far as Nikki knew, Gram didn't know—and wouldn't be told—about the shooting at the safe house. Not now, for damn sure. "Thank you, Dr Bishop. Call me if there's anything else. Even something little, please?"

"I will."

Nikki trembled as she ended the call and pocketed her cell. *How much more can I take?* Gram had to be okay.

She dumped the chicken she'd been seasoning for dinner into a container. After the lid gave a snap, she shoved it into Pete's fridge and hipped the door shut. Swallowed back some tears.

Sauntering into the living room of what had turned into her prison for the past two days, she steeled herself for a fight. He would say no. Probably wouldn't even hear her out. But it wasn't going to fly. Not this time.

Nikki had no clue if she was coming or going with her detective. On top of the stress of worrying Caselli's men would appear guns blazing at any moment, Pete had pulled completely away from her.

After sleeping in his arms and getting the best night's rest she'd had since before all this crap had happened, he'd not slept with her again, despite the fact Lee had gone back to her hotel.

He hadn't kissed her. Barely touched her at all. If they accidentally brushed shoulders or hands, he'd move away as if she was made of fire. Would hardly make eye contact.

What the hell had she done?

Hot, cold, hot, cold.

She'd failed at her attempts to understand him, even read him. Sure as heck couldn't tell what he was thinking.

It...hurt. Physically. Nikki's chest ached. It was hard to breathe.

Stop thinking about it. Focus on Gram.

She'd bawled the night before. Tears had soaked the pillow that still carried Pete's clean, woodsy sent. That made it even worse. He hadn't been there. Somehow it'd made her feel even emptier.

But had she really been crying over the detective? Or had she finally broken under the stress of her world being tossed upside down? Was it even normal to feel as if he'd rejected her?

Nikki wouldn't admit she was losing it, and she sure as hell wouldn't confess to her tears being Pete-related.

Grow up, Nikki Harper. This, too, will pass. Gram's familiar phrase came with the memory of her voice.

She just needed to forget about him. Or at least stop dwelling on what had happened between them.

Yeah, right. She still wanted him.

The way he kissed, the way he'd made her feel when they'd been on the couch in the safe house—no man had ever made her blood boil like that.

An orgasm in a few minutes? It'd never happened for her like that. Ever. Sex had always been pleasant, something she'd enjoyed. But Nikki had never even come close to feeling the way Pete had made her feel. And that was just foreplay.

God knows, had Caselli's men not burst in, she would have been naked in his arms in seconds. Demanding, begging him to come inside her.

Squirming, she squeezed her thighs together. Now was a bad time for those memories. Her desire for him could do nothing but torture her.

"My grandmother's in the hospital."

Lee and Pete looked up collectively from the laptop perched on the ottoman between them. They sat side by side, heads and bodies close together—too close. Nikki swallowed back a scowl and stepped toward them.

Her detective was on his feet in seconds, resting his hands on her shoulders. "Nikki—"

"Oh, my God. You knew. You *knew* and you didn't tell me?" Nikki shoved his hands off her. "How could you not tell me?"

Pete winced and glanced at Lee, but the FBI agent shook her head. Like she was saying the detective was on his own. Good.

"I did know." The regret in his expression should have made her feel a little better, but it didn't.

"How could you keep that from me?" Nikki meant to prop her hands on her hips, but ended up wrapping her arms around her middle. Hurt assaulted her. Was it over Pete or Gram?

"Crowley called me this morning. He and Walton went over there. They're both with her. She's okay."

"This *morning*? It's not okay. Gram's been alone in the hospital all day. Without…me." *Do not cry.* She bit her bottom lip to keep it from trembling.

"Darlin'—"

"No." She made a cutting gesture. "You do not get to lie to me and call me that."

"I didn't lie to you." Pete squared his shoulders. His green gaze burned into her. Nikki couldn't look away.

A lie of omission is still a lie. How many times had she heard that as a child? But it wasn't worth saying. "It if involves my gram, I have a right to know what's going on."

"I did what I needed to do to keep you safe. I won't apologize for that." His voice was hard and he glared.

Nikki scowled right back, heat creeping up her neck. She clenched and unclenched her fists at her sides. "How dare you treat me like a child?"

The squeak of shifting leather sounded in the momentary silence but she didn't spare a glance for the obviously uncomfortable FBI agent.

Screw Lee, too. No doubt Pete's temporary partner knew about Gram getting transported to the hospital. She could have told Nikki. Should have. Was there no such thing as woman code? Men seemed to insist on it.

Pete's chest heaved as if he'd taken a calming breath.

Nikki glared harder. "I'm going to the hospital."

"The hell you are." His tone was low and deadly. And pissed her the hell off. How dare he talk to her like that?

Lee stood up as Pete took a step closer to Nikki.

Instead of backing away, Nikki moved toward him. So close they almost touched. She could feel the heat, the anger coming off his muscled body. They stared at each other.

Pete narrowed his eyes.

"I'm going to the hospital," Nikki repeated.

In her peripheral vision, she saw Lee tense, eyes darting back and forth between them. As if she didn't know who to grab first if they came to blows.

Nikki wasn't afraid of Pete. He was angry, yeah, but he wouldn't hurt her. She knew it in her gut—and her heart.

"Pete." Lee's voice jolted her.

She looked at the FBI agent, then back at Pete. His hazel eyes widened and his shoulders loosened, as if Lee had surprised him, too. He didn't move away from Nikki.

"We can take her."

Relief that Lee was on her side washed over Nikki. She blew out a breath and told her body to relax. Blinked away tears that threatened. She didn't want to look back at her detective. Cursed the part of her that wanted to throw her arms around him.

Why? He just ordered you around and tried to control you. Made decisions for you again. Lied to you.

"We're not staying long." His voice was gruff, grudging.

"Being stuck in the house is affecting all of us," Lee continued as if the detective hadn't spoken. "It might be good to get out for a little bit. We can get something to eat, too."

Nikki nodded, not mentioning the chicken she'd marinated. They could eat it tomorrow. God knew, they'd still be stuck at Pete's.

Chapter Sixteen

He didn't like this. At. All. Pete looked around the hospital corridor outside Mrs Jenkins' room. Nothing seemed out of place as hospital staff bustled with trays and carts. Phones rang, the hum of voices carried and faded as people traversed back and forth.

The ding of the elevator around the corner made him jump.

"Relax." Lee's voice was meant to soothe, but the one word did nothing for his twitchiness.

Pete forced a nod and resisted the urge to palm his SIG. His gut said something was wrong even though he could see nothing out of the ordinary.

"Damn, dude. I'm wondering if there was crack in your lunch. What'd your chick feed you?"

He met the FBI agent's dark eyes. Humor danced there.

"She's my witness," he said automatically. "I need to make sure she's safe."

"Okay, now you're insulting me and the two boys in blue in that room. We all got guns. We all got her back—and yours."

Sighing, Pete shoved his hand through his hair and screamed at himself to calm down. Lee was right. He was just revved from the argument with Nikki.

What a hell of a turn-on when she'd gotten up in his face, seething, fire in her brown eyes. The demand in her expression. The hard set of her luscious mouth. Was that wrong?

He'd wanted to kiss her until neither of them could breathe. Clinging to his anger at her insult had been the only thing that'd kept his hands to himself. Pete was a lot of things, but he wasn't a liar.

"Why don't we go get a bite? I thought I saw an Italian place across the street," Lee said.

"Hell no. I'm not leaving her here."

"Earth to Pete. You need a breather." Lee gripped his wrist and tugged, forcing his gaze down into her face.

"I'm fine."

"Bullshit. I've never seen you lose it like that. Thought I was gonna hafta whoop your ass." Lee quirked a half-smile, but she was as serious as a heart attack.

"I wouldn't hurt her. Or any woman for that matter."

The FBI agent nodded, despite the solemn look in her eyes. "I thought she was going to take a swing at you."

"Nah."

"Let's get out of here. In the time it takes to have a meal, you can calm down and she can have some privacy with her grandmother. Threaten the cops in here, chew on them, do what you need to do, but you're coming with me to that restaurant."

Pete was about to growl a no, but her shrewd gaze narrowed. Lee dared him. He didn't want to argue with his temporary partner. And he *was* hungry. A voice whispered that space from Nikki would cool his ardor. He ignored it. He'd still grab her up and kiss her if given the chance. Even if the choice should be hands-off. "I could eat," he admitted.

Lee smiled slowly. Patted his forearm. "Good boy."

He chuckled in spite of himself, pushing the door open just enough to enter. He left the FBI agent posted outside.

Nikki looked up and glared his way, but her grandmother gave a wide friendly smile. Officer Mark Rodriguez threw a nod that Pete returned. The other officer, the newest of Sergeant Chloe Stein's guys, Officer Joe Benton, smiled. The guy wasn't a rookie, but close.

Pete didn't like it. Wanted another of the experienced guys instead. Even if that wasn't fair to Benton. He swallowed back his frown and took Mrs Jenkins' outstretched hand as soon as he reached her bedside.

"Evening, Detective," Nikki's gram said.

He pressed a kiss into the soft, nearly transparent skin of her knuckles. "Evening, Mrs Jenkins."

"Oh, you charmer, you." The elderly woman grinned while her granddaughter glowered.

Nikki made a disparaging sound and crossed her arms over her breasts. Pete forced his eyes away, though he didn't miss the scowl that seemed to have taken up permanent residence on her gorgeous face.

If Gram noticed, she ignored Nikki and met Pete's eyes. "Are you taking care of my granddaughter?"

"Yes, ma'am." He expected a snarky remark from Nikki. She said nothing, and she wouldn't look at him.

Mrs Jenkins squeezed Pete's hand in a grip that belied the appearance of her fragile-looking fingers. "Good. I know she's in good hands."

"Thank you. How're you feeling, ma'am?"

"Stop this *ma'am* stuff. It makes me feel old." Gram mock-glared and Pete couldn't help but smile.

Mrs Molly Jenkins might be diminutive and elderly, but the word *weak* didn't apply, despite a stroke and heart problems. It was no secret where Nikki had gotten her strength.

"I would never want to make a beautiful woman feel old. I apologize."

Gram laughed, her pale blue eyes twinkling. "Nikki-baby, I like this one."

Nikki closed her eyes for a split second and cleared her throat. "I like him, too." Her voice was breathy and made his stomach jump. She leaned closer to the bed and grabbed her grandmother's free hand. Still wouldn't look his way.

Pete felt like a heel. *Pissed* he could handle. Hurt was another matter entirely. And Nikki exuded hurt. His fault. Just one more way he'd failed her.

"Uh." He cleared his throat and tried again. "I'm going to step out with Agent Dawson. Spend some time with your gram."

She finally met his eyes. Nikki nodded, remaining silent.

"I won't be gone long. Rodriguez and Benton will be here with you. They won't let anyone come into this room." He raised his voice and glanced at the two cops. They both nodded. "You call my cell every ten minutes. I'll be back for you in a bit."

Pete made himself turn and leave even though there was a weight on his chest he didn't want to acknowledge.

She'd be fine for an hour. They'd order her some food to go, too.

Rodriguez and Benton would protect her. Everything would be fine.

He met Lee in the hallway. "Let's go."

* * * *

Pete cleared his throat and tried not to shift under the weight of Lee's gaze. This suddenly felt like a date.

The place was dark and they were surrounded by couples. Masculine arms around feminine shoulders in booths and heads bent close together all around. People sitting against each other like the lovers they probably were.

He felt keenly out of place. As if he and Lee had a spotlight over their table.

Rizzoli's buzzed with life around them. Wait staff worked the room, plates and silverware clinked from all angles. Old Blue Eyes crooned from the speakers. Garlic permeated the place, but the mix with other Italian spices was pleasant. Mouth-watering. Made a guy crave lasagna from the moment he walked in the door.

Something was missing. Or more like *someone*. He half expected to look up and see her striding in the entrance to join them at the table. She'd been at his side for almost a week now. His new constant.

You should have never left her. Alone. But Nikki wasn't alone. He'd just have to keep reminding himself of that.

It didn't help. No matter how many times he repeated it in his head.

The whoosh of the kitchen doors swinging past each other offered a distraction. Conversation with Lee had never been difficult. He wasn't about to let it start. "Thanks for going over the database with me. If we could just tie Marchetti or Donati to the blood on the windowsill at Health Solutions through DNA, we'd solidify things all around."

"No problem." Lee nodded, a smile playing at her lips. As if she could see right through him. As if she *knew* how awkward he was feeling. "But science shit or not, we'll get him, I've no doubt."

"Yeah. We will."

Silence descended and she reached for her water glass. Pete watched her slender hands. Manicured nails, but plain and neat, no polish or color. She wore no rings, but had a small gold bracelet on her right wrist. Her tanned skin spoke of her heritage, and his eyes followed her wrist up to her elbow.

Lee wore a short-sleeved dark top that displayed her full breasts and was tapered and form-fitting at the waist. Somehow dressy and casual all rolled into one. Her jeans were tight like always, and navy denim. She was dressed as normal at work—still gorgeous, even with her black hair in a ponytail.

He liked her. Had liked her from the moment she'd walked into the briefing room last year when he, Andi and Cole had been after Carlo Maldonado. She had balls. Lee was easy on the eyes, too.

She isn't Nikki.

"What's going on with you, Pete?" She shelved her chin on her hands, both elbows on the table. She appraised him, her gaze keen.

"What?"

"You're wound so tightly I'm afraid you're going to blow at any second. Granted, we haven't been working together too long, but I read people pretty well. And I haven't seen you like this before. Not like you were before we left the house tonight. It's not the case. That's not what's getting to you."

"I don't know what you mean," Pete said.

"Bullshit." Amusement flickered across her face.

Damn. She was as shrewd as he was. Now he understood why Andi hated when he put her in the position Lee was currently slamming down on him. He sighed and averted his gaze.

"If you don't want to open up to me, so be it. Call your partner. I know you're close to her. Run ten miles. Do *something*. 'Cause you need a release, dude. Or we're not gonna get anywhere else on the case. You're gonna pull a Mount St Helens."

Shaking his head, he bit back a snort. He needed a release, all right. A ten-mile run—or all the cold showers in the world—wouldn't fix it. Not since he'd tasted her. Craved her.

Nikki. She was what he needed.

Nikki not angry at him. Nikki in his arms and in his bed, but *with* him instead of alone like the last two nights. Shifting in the chair, he cursed himself as his cock stirred.

Desire warred with conscience. It was hard for any of it to matter—how his boss had said hell no, how he was too old for her, how he couldn't love her like she deserved, it all went unnoticed in the back of his mind.

"Pete?" Lee's voice dragged him back to reality.

He cleared his throat. "Thanks for your concern, but I'm fine, darlin'." Pete flashed his best smile.

She reclined in her chair and cocked her head to one side, a smile playing at her full lips. "Since you're so charming, I don't think I should call you a liar."

"You kinda just did." He laughed.

Lee's grin was impish. "Now that's better. Pete back in the home team's dugout."

"What a relief." He gave an overdramatic sigh that had his new partner laughing again.

Their waitress appeared to check on them, so Lee didn't answer him.

He watched her. She was direct in everything she did, even eating. With Lee, you saw what you got a mile away. There was no subterfuge.

Pete admired that. Hell, he always tried to present the same front. Andi was probably the only one who could see right through him.

His observation of her didn't go unnoticed by Lee—she was too keen for that—but she didn't say anything. They fell into a nice rhythm. Laughing and talking. Natural. No spark...like when he was with Nikki.

Jesus, get her out of your head. He couldn't follow his own damn orders, though. If he closed his eyes he'd see her mussed red locks, heavy-lidded brown gaze and pink cheeks, kiss-swollen lips. He wouldn't let his memory go south—in any stretch of the word. His jeans were already a bit tight.

Cursing himself—again—Pete forced his eyes to Lee's. "Your partner missing you?"

Lee laughed. "Not that he'd ever say. He's not really the touchy-feely type, but I'd consider him a friend. Today they busted up another buy. Arrested a few guys. Caselli's dealing with Mexicans heavily now. They got three girls out."

"Damn. He's expanding things?"

"Right. We need to take him down. There're also rumors of collaboration with Russian traffickers. Girls from Russia, the Czech Republic, and especially Ukraine. They're selling for more than any other nationalities. Bastards." Her tone was firm and Lee made a fist.

Pete shook his head. "I'd like to shoot each and every one of them."

"They're better off getting raped in prison." Lee smirked.

"Yeah, I wouldn't lose sleep over it."

"We're taking them down. Already put a dent in his organization. It's only a matter of time before Caselli's behind bars."

"So you're missing New York?" Pete asked.

"Maybe my unit. Texas is a break from the constant action of the past few months, though."

"Might be a good thing."

"Well, every time Caselli's guys come into town, little Antioch gets some action."

Pete chuckled. "Something I could do without. Makes our murder rate go up."

Lee winked. "At least my partner in Texas isn't so bad." Her dark gaze was inviting.

He stared, trying to decide if the innuendo in her expression was his imagination. She regarded him steadily, as if daring him to call her out. He didn't.

The moment passed and soon he was leading her back to his unmarked, hand at the small of her back. Pete opened her door and Lee glanced at him.

"Detective."

"Hmmm?"

Their eyes locked. Pete shifted on his feet like he was seventeen.

Lee grabbed his wrist and pulled him to her, standing tiptoed to press her mouth to his. Instead of pulling away, he lowered his head and met the FBI agent's lips halfway. Pete took control and wrapped his arms around her.

She kissed him thoroughly, opening for him. Their tongues mingled, but Pete didn't pull her closer and Lee didn't push her way against his chest.

She was a good kisser. It was…pleasant. But it didn't fire his blood or stir his cock. He didn't need more.

Like with Nikki.

He pulled away on a sigh.

Lee stared up at him, one corner of her mouth lifted. Her brown eyes were clear of passion and amusement rippled across her gorgeous face. "Well, it was worth a shot." The diminutive FBI agent patted his pecs with a flat palm.

Pete reared back. "Excuse me?"

"I thought I might be able to help you relax, but I'm not fool enough to think that kiss did anything more to you than it did to me. Guess you kissed the wrong girl." Her gaze darted toward the hospital before meeting his again.

So his new partner wasn't so oblivious after all. Then again, she *had* caught him with Nikki in his room. Probably hadn't believed a word he'd said about nothing happening.

Speechless wasn't often something he claimed. However, as Lee observed him, he couldn't have kicked himself harder. She was beautiful, sensible and in law enforcement, for God's sake. Could see eye to eye with his daily life. She *liked* him.

She would've taken him into her arms, and into her body. She might not have been turned on by their first kiss, but Pete could've convinced her. He was a good lover. He could make her feel good.

Why couldn't he want her?

She's not Nikki.

He swallowed a cringe. "I got nothing," Pete whispered.

Lee laughed, actually laughed. "Oh, I wouldn't go that far, Pete. You're a great guy. I like you. But someone else likes you more. Pretty damn good chance you feel the same way. There's nothing wrong with that." Her gaze was pointed. No emotion detectible in her voice. No sadness, no regret, just pure fact as she saw it. That was completely Lee.

He dragged his hand through his hair. "Dammit." *She's my witness* was on his tongue but Pete wouldn't admit how spot on Lee was.

She smiled, throwing him off even more. "It'll be okay."

The *shhht* of the radio caught Pete's attention, though the volume was low. He missed the first half of the transmission. "...fired. I repeat, shots fired."

"Shit. That's Mark Rodriguez," Pete said. His stomach roiled, threatening to eject the lasagna. Without a word, he ran around to the driver's side.

Lee yanked her gun from the holster as she climbed in the car. "Son of a bitch."

Chapter Seventeen

Luciano Marchetti was the last guy Berto had ever expected to see again. But as he threw himself over his wife's form on the hospital bed and fired his .357 Magnum Ruger, it occurred to him that Luca might be the last guy he saw, period.

Hell no. I'm gonna kill him before he kills me.

His arm burned where the first bullet had torn through. He'd taken a hit Maria's battered body wouldn't have survived. Barked at her to stay low and covered as much of her as he could.

Berto fired three more times, praying he hit the bastard. He only had two remaining shots in the revolver, though he had a nine-millimeter Glock in his ankle holster. Could he pull it in time?

"Fuck." He gritted his teeth as a bullet ripped through his left leg.

The cop who had been guarding Maria's room from the corridor wasn't coming to the rescue.

Pain seared his side and the bed spun. Maria clutched at him, screaming. He heard pops and bangs as he concentrated on pulling the trigger for the last time.

Berto fought to stay awake.

Luca swore and backed from the room, grabbing his upper arm. He swiveled his body and Beretta, shooting in the other direction.

Maria was cursing in Spanish and English, begging Berto to live. Screaming she loved him. Held onto him until her nails dug into his wrist and forearm. But feeling was good. His other arm, his side, even his leg were numb.

He started to slip sideways from the hospital bed, but his wife's arms encircled his chest. Maria did her best to keep him still and on the bed with her.

Other people were screaming—women wailing and deep voices shouting orders. Heavy footfalls were everywhere—some sounded as if they were coming closer, but others faded away. People must be running.

Everything echoed and his vision blurred. Maria's bed became a Tilt-A-Whirl.

"Berto, please. Berto, *por favor*! *Te amo*, Alberto Carbone! Do not leave me!"

He opened his mouth to assure the love of his life he was right with her, even though he was having trouble focusing on her beautiful face.

Berto tried to wipe the tears from her cheeks, but his arm wouldn't lift, his fingers wouldn't move.

Everything went black.

* * * *

"He's just *gone*. I gave chase. He's hit in the arm so the blood trail was easy to follow at first. Not sure who shot him. No idea where I lost him. I'm sorry,

Detective." Mark Rodriguez shook his head when Pete met his dark eyes. The guy looked about as haggard as Pete felt. "I can't believe this."

"You fought as hard as you could. We'll get him," Pete said, wanting to make the fellow cop feel better. "I'm glad you were here, though, dude. Got here quick, and Bobby's gonna make it."

Officer down. Rodriguez's call on the radio was something no cop ever wanted to hear. But Officer Bobby Roper had had on a vest. He'd been hit in the hip and shoulder, but his vitals were covered. He'd live. Thank God.

"He was already laid out in the hall when I got here. Gunshots brought me downstairs. But before that, my gut screamed something wasn't right. Roper didn't even get time to call out."

Pete nodded and patted Rodriguez's shoulder. "You did good, seriously. Your arrival saved his life...all three of their lives, actually. Get back down to Mrs Jenkins' room. I'll be there shortly."

"You sure you don't need me here?"

"Nah. The cavalry's here. But thanks. Appreciate the offer."

Cops hovered. CSI rounded the corner with black evidence kits. Neil gave Pete a nod.

"I'd offer my Spanish speaking skills, but looks like your FBI agent's got it." The cop gestured to Lee hovering over Maria Mata's hospital bed.

The two women were speaking in rapid-fire Spanish.

"Dawson's got it for sure. Just make sure Nikki and her gram are all right."

"Gotcha, Detective. See you in a few."

He'd let Rodriguez gain his bearings a bit more and take his statement as quietly as he could manage

outside Mrs Jenkins' room. The guy was a good cop—
had been around for a while, but like most of APD,
tonight was probably the guy's first shooting. Would
rattle even the best veteran cop.

Pete sighed. His heart hadn't returned to his chest
from his stomach until he'd heard Nikki's voice on the
phone. She was fine. Gram was fine. Officer Benton
had them in the room.

Protected.

She'd told him to handle his business.

It'd been the first real conversation they'd had since
their argument. She'd sounded concerned, but not
scared. That was good. Helped him deal. Pete wanted
to be back upstairs, with her in his sight…in his arms.

A woman with blonde hair, wearing a white coat
hovered. "Are you in charge here?"

"Yes, ma'am."

"Mrs Mata is my patient. I need to move her."

"As soon as Agent Dawson is through, I don't see a
problem with that, Dr…"

"Holmes. Thanks." She gave a curt nod.

"How's the husband?"

Neil and his team discreetly slipped into the room
behind Pete.

"He had four GSWs and one entered the abdomen.
It's a good thing they were here at the hospital. We got
him right into the OR. I can't say for sure, but the
blood was dark. Stomach or liver." Dr Holmes'
expression became grave.

"Dammit," he muttered. He should've never
dragged his feet on talking to Carbone about WitSec.
They could've already been out of Texas. "Will he
live?"

"We got him mostly stable before he went under the
knife. He's got a shot."

Pete wouldn't sigh in relief. It was too soon. "If you'll excuse me, I'll check on my partner and the wife. Give you a holler when we're through."

"Thank you, Detective."

"Pete Crane. Here's my card."

The doctor nodded, slipping his business card in her lab coat's pocket after a glance.

Chloe made scene and was already questioning hospital personnel. Pete gestured to her. "Sergeant Stein over there will probably speak with you, but if you need anything, don't hesitate to call me."

He was at Lee's side in a few strides. They made eye contact, then the FBI agent looked back at Alberto Carbone's woman. Pete followed her gaze.

Maria's face was streaked with tears. He could feel her anguish. His gut tightened. *Let Berto make it, please.* He wasn't usually so empathetic—especially considering the man's past—but the look on the wife's face was enough to slay him.

Nikki kept popping into his head and he remembered hovering over her too-still form, unconscious and bleeding. Maria Mata was in the same position.

Maria sobbed, sucking in great gulps of air.

Lee grabbed a box of tissues and handed it to her. "Shhh, it'll be okay. He's going to be okay." She threw a glance at Pete and he nodded.

"I just talked to the doc. He's in surgery, but he's gonna be all right." *Please, God, don't let us be lying to this poor woman.*

"Luca… He's a cruel man. He…hurt me…before my Berto found me." Maria wiped her face and blew her nose, taking another tissue when Lee offered the box again. Her heavy accent combined with emotion shook him as much as her expression. This beautiful woman had really been a trafficking victim, like Cole had told him. She didn't need to deal with that world all over again. Much less lose the man who'd saved her.

"He won't hurt you again."

Lee's dark gaze bit him. She clenched her jaw and frowned.

Yeah, yeah, Pete had been on the job long enough to know better than to promise something, but he knew in his gut they'd get Marchetti. Right now, dead was looking better than alive.

No doubt his FBI agent partner would lay into him later.

"The doctor would like to move you to a new room, Maria," Pete said. "All done?" he asked Lee, keeping his tone light.

"I think so." Lee took Maria's hand and squeezed. "It'll be okay." She reverted to Spanish. Pete didn't understand her words, but they sounded encouraging and Maria's mouth even turned up in a small smile.

Lee sighed and shook her head as they hit the corridor. "Dude, you know better than that."

Pete made a fist. "I didn't lie to her. We're going to get the bastard. Hey, do you know anyone in the Marshal's Office?"

Her dark brows drew tight. "Witness protection?"

"Damn, you're good."

She smiled a little, but Pete could tell he wasn't quite off the hook. "I do, actually. But don't tell your partner."

"My partner?"

"My friend used to…date…Cole Lucas."

"Date?" Pete laughed when Lee rolled her eyes. A four-letter word came to mind, but it didn't start with a *d.* He wasn't going to say it out loud, though.

"Anyway, I'll give Madison a call. She'll probably fall over if I tell her Lucas is married. With kids no less." Lee palmed her cell.

Pete grinned. "Good deal. I was worried about Carbone agreeing to WitSec when Chief and I talked about it. Hopefully when he's out of surgery and we can chat, he'll agree."

"No doubt his wife will." The phone rang a few times. "Hey, Maddie, it's Lee."

He left Lee to talk to her friend, crossing his fingers the woman would help. Strolling back to Maria's room, he looked at the blood trail leaving the room and leading down the wide hallway. Mark had said the bastard was hit in the arm.

Neil was already on it, gathering samples. "Think it'll match what we found at Health Solutions?" the guy asked, looking up at Pete.

"You know it. Damn I want this bastard."

"He is doing a great job of tearing up our city."

"Tell me about it." Pete shook his head.

"Pete," Lee called.

"Yeah?"

"Madison said she'd be happy to help."

Chapter Eighteen

Pete sank into the couch, leaning his head back and closing his eyes. After the day and night they'd had, he just wanted to sleep. His shoulder ached dully. The old wound hadn't bothered him for a while, but he should've known better than to assume it was gone. An adrenaline dump always brought it to life again.

Lee had gone back to The Covington after some convincing that they'd be all right without her at his place for the night. Marchetti was going to lie low, at least tonight. He was hit and bleeding. Pete had checked in with Raleigh Carter. Told him to be on the lookout for the guy. Even though his CI was shaking in his boots, he'd agreed to let Pete know if Marchetti crossed the Antioch scum radar. One good thing about Raleigh was that the meth-head knew them all.

He'd bade Nikki goodnight and she'd headed up to his room. Pete could have slept in his guest room, or let her take it when she'd offered, but had thought it better they had one story between them. Although a staircase and a hallway did nothing to his want. It was still killing him to know she was up there. In his bed. Alone.

"Pete?"

Eyes flying open, his heart thumped and he startled, one hand on the butt of his gun. "Jesus!"

Nikki slid closer, her palms flat and high. "Sorry. It's just me."

Shit. He hadn't heard her come back downstairs.

Forcing himself to relax and let go of his weapon, he took a deep breath. "Are you okay?" he croaked.

"Me? Sure. I wanted to make sure you are. Tonight was crazy. And... I needed to apologize."

"For what, darlin'?" Pete sat up straighter and made himself scoot back a little when she took a seat beside him.

"Our argument."

"Don't worry about it. We're cooped up together — no surprised things can get heated."

She smiled and gave a small nod. Nikki tucked an errant strand of hair behind her ear and leaned closer.

Heated. Sure as hell the wrong choice of words.

His gaze traveled her gorgeous form. She was dressed in her same outfit of barely-there sleepwear — a pale green spaghetti-strapped tank and matching shorts that stopped at her ass. Smelled good, too. Something clean and floral.

Damn, she had great legs...arms, neck, everything.

Nikki moved closer, her thigh touching his. She put her hand on his leg. The warmth of her touch sank into the jeans.

Pete's cock jumped, begging her to move closer to his crotch. To touch him. Stroke him. Free him.

Their lips met on a mutual groan and he yanked her onto his lap, deepening their kiss. Nikki straddled him, her thinly covered sex hitting him with enough impact he was rock hard in less than a second.

She pushed her hands up under his shirt at the same time he spread his palms beneath her tank across the soft skin of her back.

He needed her bare. *Now.*

She rocked in his lap, her tongue mingling, dancing and dueling with his.

His abs quivered under her seeking fingers and Pete's heart hit overdrive. He kissed her harder, pressing her into his chest until her hands had no room to roam and her breasts were flat.

Nikki moaned and kept his pace, slanting her mouth against his again and again.

A voice popped up in his head to stop, reminding him this wasn't right, but there was no saying no.

She was passion and heat, and he *needed* her.

"Pete," Nikki breathed against his mouth.

He stopped kissing her though his body screamed a protest, and pulled back to meet her eyes. Heavy-lidded and almost black, he read desire as strong as his. Pete's cock throbbed.

They panted against each other.

"Darlin'? Did I hurt you?"

She shook her head. "I want to go to your room. Now."

Conscience broke through from the back of his mind, and he sucked in a breath. "We shouldn't do this," he whispered.

"I want you."

Pete's whole body stuttered. God, she was going to kill him and she hadn't even touched his cock yet.

"Are you okay?" Nikki whispered.

"Yes. No. I don't know."

Hurt crossed her gorgeous face.

If he rejected her, it would be it for them. Dead in the water before they could even be. Pete would never have another shot with her, forbidden or not.

Nikki put her hands on his shoulders and squeezed. "You want me, too." Statement, not question.

Pete didn't say anything. Opening his mouth would result in a resounding *yes* and he wasn't ready to admit it.

It's wrong. So wrong.

Irritation flashed across her expression, and she pulled away. "Are you denying what's between us?" Her whisper was thick and he bit back a wince.

He wouldn't hurt her again.

She rocked in his lap, tearing a moan from his lips. "Because this feels like we're on the same page. Am I wrong?"

"Damn, that's unfair," Pete groaned.

Nikki grinned.

Fuck it. Cupping her face, he devoured her mouth. She wrapped her arms around his neck and kissed him back hard, like she wasn't done proving her point.

"Upstairs, now," she ordered against his lips.

He stood without breaking their kiss, gathering her up in his arms and hitting the stairs.

When he set her to her feet in his room, Nikki looked up at him, her expression open and earnest. "Pete, I—"

"Shhh." He pressed his finger to her kiss-swollen lips. "I want you, Nikki. Never doubt that."

She threw herself into his arms and Pete laughed as he caught her up. He took her mouth and carried her to his bed, then set her down at the center. He took a step back to rip off his shirt.

Nikki stared. "You have a tattoo."

"Yeah, I was young and dumb once." He gestured to the badge and gun on his chest, wishing he had enough chest hair to obscure the thing.

She laughed. "Oh yeah, you're just so ancient, Detective."

Old enough to know better than this. But he couldn't say it. Nikki was in his bed. She wanted him. He wanted her. Pete was going to have her.

"Lose the clothes, Ms Harper," he said, ignoring her jibe.

Giggling, she nodded. "You, too, Detective Crane."

Pete grinned and slid the holster off his belt, setting his SIG on the nightstand. He tried not to stare her down when she lifted her gorgeous bottom and pushed the pale green shorts off her hips. Tried not to gulp at the first glimpse of her sex.

Her tank followed and she was in his bed, naked.

Body supple, curvy in all the right places. Breasts perfect, round and high. He would taste them again— and the rest of her. The trimmed strip of red curls between her legs made him groan.

She made no efforts to hide herself from him. Looked in his direction with desire and heat in her brown eyes. Waiting for him. Wanting *him*.

Pete itched to touch her. His mouth went dry. He swallowed hard, fumbling with his zipper, but he refused to look away from Nikki.

"I don't think I've ever seen you this quiet," she whispered, holding out her hand to him. She rose to her knees.

"Because you're so damn gorgeous," he managed, kissing her knuckles as he stopped at the edge his bed.

She blushed and flashed a smile that had his heart thundering in his ears.

"You're not so bad yourself, Detective." Her hand skimmed his chest and the sparse blond fuzz.

His nipples peaked as her fingertip traced his pec.

He clenched his jaw. "You're killing me."

"Well, we're just getting started, but it looks like you need some help."

Pete let her open his belt and lower his zipper. His abs and cock jolted at the same time, but she didn't pause, pushing the jeans off his hips and down until he could step out of them. He made quick work of his cowboy boots and socks.

With a strength that surprised him, Nikki snaked her arms around his neck and pulled him down. They moved onto the bed in unison, Pete fusing their mouths as he settled into the cradle of her body. His cock threatened to blow when her bare skin met his.

Kissing her harder, he rocked his hips. His erection was trapped pleasantly between them, throbbing against her hot core.

She moaned and writhed under him. Her arms tightened as he dragged his tongue in a path down her neck. Whimpering, Nikki rubbed her pelvis into his.

After he suckled one nipple, she arched, burying her hands in his hair and holding him to her. Prevented him from continuing.

Pete chuckled. "I need to breathe."

She panted, wiggling. "Sorry."

He smiled as he circled the hard peak with his tongue, blowing gently before nibbling.

Nikki moaned his name, tugging his hair with tight fingers.

"Smother me against your beauty anytime." He licked his way downward, lavishing the soft part of her belly before urging her thighs wider.

He parted her curls with his tongue. She was hot, wet. Pulling her swollen clit into his mouth, he sucked hard until she screamed and yanked his hair again.

Pete didn't care if she made him bald as her essence greeted his tongue, he just needed more. He licked and nipped up and down her slick folds, sliding one finger inside, then two.

Moving his hand in rhythm with his tongue, he tasted her fresh arousal as more moisture rushed her sex and her core pulsed around his fingers.

She threw her head back and yelled, lifting her hips off the bed. Her muscles tightened, and she panted his name. "Pete, I'm...I'm..."

"Let go, Nikki. Come for me, darlin'."

He looked up at her, gloriously laid open for him on his bed, flushed pink from head to toe, her thick red locks spread out in waves on his pillow.

Pete gulped. His balls tightened like he was about to climax. His cock jerked. Fighting for control, he whispered her name as her inner muscles gripped his fingers.

He stroked her thigh and helped her ride out the orgasm. She clutched at him, hands grasping for purchase on his forearm.

Nikki's brown eyes were almost black as her gaze collided with his. "I...need...you...inside."

Dropping his body over hers, Pete stared into her flushed face. "Condom?"

"I'm on birth control."

"I know, but—"

"I trust you. I...don't...want anything between us."

His heart thudded and he studied her. "I don't know what to say," he whispered.

"Do you trust me?"

"Yes."

"Then get inside me. I need you." Nikki raised her pelvis.

Pete didn't wait for another word. He gripped and positioned himself, pushing into her in one full stroke.

He stilled, looking down when she gasped. "Did I hurt you?"

She shook her head.

He let the sensation of her contracting muscles wash over him. Damn good thing he took a moment to breathe, it was the only thing that kept him from losing it before the first thrust.

Nikki was perfect surrounding him, holding him snug within her.

He groaned and his blood pounded in his ears. His body screamed and throbbed, begging him to move forward. But he needed to taste her mouth first.

Leaning down, he let her pull him close as his lips took hers. He kissed her long and thoroughly, starting to move his hips.

She didn't disappoint, tilting to take him deeper and meeting each thrust.

Slow and tender was what he'd been aiming for. It didn't matter, because as they moved together, each thrust was more frantic. Her nails sank into his ass as she squeezed and urged him on.

Pete grunted as he propelled forward again and again. She begged him for more and he gave her what she wanted.

Sweat covered them both. Nikki kept up with him, shifting under him, with him, shoving her hips up to meet his when he moved away.

When her body stiffened and she screamed his name, it was too much. The tingling in his spine shook his balls and took his control. He thrust forward one last time hard, pleasure hitting him like a ton of bricks as his release shot into her.

Her sex squeezed him like a vice, milking him as he rocked his hips, and Nikki continued to writhe against him.

Pete panted, freezing above her. Sensations threatened to bowl him over and he locked his arms to keep from collapsing on her, crushing her.

Her brown eyes were hazy with passion. Her gorgeous breasts lifted and fell, tickling his nipples as she panted.

Nikki's arms shot around his neck, yanking him down.

Pete took her mouth without thought. He deepened the kiss, exploring, plundering. She mated her tongue to his, her moan spreading a languorous heat over his sated body.

God, she was fantastic. His cock was softening inside her, but he wished he was ready to go for round two.

Sex had always just been sex.

But this—the difference made his heart stutter.

He pushed the feeling away. Lust was better. *Focus on the lust.*

She pulled away from him, color spreading across her lovely cheekbones. "What's wrong?" The whisper was worried, belying her expression.

"Nothing, darlin'." He kissed her again.

She made a grab for his face, forcing him to meet her eyes. "Your kiss changed. What're you thinking?"

Damn, she's spot on. Pete bit back a gulp. "I'm thinking I wanna stay here with you tonight." He shifted, slipping from her body and rolling over. Tugging her to his side, he wrapped his arms around her.

Nikki stared. Her beautiful eyes asked, *Are you sure?*

"I've wanted you for ages, I'm not pulling couch duty now," Pete said, praying he sounded sincere. He meant every word, but it scared the shit out of him.

"I want you to stay here with me. Your bed, after all," she whispered, her shoulders relaxing as her body loosened over his. She sighed and kissed his chest at the same time he pressed his lips into the crown of her red hair.

He flashed a smile and met her eyes again. "Good. I'm not done with you."

Finally grinning, she scooted closer.

Pete cradled the back of her head and held her to him, nibbling her bottom lip and deepening the kiss when she opened for him. Nikki moaned, and his cock stirred.

She's exquisite. God, he could get lost in her perfection, her taste, her everything.

He pulled away before he wouldn't be able to, struggling for coherent thought as his chest heaved.

"I hope you're never done with me," Nikki said.

Resting his forehead against hers, he ignored the fluttering in his stomach as he met her half-lidded dark eyes.

He didn't answer. What the hell could he say?

Pete was so screwed.

Chapter Nineteen

Nikki closed her eyes and sighed. Hot water sluiced down her body, melting away tension in her muscles, but she was sore in a good way. Pete had made love to her twice throughout the night, and she wouldn't have changed the tightness in her arms and thighs, and certainly not the throbbing between her legs, for anything in the world.

She smiled, tilting her head back under the spray of his massaging showerhead. Burying her hands in her hair, she rinsed away conditioner.

Despite having her own bath stuff in his shower, she was surrounded by his masculine clean woodsy scent. Nikki loved it. It was like being encased in Pete.

The door to the bathroom closed and she stilled, but when the glass door to the wide shower stall slid open, a tremor shot down her spine. A tremor that had nothing to do with cool air accompanying Pete's entrance from the bedroom.

He said nothing, just closed them in together and came up from behind her. His muscled chest pressed into her back and his hand settled below her navel.

Pete tugged her bottom against him. An erection pushed into her.

"Hmmm..." Nikki murmured, laying her head back on his chest.

His hands rose, exploring her stomach and breasts as if he hadn't touched her a hundred times. Pete kissed her neck, stubble teasing her hot skin, the water from the shower intensifying things.

He teased her nipples with his thumbs. She already ached for him in any place with nerve endings. Nikki wiggled her ass against his erection and Pete moaned in her ear.

"Don't you want to wash?" She turned in his arms.

Pete lowered his head for a kiss, but she pulled back before he could deepen it. He nipped her bottom lip, then licked the spot.

It was her turn to moan.

"I need to get dirty, first." Despite his wink, his green gaze was intense.

Nikki wrapped her arms around his neck and crashed her lips to his. He took it from there, kissing her so long and hard her belly quivered from the inside out and her legs threatened to wash down the drain like the water.

He held her up, pinned to his chest, kneading her bottom until they fell into a natural rocking rhythm that wasn't enough for Nikki. Her thighs shook and her core begged for him.

Pete's kiss turned her into a ball of need.

The shower didn't help. Her muscles were lax and her overheated skin super-sensitive. If he touched her clit, she would come in two seconds — she wanted him that badly.

"I need you," Nikki breathed against his mouth.

In answer, Pete pressed her back to the tile behind the showerhead. The water beat down on him, soaking his sparse chest hair, rivulets running down his gorgeous pecs, down his defined abs and his beautiful jutting erection.

Nikki bit her lip. His thighs were thick and powerful and all she could remember was the feel of his rough hair against her legs when they were entwined in bed.

"Darlin', don't look at me like that." Pete's chest rose and fell with his effort to speak.

She wanted to lick the water droplets off his chest, suck his nipples then tell him to get back in the shower so she could do it all over again. Then she'd taste the rest of his body, too.

Why wait?

Dragging her hands down his chest, Nikki knelt in front of him, cradling his penis in both hands, running her hands over his soft skin, cupping his sac.

Pete gasped when she enfolded him into her mouth. She sucked the thick head of him, tracing the underside with her tongue. His whole body shuddered and he buried his hands in her wet hair. She took all of him, moving slowly up and down on his shaft. The water caressed her head and shoulders and Nikki closed her eyes, tasting every inch of him.

Saltiness tinged her taste buds—he was close. Her sex pulsed, her blood pounded in her ears. Making him feel good was a total turn-on. She wanted to finish him, give him ecstasy like he had with his tongue on her, but she didn't get the chance.

Pete grabbed her arms, yanking her up against his chest. His mouth descended hard. He kissed her until she was dizzy, the hot water and steam surrounding them arousing her even more.

"Inside you...now..."

Nikki didn't need another invitation. She wrapped her arms and legs around him.

He shoved inside, filling her completely even before the cool tile hit her back again. Panting his name, she tilted her hips to take him deeper, holding on tight when his thrusts became desperate.

Neither of them lasted long. The arousal and heated haze had Nikki so wrapped up in Pete she had no chance of drawing out her pleasure. With only two more lunges of his hips, she was screaming his name and gripping his biceps until her nails sank in. Her whole body contracted.

He shouted when he came, his erection jerking inside her, and he buried his face against her neck. Pete's wet, blond locks brushed her cheek and she clung to him so hard her breathing was labored. She didn't care. Nikki could die at the moment and be content.

Pete pulled her away from the tiled wall, caressing her back with such tenderness she shivered.

Nikki lowered her legs from his waist. They shook, threatening to dump her on her ass, so she stayed close to his chest, smiling as he pressed a kiss to her cheek. She felt a sense of loss when he slipped from her body. Pete held her tight.

Safe. Warm. No cares in the world.

He tilted her face up so gently a wave of emotion took her by surprise and she had to blink tears away. *Please think it's shower water.*

Pete kissed her tenderly and it melted into something deep, languorous. Made Nikki yearn for more. For him. Forever. She moved as close as she could get, kissing him back with all her might.

Their mouths parted and he studied her face until she almost squirmed. He caressed her cheeks with both thumbs. "Are you okay?"

She nodded. "Perfect. You make me...feel better than I ever have."

He smiled and her heart stuttered. "You too, darlin'. You make my blood boil I want you so bad. Even after I just had you."

"I want to stay here with you." She left *always* off her statement.

Pete spoke of lust, physical need, want. She felt that for him, definitely. But...there was more.

Nikki couldn't put a word to the feeling. Not even in her own head.

"Damn good thing you're not going anywhere, then." He winked and she couldn't help the smile that curved her lips.

"You know you're adorable, right, Detective?"

He reared back as if she'd slapped him, green eyes wide. "Adorable?"

"Yup. Adorable." Nikki kissed his chin and his chest.

"Hmmm, that seems like a word much more appropriate to describe *you*."

"Well, instead of arguing with me, why don't we get you clean? It seems like you're more than dirty, now."

Pete laughed and kissed her.

They made love in the shower once more before Pete finally shut the water off and gathered her up in his arms.

Drying their bodies didn't result in getting dressed because of wandering hands on both their parts. So in a tangle of lips and limbs, Nikki gave herself to him again.

They could stay in bed all day as far as she was concerned. Pete's body could sure use more nips, licks and kisses. She hadn't touched him enough. Every time she tried, he'd end up taking over, and taking *her*.

She'd complain, but who could be mad at a selfless lover?

Nikki traced the police badge tattooed on his chest, going around, down the side and back up, moving on to touch the black gun next to it as well as the decorative ribbon that announced a date in a flourish of gold lettering. "What does this date mean?"

Pete lay with one arm around her and the other tucked behind his head, elbow bent. His expression was content, and about as relaxed as she'd seen him lately.

One corner of his delicious mouth lifted. "The day I started at APD. Patrol Officer Pete Crane. A long time ago."

"Well, it's gorgeous work. Detailed. It doesn't look old at all. And neither do you, Detective."

He winked. "Well, you were, what, nine?"

"Ten, thank you very much. So what?"

He sighed and broke eye contact.

Her heart sank.

Pete must be bothered about their age difference, because he was the one who kept mentioning it. Nikki didn't give a crap how old he was. She loved him anyway.

Freezing against him, she was suddenly glad that he wasn't looking her way for her little revelation. Being shocked was a copout.

She *did* love him.

It'd happened fast and should've taken her by surprise, but it hadn't. Her detective was a great guy. She'd known that for years. Spending a little time with

him, despite the circumstances, was all the
encouragement her heart had needed. And now it
belonged to Pete.

Did he want it?

Blinking back tears, she refused to acknowledge that
he'd most likely crush it. She stared at his profile. His
strong jaw line, patrician nose, fair stubble, piercing
green eyes. Nothing *didn't* appeal.

"Pete?"

He swung his head back around and their gazes
locked.

Nikki sucked in a breath. "I don't give a damn how
old you are. You know that, right?"

His eyes widened, but he didn't say anything.

"And besides… I'm a woman. Not a child. A woman
who knows what she wants."

She dragged her hand down his chest, traced his abs
with her fingertips until he was panting. Continuing
to move downward, she encircled his growing
erection, stroking him until Pete was whispering her
name like a mantra.

"What…does…she want?" he breathed.

"She wants her detective. Inside her."

Nikki's belly fluttered as desire unfurled for him
again. Her core quivered at the intensity in his eyes.
Pete sat up, resting his hand at the back of her neck to
pull her closer.

She met his heated kiss halfway and slid her tongue
into his mouth. She'd show him with her body what
she couldn't tell him in words. For now, it was all she
could do.

He shivered when she touched the puckered skin of
the round scar under his arm.

"The bullet went in right there?" Nikki's voice was concerned. Like he'd been shot yesterday.

"Yes. And out my back. Collapsed my lung on the journey."

She gasped. Her eyes welled with tears that clenched his heart.

"Darlin', don't cry for old wounds. I'm fine." Cupping her face, he pressed a kiss to her mouth, but her expression didn't soften.

Her hands spread over his right shoulder, examining the scar of the less lethal result of his run-in with Carlo Maldonado last year.

"What about your arm?" she whispered. "Sometimes you hold it like it hurts."

Pete frowned. How the heck had she noticed that? Had his little redhead been watching him at work? "Sometimes it's stiff," he admitted.

"I'm sorry."

"What the heck for?" He made her look at him again.

"I don't like that you got hurt. And my...situation...puts you in danger, again."

Pete laughed. "I'm a cop, Nikki. Besides, I'm the one who got *you* shot." His fingers brushed the bandage covering the stitches on her upper arm. "You had nothing to do with what happened to me last year."

Nikki's auburn eyebrows drew tight and he tried to focus on that instead of her bare breasts propped on his chest.

"*You* did not get me shot, Pete Crane."

"I shouldn't have let my guard down. It got you hurt."

"Let your guard down?" Now hurt crossed her gorgeous face and he could have kicked himself.

Why did that tumble out of your mouth, idiot?

"Nikki—"

When her eyes misted over, his gut tightened. "Do you regret what happened at the safe house? Before you open your mouth, you damn well know I'm not talking about the shooting, so don't play stupid."

"No." *The truth.* "I don't regret what happened between us. I regret that my screw-up got you hurt."

She didn't relax. "Pete, I wanted to be with you then. I want to be with you now."

He gripped her shoulders and pulled her closer, ignoring how her nipples brushed his. His cock twitched. "You are with me, sweetness."

"Do you want to be with me?" The whisper was heavy, hesitant. Pained.

How could she even ask that after he'd made love to her more times than he could count? Was he that much of an ass to make her so insecure? "Yes, darlin'. You can't tell by now?"

The tease had missed its mark. Her face was still tight, hurt.

His cell blared from his nightstand and Pete cursed it to hell and back. He wanted Nikki's answer. It mattered. How she felt...mattered. More than it should. It didn't matter—even if he'd let the call go to voicemail, the moment was gone.

She moved away, backing off his chest. He was cold, and it wasn't because of the loss of her body heat.

"Crane."

"Today's Sunday."

"Aren't you the observant one, little brother?" Pete said.

Nate growled.

Damn, you're losing your touch all around today.

"Are you coming to Mama and Pop's?" Nate barked before he could answer.

Nikki's eyebrows shot up and Pete pulled her back down, rubbing her back in long strokes. He wanted her close. He wanted things okay with the two of them.

She didn't fight him, resting her cheek on his chest and looking much too interested in his phone call.

"Uh… I'm working a case."

"It's Sunday."

"So you've pointed out."

"Pete, seriously. I *will* come over there and kick your ass all the way to Mama's. Don't leave me hanging with my balls out."

Nikki stifled a giggle and Pete winked.

"Balls out? Would hope they'd be all put away when you grace your parents' house with your presence."

Nate sighed. "Gonna make me beg?"

"Gonna tell me what your issue is?"

"Your mother."

"Ah, you mean *your* mother? What'd she do?"

"She's bugging the crap outta me and I need backup."

Pete winced. He hadn't been to his parents' for Sunday dinner in three weeks. If he did go, his mother would bug the crap out of *him*. And besides, he'd have to take Nikki. God, his mother would never let him hear the end of bringing a woman home. She'd have them engaged before end of dinner and married off by the end of the week. *Shit.*

She'd been after him to marry Andi for years. Until Cole had done it for him. Only then had his mother calmed her jets about his partner. Turned out she liked Cole, though, so he could live in peace instead of having to hear 'I told you to marry that girl' for the rest of his natural life.

But Nikki... His mother already adored her. They'd met at one of the APD-hosted family picnics.

Pete was doomed.

"What time do we need to be there?" Nikki leaned up, her mouth next to his.

He wanted to kill her, not kiss her.

"Who's this?" Nate asked.

"Nikki Harper."

"Nikki Harper... From the police department?"

"Yup. What time do we need to be there?"

Pete mouthed *I'm going to kill you* but she only flashed a grin and kissed him silently.

"Well, didn't my day just get interesting?" Nate mused.

"Kiss my ass, little brother."

Nate and Nikki laughed at the same time.

"See you *two* at four. You know Mama likes to socialize before we eat. Especially when someone brings a *guest.*"

Sighing, he dragged his hand down his face. "See you at four then, you bastard."

Nikki giggled again, but she was gloating. No doubt Nate's expression could mirror his redhead's.

"Bye, big bro. Bye, Nikki Harper." His brother's voice was wrapped in laughter.

"Yay! I love your mother," Nikki said after his brother disconnected the call.

Pete tossed his phone on the bed. "Yeah, yeah, she loves you, too."

She beamed and his heart missed a beat.

Nikki was happy. He'd do every damn thing she wanted if he could keep that silly grin on her face.

"I'm excited. We get to do something fun."

He waggled his eyebrows. "We haven't been having fun?"

She made a playful swat at his chest. "You know what I mean."

"Well, laugh it up, sweetness, but the last laugh will really be on Nate."

"How's that?"

"I'm calling Lee."

Chapter Twenty

The look on his brother's face when Lee stepped into their parents' house was priceless. Had him grinning like an idiot. Who knew Nate could gape?

He was up off the couch as Pete threw a nod to their father, who was involved in the Rangers game on the big screen.

"Agent Lee Dawson." Nate crossed the room in two strides. Hugged her.

Pete arched a brow. They knew each other, sure. Had met during Maldonado's trial. But a hug like *that*? His brother was usually the consummate professional—no matter what.

Lee looked comfortable in Nate's embrace that lasted a few seconds too long. Not at all like when she'd hugged Pete in greeting the day she'd come to town.

"It's nice to see you again, Counsellor," Lee said.

Hmmm... Was Pete's plan to make his younger brother feel uncomfortable going to backfire? He stared at Lee and Nate. They fell into easy conversation.

If she was into his brother—and it was a big maybe—why had she kissed Pete last night? Would Lee have really slept with him if there'd been something to that kiss?

Nikki tugged on his arm and heat crept up his neck as if she could read his thoughts. His stomach was a lead weight.

Pete had kissed Lee then had gone home and made love to Nikki.

Shit. He rubbed his neck. Why did he feel like he'd cheated on Nikki? *Ridiculous.*

"Uh, Nate, you know Nikki?" Pete said.

She smiled as his brother pulled her into a quick hug—nothing compared to the one he'd given Lee.

"So nice to see you again, Nikki."

"Nice to see you, too, Nate."

His brother grinned. "Want a beer, guys? Pop, you need a fresh one?" Nate called.

"Nope, I'm good." Their dad didn't move from the end of the couch and Pete shook his head, smiling. The game must be good to override his good old Southern manners.

Lee declined the beer and followed Nate into the kitchen for an iced tea instead. Pete watched them go. Their mother was in the kitchen, no doubt. Why would Nate take her into the lioness's den?

"Well, that's interesting," Nikki said.

"I know it."

"They look good together."

He looked into her pretty brown eyes. "You think so?"

"Yes. We do, too." She smiled and grabbed his hand.

Letting her entwine their fingers, he fought the urge to kiss her knuckles. If she planned on touching him, holding his hand, staying close to him all day, it would be no secret to his family that Nikki and he were together.

Somehow, that didn't bother him as much as it should.

Pete gulped. "Nah, you're too good for me."

Nikki frowned. He'd meant it as a half-joke, but shifted on his feet as she stared him down.

"C'mon, I don't think you've ever met my dad."

She nodded, but her expression didn't soften. Where was the happy grin he'd seen before?

"Dad."

"Peter Allen Crane. Why didn't you tell me you were bringing two lovely girls to dinner?"

Pete winced. His father hadn't even had a chance to speak, though the man did stand and put his hand out to Nikki.

He turned to see his mother—all four feet eleven inches of her—striding across the living room in her Sunday livery of a frilly pink apron over a red dress right out of 1955. Her puffy blond hair was piled on top of her head, larger than life. She had on matching red hoop earrings and high heels. Like always, his mother looked great. Ready for church or a night on the town. She'd told him many times that one always needed to look one's best. Marilyn Crane was as vibrant as the clothes she always wore.

But damn, *nothing* was worse than her leaving the kitchen in mid-meal preparation.

"Hi, Mama." He hugged her tight.

His mother cupped his cheeks and dragged his face down to her level for a loud, smacking kiss. Pete just hoped he survived the incident sans the bright red lipstick that was her staple.

He glared at his brother, who was smirking from the archway with Lee beside him. His temporary partner had amusement written all over her expression as she watched the torture.

"Nikki Harper, you look fantastic." His mother held both Nikki's hands out and perused her outfit.

Nikki beamed and his heart jumped. She did look fantastic in the multi-colored bright sundress.

Pete couldn't help but wish they were alone so he could get her out of it.

"Petey, how did you get this gorgeous little thing to come with you?"

Petey? Fighting the urge to close his eyes, he ignored Lee's snort. He'd never live that down.

Nikki saved him from answering — thank God.

"Thank you for having me, Mrs Crane."

"Oh, sugar, Mrs Crane was my mother-in-law. Please call me Marilyn."

She smiled and nodded, shifting on her sandaled feet. Mama's gaze appraised them both. He wanted to squirm.

Dad slid his arm around Pete's mother's shoulders and smiled at Nikki. "Nice to meet you. I believe you work for Chief Martin?"

"Yes, sir." Nikki moved closer to Pete after shaking his father's hand.

He wanted to throw his arm around her, but made his hands remain at his sides. His mother was already doing the stare-down. If he touched her, it'd get worse.

"I had no idea you two were dating," Mama said.

"We're not." Pete's answer was fast. Quick denial was easier than acceptance he was starting to feel. Starting to want?

The look Nikki flashed him was full of pain. He cringed but she schooled her expression quickly. *God, please don't let Mama notice.*

"Ah," Dad said. Retired Lieutenant Dennis Crane had put in thirty years at Antioch Police Department. His father would catch on fast it was work-related and he couldn't discuss an open case.

Not that his mother would care. Her quiet stare was already matchmaking.

"Well, let's eat, shall we?" Nate asked, much too brightly.

"Great idea, son. Let's eat on the patio, since it's just a mild day."

* * * *

Nikki grinned at Nate's ribbing Pete about something as the guys set the picnic table on his parents' sprawling, covered patio. They pulled the white and red checked tablecloth tight then set silverware and plates down.

Nikki and Lee were told by all of the Cranes to have a seat and relax, they weren't allowed to help. Mr Crane brought the large platter of smoked brisket to the table and set it at the center. The aroma was fantastic, teasing her nose and causing her stomach to rumble.

Watching the brothers interact as they brought the rest of the food out of the house was enjoyable. Pete was laughing and quipping back as soon as Nate could fling teases at him. The most normal she'd seen him in days.

This Pete was the one she was used to seeing at work. The jokester. The lighthearted guy who always had something witty to say.

He was gorgeous and fun, and she loved him even more.

She couldn't stop staring. He was aware she was watching him. Every glance he spared her — the way his green gaze would heat sent tingles down her spine, warmed her limbs. Made her want him.

They'd made love so many times she was sore, but it wouldn't stop her if he wanted her tonight. She wanted to sleep in his arms again. Tonight. Tomorrow night. Every night.

Even though he'd crushed her when he'd too-quickly corrected his mother. But it was true — they weren't *dating*. Having sex wasn't dating.

So why does that hurt so much?

"Why are you so quiet?" Lee asked from her seat next to Nikki at the picnic table. Her dark hair was loose today, and she wore a short-sleeved, scoop-neck maroon top with layers of fabric at the front. It was tapered and hugged her curvy figure. Her gray skirt stopped at her knees, but Nikki would bet money the woman had a gun strapped to her thigh — even on Sunday. The outfit was simple and gorgeous. Like Lee. Fitting.

Should Nikki still be jealous of Lee's interaction with Pete?

Dismissing the thought, she smiled at the beautiful FBI agent. "No reason. Just soaking in our surroundings."

Lee smiled back and gestured to Nate and Pete. "They're something else, huh?"

Nodding, Nikki looked back at the two brothers. Both too handsome for their own good.

Nate was an inch or two taller than Pete's six-foot-one-inch frame, and his eyes were hazel more than green, but they both had the same lean muscular build. Both had the thick blond locks of their mother and resembled their father in looks — chiseled jaw lines and high cheekbones.

Although his brown hair was receding, retired Lieutenant Crane was still just as tall and good-looking as his sons, even though his wife's cooking had filled out his middle.

The family got settled at the table and Nikki had to stifle a few laughs at the fussing Mrs Crane threw at her sons. Like they were little boys, instead of thirty-two and thirty-five.

When Pete took a seat beside Nikki, and Lee moved to sit across from her beside Nate, all she could focus on was the warmth of his thigh next to hers.

"So did you catch that murder at the trailer park?" Mr Crane asked as he handed Nikki a full plate of steaming brisket.

She thanked him and passed the large bowl of mashed potatoes when Nate asked.

"Nope," Pete said after taking a sip of beer. "Manning's on the case."

"I didn't get a call just yet, either, so I don't know if I'll be on it," Nate said.

"We have to catch him first," Lee said.

"Please, let's not talk about this at dinner," Pete's mother said. "It's uncomfortable talk for Nikki, I'm sure."

Before Nikki could assure her the guys and Lee were fine, their father nodded and apologized.

"We can talk shop after supper."

"Petey, can you pass me the salt?" Lee asked, dark eyes dancing.

Nikki swallowed back a giggle at the look Pete threw his FBI partner. His brother snorted, reaching for a drink.

His father looked amused when Nikki glanced his way, but evidently Mr Crane knew better than to remark.

Nikki reached for the salt at the same time Pete did, because she was closer, but their hands bumped. Eyes locked. She relinquished the salt shaker.

His expression softened and she suddenly *needed* to kiss him.

The moment passed when someone cleared his throat and her eyes inadvertently collided with Nate's hazel gaze.

He gave her a half-smile and grabbed the salt from his brother for Lee.

She shifted at Pete's side, heart racing. Heat crept up her neck. If he didn't want his family to know about them, he'd have to stop looking at her like that. Her blood sang for him and her belly warmed.

When his hot hand settled on her upper thigh under the table, Nikki jumped. He patted her leg without looking her way, without stopping the conversation about sports he'd struck up with his dad. But his touch made her calm and burn for him at the same time.

Nikki felt a stare. Pete's mother was studying them. She fought the urge to gulp and flashed a smile.

"How's your grandma, sugar?" Marilyn asked.

Good. Something she could focus on. Easy conversation. "She's coming around from the stroke nicely. But the doc has her in the hospital to monitor arrhythmia. She's tough. Gram will be fine."

"We'll pray for her."

"Thank you, ma'am."

Mrs Crane smiled and clapped her hands. "Are ya'll ready for dessert? I made my famous apple pie."

Nikki shifted on her feet as she watched Pete's mother bustle around the kitchen after dinner. They'd left the guys, Lee and Lieutenant Crane on the patio. "Are you sure I can't help you, Mrs—I mean, Marilyn?"

"Oh, no, sugar." The older woman rinsed off a pan and shut the water off. "I brought you in here so they could talk about horrible police stuff. And my mama taught me you never put guests to work."

"I really don't mind." Heading to the sink, she grabbed a kitchen towel and started wiping the dishes Marilyn had hand-washed.

Pete's mom laughed and shook her head. "Looks like your gram raised you to be as stubborn as she is."

Nikki grinned. "I guess so. Where does this go?"

"Put them in a stack next to the dish drainer and we'll put them away afterward."

"Yes, ma'am."

"I knew I always liked you, Nikki Harper."

"I like you, too, Mrs Crane."

Marilyn stopped washing the pan she was working on. "What did I tell you about that *Mrs Crane* stuff?"

"Sorry, Marilyn. Gram raised me to be polite, too."

"Good thing you're so stubborn. You're going to need it."

"Ma'am?"

"My boy is stubborn, too. You'll have to fight for him." Her green gaze—just like Pete's—evaluated her.

Nikki almost dropped the dish she'd just dried. "I-I-I don't know what you mean."

"Nonsense. I'm not blind, sugar. I see the way you look at him. But more than that, I see the way *he* looks at *you*."

Her limbs warmed and words dissolved. She'd noticed how Pete looked at her, too. He cared about her—he had to. His touches, kisses, they weren't totally lust, were they? Was it too much to hope he planned on keeping her around? Probably.

She swallowed back a gulp. Had Pete's mother pulled her into the kitchen to ambush her? "I'm...kinda stuck with him right now because of his case. Pete said I can't really talk about it."

His mother's gaze called her on the bullshit she'd just spewed. "It's always under the veil of the blue line, isn't it?"

"Well, it's an open case—"

"Tell yourself what you need to, to get through the night, sugar. Just don't let him go if you don't want to. You'll regret it. And so will he."

What the heck could she say to that?

"I love him," Nikki blurted. *Shit.* Why the hell had she said that?

Pete's mom smiled—no, beamed was more like it. "Good." She went back to scrubbing the pan.

Frozen by the counter, Nikki fiddled with the glass she'd just dried, bit her bottom lip and waited for Marilyn to speak. But Pete's mom said nothing for a good five minutes.

"Plates go in the cupboard on the right above the microwave."

Nikki jumped.

"Well, sugar, you said you wanted to help, didn't you?"

Nodding hastily, she grabbed the plates and put them away.

"I love my Pete," Marilyn said after handing her the pan and directing Nikki to its home. "But he's just like his father. Can't tell a good thing if she's staring him in the face."

Nikki paused. Should she comment? But Marilyn saved her the need.

"My point is, sugar, he can be stubborn and foolish."

"Why are you telling me this?" Nikki whispered.

"Because if he hurts you, I want you to know I'll kick his behind."

Chapter Twenty-One

"Suck harder, bitch. I paid extra." Luca buried his hand in Prostitute Barbie's bleached hair, making her take all of his cock. Pleasure from her hot mouth rolled over him. Damn, the girl didn't have a gag reflex.

He hissed when her teeth grazed over-sensitive skin, but he liked it. Rocking his hips, he fucked her face until his balls tightened.

Hand at the back of her neck, he moved her head up and down the length of his dick, biting his lip to keep his moans and groans to a minimum. It might feel good as shit—however, there was no reason to let her know that.

She put her hands on both his thighs and raised herself on her knees, making sure to press her fake tits into him.

Luca grinned and put his hand around her throat, squeezing slightly as she sucked him off.

Pale blue eyes widened when he increased the pressure, and that just got him hotter. He lifted his hips and shoved his cock down her throat.

His spine tingled and his dick jerked in her mouth. "Unnnggh, I'm coming."

Prostitute Barbie gripped his thighs until fake nails sank through the fabric of his slacks and licked every last drop of him like he was a popsicle.

What a good little whore.

She flashed a satisfied smile when she leaned back. "Did you like that, baby?" She dragged her fingers down his chest—like that was supposed to turn him on.

Suddenly, he didn't want her hands on him. Post-orgasmic haze faded. Caselli was after him. He needed to get the fuck out of this cheap motel. Find another. Stay close. They—police and his boss alike—would assume he'd hightailed it out of the city.

Luca needed to make sure Berto was dead. He'd shot him three or four times. Had he hit the woman at all? Berto's whore had screamed, but he couldn't be sure.

Shit. Why the fuck did he keep failing?

Leaning up, Prostitute Barbie made like she was going to kiss him, but Luca turned his head. "I didn't pay for that."

The hooker pouted and plopped down on the bed beside him. "But I fixed your arm and everything."

"I paid you for it."

She said nothing as Luca stood and shoved his dick in his pants. His right arm smarted but he ignored it. He needed to get rid of Prostitute Barbie. Needed to look around and make sure no one had found him. Glancing around the room, he took comfort in the three guns he spotted. Damn good thing he'd stuffed one of his duffles with ammo.

"What about me?" She frowned.

"What *about* you?" Couldn't the bitch tell he was done with her?

Those blue eyes flashed and she crossed her arms over the fake double-Ds. They sat high in the black pleather corset, threatening to pop out.

Luca liked big tits like any other man, but this girl wasn't his type. She'd just been available. He liked them dark, Italian-looking.

Ah, so this one actually enjoys sex. "I don't remember paying to get *you* off."

The girl huffed and puffed.

Luca leaned down over her plastic body, forcing her to lie back. He wrapped his hand around her neck. "You have a problem, sweetheart?"

Applying pressure caused her eyes to widen again. Her cheeks flushed red and it had nothing to do with arousal.

Her fear made his dick twitch. Maybe he'd fuck her after all. She'd gotten an extra hundred bucks for getting the medical supplies from the pharmacy and dressing his wound and she'd even dug the bullet out. Like she'd done that a time or two.

"Hmmm, who would miss you if you were gone, babe?"

She sputtered and struggled beneath him. Clutched at his wrists, her nails bit into his skin. Luca didn't care.

Now his cock was hard as hell, the zipper of his slacks cutting into him.

He released the girl and she rubbed her neck. Glared at him. "My pimp will kick your ass."

Luca laughed. "Not likely." He moved off the girl.

Her eyes raked his form, stopping at his tented pants.

"I changed my mind. Get naked. You want fucked, I'll fuck you."

When she touched her neck and hesitated, he growled.

"Take 'em off, or I'll rip 'em off. I only need your cunt."

* * * *

"Someone reported a big black Hummer abandoned behind an empty rent house down the street from the trailer park." Jared Manning jogged over from his work area in CID, a small piece of paper in hand.

"Oh yeah?" Lee asked.

"Just wait for the best part."

"What's that?" Pete reclined in his chair.

"Guess whose prints were all over it."

Pete met Jared's dark eyes. "Whose?"

"Billy Madden's."

"Not a shocker," Lee said. "We knew he was the getaway driver."

"Yeah, but now we have some physical evidence," Pete put in.

Lee nodded.

"Anything else interesting inside?"

"Lieutenant Wells had it impounded. You want to process it? Or you want me to?"

Pete shrugged.

"What'd ya say, Petey, shall we go and check it out?" Lee winked.

Jared snorted.

Pete frowned, but let it slide. "Sure, why the hell not?" Pete looked at Jared. "Thanks, man."

"Anytime."

Although the impound yard wasn't far, Pete didn't want to be gone for an extended amount of time. He'd told Nikki not to move from the station. A part of him didn't like leaving her, even though processing one vehicle shouldn't take too long.

"So, how's it going?" Lee asked as she strapped the seatbelt on in his Crown Vic.

"You've been with me all day..."

"Not talking about the case."

Pete sighed. "Then what are you talking about?" He started the car, not looking in her direction.

"Right."

"How's my brother?" Pete fired back.

Lee fidgeted — actually fidgeted — and stayed silent for way too long.

"Ah, I see. You can pry, but I can't." He grinned. It wasn't often he could make her feel uncomfortable.

"Not prying."

"Right." Pete smirked.

"Fine." She crossed her arms over her breasts. "Let's just say when I kissed you, I kissed the wrong Crane."

Pete laughed. "Okay. I don't want to know more."

"Didn't think so."

He pulled out of the PD lot. Radio chatter was the only noise in the car.

"Your turn," Lee said.

"For?"

"No, no. I share, you share. It's only fair. And don't say shit about me rhyming. It was an accident."

One corner of his mouth shot up. His heart skipped a beat. Pete tightened his grip on the steering wheel. "It's...complicated."

Lee frowned. "As complicated as sixteen hundred miles?"

He glanced at her and couldn't look away for a moment. Her expression was tight. Un-Lee-like. Did she care for his brother?

"Feels like it," he muttered.

"It doesn't matter, anyway." Lee's voice was low. Pained, even.

What the heck's that about?

She looked out of the window and said nothing more. He didn't push her.

By the time they'd parked and got out of the car, Lee had a smile back in place.

Something lurked below the surface, but what? His gut told him Lee was a deep, complex person, despite the constant humor and appearance of a perpetual light nature. He'd suspected she was a former alcoholic, but only because she never drank. Declined all offers at his parents' and every evening they'd shared a meal at his place, or even at Dixie's. But every time Pete or Nikki or even Nate had touched a beer, Lee's eyes would dart to the bottle or can then away. Like even looking was too much temptation.

When curiosity had gotten the better of him, Pete had asked Cole, only to get nowhere. Lee's former partner hadn't a clue. Cole had just affirmed he'd never seen her drink, either.

If she wanted to open up to him, Pete would listen. He wouldn't push her. He liked her too much to lose an argument about something that wasn't his business.

He gestured for her to walk in front of him, watching her figure. If Lee wanted Nate, so be it. Good for his brother. Pete could see it. Nikki was right—they looked good together.

If they wanted a relationship, they'd make the distance work.

What about Nikki? Him and Nikki...

No, don't think about it. The sex was great. That was all he needed to know right now. Or ever. It wasn't like they could actually be together long term.

She was young and vibrant. He was inappropriate for her all around.

And Chief... His boss was going to kick his ass if he found out they'd slept together. Were still sleeping together. God knew Pete wasn't letting her out of his bed until he had to.

Until the case is over.

Then what? It wasn't like he could go back to normal. He'd had her. He...cared...about her. Pete almost choked when another word came to mind, but he shut it down, put it in a vault and threw away the combination.

Of course he cared about her. She was his lover, his witness, but more than that, she was his friend. Sure, he'd known her for a few years, but she'd been a work acquaintance. The case had forced him to get to know her. She was strong, passionate in and out of the bedroom. She cared about her friends, her job. Loved her gram. She was funny, sexy and adorable. Gorgeous inside and out.

Nikki was...perfect.

Lee stopped to open the office door, and Pete came up short, almost bowling her over. He turned his body and ran into the side of the building instead. His forehead smacked the doorframe. His vision blurred and his temples throbbed.

"Shit!"

"Pete, crap. What happened? Are you okay?" Lee grabbed his arm. She steadied him when he wobbled on his feet, her grip surprisingly strong.

"I'm fine." *Jesus.* He rubbed his head. No chance to even play it off.

What a fucking jackass.

"What happened?" His temporary partner stared at him, her gaze raking his face then his body. "Did you trip?"

Pretty bad when your knee-jerk is 'I wish.' "I must have." Heat burned his neck and he fought the urge to tug at his collar.

"Hope you don't end up with a shiner. You hit pretty hard."

"Shit. No one will believe I actually walked into a door."

"A building, actually." Lee flashed a crooked smile.

"I'm glad I can entertain you."

"Hey, we can always tell people Nikki beat you up. She does have a temper."

Pete glared. "Let's just get this done."

"Here, let me open the door for you. I don't want you to walk into it."

He ignored her laugh at her own joke and followed her into the building.

They were able to bag some hair and collect some fiber particles that were a possible match for what had been found on Billy's clothes and body, but the Hummer had been wiped clean by someone who'd known what they were doing.

Not one fingerprint on the leather seats, door handles or console. The only place that had prints was the steering wheel, and like Manning had told them, they were a match for Pete's dead informant, Billy Madden.

They'd been left on purpose. Pete didn't buy that Billy was the one who'd wiped the car down and accidentally left his prints on the wheel.

"What a fricking waste of time." He sighed.

"Not really," Lee said, hipping the door shut. "We got these." She held up the bags of fiber and the dark hair they'd found in the carpet on the driver's side of the big SUV. "And we've learned that the prints on the steering wheel were left deliberately."

"The hair is black. Could be any one of them."

"Right. But it could actually place Marchetti or Donati *in* the car. Goes from circumstantial to physical."

"True."

She smiled and tucked the sealed bags into the black case.

Pete hefted the kit after trashing his latex gloves. Lee followed suit, and tossed hers into the trashcan in the garage.

"They got those plates in Texarkana." He pointed to the stolen Texas plates on the Hummer.

"It sure as hell isn't a 2004 Nissan."

"Right. But knowing where they stole it and what car it belongs to doesn't help much either."

"Nope," Lee agreed. "Just tells us they weren't very far into the state when they jacked new plates."

"Well, let's go. We can swing by the lab and I need to get back to the station. I want to write all this up." He needed to check on Nikki, too.

His temporary partner gave him a long look and arched a brow. "Sure. That's why you want to get back."

"Right."

"You keep telling yourself that." She smirked.

Chapter Twenty-Two

Nikki shut the filing cabinet and paused. Voices from the corridor drew her attention. That in and of itself wasn't odd—people walked by Chief's office all day, every day, and the door was always open, as was the boss's policy. But giggling? Kids?

"Nikki!"

She whirled around in time to see a familiar little redheaded boy as Ethan rushed into her office.

Grinning, she met him in front of her desk and ruffled his hair. He opened his arms, so she swept him up in a hug.

"Ethan, don't yell." Andi winced as she came into the office, baby carrier containing Micah in one hand.

A pretty dark-haired woman and two little girls were on her heels.

"Oh, he's fine. Chief's out this morning." Nikki propped Ethan on her hip as Andi set the baby down.

"Bummer. I wanted him to meet Micah." The detective gestured to her sleeping son.

Nikki smiled at the tiny gorgeous infant, then met Andi's blue eyes. "Oh, no. He won't be in until after lunch, said he had some things to take care of."

"Well, I should have called. My fault. Just had to get out of the house, so I brought Cass and the kids to see where Cole and I work." Andi gestured to the other woman and little girls. "Nikki, this is Cass, Cole's sister. Her daughters, Kelsey and Lacey."

The girls—who looked about eight and ten—waved when Andi said their names. The older one, Kelsey, looked just like her mother—and her uncle. They were adorable.

Actually, Cass looked like the female version of Cole, gray eyes, dark hair, high cheekbones. Her face was soft, feminine. Beautiful. She flashed dimples when she smiled. But her brother was very tall, and Cass was petite, probably only about five-three. Andi and Nikki both had five or six inches on her.

Nikki set Ethan to his feet and he rushed to his cousins, reaching for Kelsey's hand.

"Nice to meet you, Nikki." Cass put her hand out for a shake.

"Nice to meet you, too." Nikki smiled.

"Where's my partner gotten off to? He didn't answer his cell," Andi said.

"Pete poked his head in here about an hour ago and told me to stay put. He had to run out with Lee. Said he'd be back as soon as he can. He didn't get specific."

"Ah," Andi said. "Guess I'll catch him later."

"Mommy, I'm hungry." Lacey, the younger of Cass' girls, tugged on her arm. Her light brown hair was in pigtails with pink ribbons to go with her pink and purple jumper.

Totally a girly girl, where her sister was not. Kelsey was dressed in jeans shorts and a printed T-shirt, her dark hair in a simple ponytail like Andi's.

"We'll go grab some lunch soon, baby. Aunt Andi wants to show us around." Cass caressed her daughter's cheek.

"Actually, if you don't mind me saying, there's a full breakfast in the break room. One of the guys' wives brought food, pancakes, eggs, the works."

Andi looked at Cass. "Wanna feed the kids here?"

Cass shrugged. "Sure."

"I want pancakes!" Ethan jumped up and down.

"You're more than welcome to it. I'm sure there's a lot left," Nikki said, grinning at the little boy.

Their voices faded as Andi led her family out of the office and down to the PD's kitchen and break room area.

Nikki smiled as she slid back into her seat. The kids were adorable.

She couldn't wait to have kids. A baby to hold in her arms and grow into a rambunctious little boy like Ethan, or a cute little girl who wanted her hair braided. Blond hair. Big green eyes.

Shivering, she shifted in her seat.

Kids...with Pete.

Nikki wanted that. More than anything.

Heart thundering, she chided herself and moved the mouse to wake up her computer.

Chief had asked her to type up a few memos, so she organized his notes and opened a new doc in Word. Wouldn't take her long. He wrote neatly and she typed fast.

Yes, focus on work. Get your stuff done.

When she finished with the memos, she needed to look at his meeting schedule for the next two weeks.

"Nikki."

She jumped in her chair, giving a yelp as heat ran up her neck and flamed her cheeks.

Andi stepped back into the room, her baby in her arms. Little Micah was awake. "Sorry, I didn't mean to startle you."

"It's okay." She cleared her throat, shifting on her mesh chair.

When the detective dragged one of the chairs over from the edge of the room where Nikki had people wait for Chief, she arched an eyebrow.

Andi plopped down at the edge of Nikki's desk, settling the baby against her breasts.

"What's up?" Nikki asked.

"Talk to me."

"About?"

"Life. Gram. Pete. The case. Whatever. You haven't called me in ages. Last time I saw you was at the house the day Cole set up the surveillance DVD."

"You *have* been busy."

"Yes, I have. But your phone works. We always talk, Nikki." Andi rocked Micah when he whimpered.

"And you're one of the few people I can talk about the case with."

"Yup. So spill. How're you doing?"

"Pete's keeping me safe."

Andi's blue eyes zoned in on her face.

Shit. What about that statement is making Andi look at me that way?

"Right."

Nikki nodded, squirming. "Right."

Her friend laughed. "Repeating what I say isn't going to tell me what I'm asking. How are *you?* Nikki Harper. My friend and fellow control freak. How are you coping with the whole witness thing?"

"'Coping' is the right word." *Although living with Pete...sleeping in his bed, in his arms...it makes it better, doesn't it?* It wasn't nearly as difficult as it had been when the whole thing had started.

Andi stared, head cocked to one side. "How's my partner? He can be territorial about his house."

"He's great."

When Andi's eyebrows shot as high as they could go, Nikki bit back a wince. Even she'd heard the joy in her voice.

"Hmmm..."

"Hmmm?" Nikki asked, going for innocence.

"You have a thing for Pete."

Heat crept into her cheeks and Nikki didn't comment.

"Oh, my God. You're blushing. You *never* blush."

"Am not." Nikki rubbed the back of her neck and looked away from her friend. But when Andi squeezed her wrist, they locked gazes.

"I think it's great."

"You do?"

Micah made a noise and Andi shifted him, cooing, kissing his little forehead, stroking his dark hair.

His tiny hand opened and Nikki caressed his soft palm. "Can I hold him?"

"Sure, but he's fussy. It doesn't get you off the hook about Pete, either."

Nikki ignored Andi as she settled the tiny baby in her arms. "God, he's gorgeous." She rocked him, patting his diapered bottom when he made a noise like he was going to wail.

Micah calmed and blinked big blue eyes.

"Thanks." Andi beamed.

The baby yawned and flashed dimples.

"Ah, there they are. The Lucas dimples," Nikki said.

Her friend laughed. "Yes, they all have them. Cole, Cass, both girls, too. It's kinda funny."

Nikki stared into the baby's face as his eyes fluttered and he drifted off. He was beautiful. She could see both Andi and Cole in his little face.

"Wow, you're a natural. He usually screams his head off when someone new to him holds him."

"Thanks. I love the way babies smell." *Do not think of Pete, Nikki Harper. Don't imagine the baby in your arms with much lighter hair. Brown or green eyes.* "How's round two of new motherhood treating you?"

"Oh, no. We're talking about you, ma'am."

Nikki cringed. "Don't want to."

Andi's expression softened. "Is he being a jerk? Do I need to kick his ass?"

She shook her head. "No. He's…great… Too great."

"Then what's the problem?"

"I love him." *Shit. Really? Blurting that again?*

Her friend blinked. Opened her mouth, then shut it. "Wow," Andi finally whispered.

"I didn't see it coming, either. But I do."

"And my partner?"

"Well…I don't know. So far it's been physical. We don't talk much. At least about feelings."

Andi smirked. "Physical, huh?"

Nikki looked everywhere but into her friend's sapphire eyes. Like she was a kid talking about sex for the first time. Thank God she had the baby in her arms to keep her occupied.

"You know that's a big deal, right? That says something about how Pete feels about you."

"What?"

"My partner. Before Cole, everyone assumed we were sleeping together. You know it never was like that with me and Pete. But…he's closer to me than anyone except Cole. Always was. When he dates, he's discreet. Always has been. Sometimes he doesn't even tell me. He's immensely private. Do you know that not even Cole and I have been over to his house more than a dozen times? The man's been my best friend for seven years."

"Oh..."

"I've been worried about him since I married Cole. He's spent too much time invested in me and Ethan since I lost Iain. But if it wasn't for Pete, I wouldn't have survived. He went over and above as my partner. Now he has a different role in my life, and it's been an adjustment for us all. But when he cares about someone, that's just how he is. He's one of the best men I know. I love him. I really do. If you're the one for him, if you can love him like I love Cole, I'm totally for that. For the both of you. I love you, too."

Nikki blinked away tears. If Micah hadn't been napping in her lap, she would have grabbed Andi up in a hug. "Thanks," she croaked.

The detective nodded. "Knock that off. If you cry, I will."

They looked at each other and laughed.

"I needed the girl-talk, so thank you. I mean it. You were right—it's been too long since we've talked." Nikki squeezed Andi's hand. "Not like I could call up Gram and tell her I'm sleeping with Pete."

Andi grinned. "No way. She'd kick your ass and grab a shotgun before she kicked his."

"Probably." Nikki laughed again.

"Well, I should probably go."

"Okay." Nikki gently relinquished the baby.

"See you soon, though, promise."

"You bet."

"Call me."

Chapter Twenty-Three

Nikki stared at Pete's sleeping form. He was gorgeous and naked, though the sheet was slung low around his waist, obscuring the view of all of his beautiful body. Tapered hips, powerful thighs, thick sex.

She'd cried after they'd made love tonight. Like a big baby. Because she loved him more than words and couldn't tell him.

Instinct told her if she'd bared her heart, he'd pull away — probably put her out of his bed.

Pete hadn't said much about it, just held her until the sobs had quieted. Maybe he'd thought she was stressed about the case, scared of Luciano Marchetti.

He'd kissed her wet cheeks then carried her to the shower, where he'd washed her body with tender hands that only made her burn for him all over again.

It might be only physical with him but she didn't want to lose that. Nikki would take Pete any way she could get him.

He still brought up their age difference too much, joking and laughing about how he wasn't good enough for her.

What the hell did that mean, anyway?

Anything to keep her at a distance, even though he kissed her into oblivion in the next breath, made her feel more than any other man ever had.

Andi's words haunted her. If Pete didn't do relationships, if he didn't kiss and tell, if he definitely avoided getting involved at work, why was Nikki different?

Her heart missed a beat and her stomach fluttered.

"Sweetness?" His voice was heavy with sleep. He stretched and yawned, his pecs heaving.

Nikki's body tingled. Flashes of his hands all over her made her limbs warm. Her breasts felt heavy, nipples hardened.

"Is everything okay? Why are you awake?" Pete drew her to him.

"Everything's good. Just couldn't sleep."

"Hmmm." Warm breath caressed her cheek as he kissed her there, then he pressed his lips to her temple and forehead. "You smell so good." Hot hands landed on her waist, urging her closer. Nikki straddled him as Pete rubbed her back in long strokes.

"You smell good, too." Leaning down, she brushed her mouth against his.

Resting his hand at the back of her neck, he deepened their kiss. Pete's chest hair teased her nipples and a tremor shot down her spine.

Nikki rocked her hips into his, already throbbing at her core. His erection bit into her bottom, but it wasn't in the right place. "I want you," she breathed against his lips.

"I want to taste you first." He nibbled around her mouth before kissing her hard and fast.

She went to move off him, to lie on her back, but Pete stopped her with a hand to her wrist.

"Not like that, darlin'. Come up here, come to me." He patted his shoulder.

A shiver racked her frame and she moaned. He wanted her where? She would've teased him about being lazy, but it was a major turn-on to know he would give her that much control. Looming over *him*. At the same time, making her feel so good.

With his hands at her waist, Pete guided her where he wanted her, having Nikki straddle his shoulders. His rough stubble grazed her inner thighs, making her blood sing for him.

Stroking with two fingers, he parted her already slick folds. Touching, teasing.

She threw her head back at the first swipe of his tongue. When he sucked her clit into his mouth, she arched her back.

He drove her crazy, licking and nibbling up and down until she pulsed on the inside. Ached for more. Her thighs shook and she panted through the pleasure rolling over her.

Pete kneaded and squeezed her ass, urging her to come closer when her body threatened to collapse.

"I won't let you fall, sweetness." His grip on her rear end tightened and he kissed her inner thigh.

Dragging his tongue up to her core, he parted her tender skin again. He circled her clit until the sensitive bundle of nerves could take no more. When he nipped gently, Nikki screamed and buried her hands in his thick blond hair.

The orgasm hit hard, locking all her muscles as he blew puffs of air against her overheated clit. That intensified her release. The bed spun and she clutched at Pete with both hands.

He chuckled and pulled her close, laying her down gently as she panted.

"I told you I wouldn't let you fall."

Pete took her mouth in a kiss that made her head fuzzier. Her own essence mixed with his minty taste as their tongues dueled, and she wiggled under him. Nikki wanted more.

He must've read her mind because he parted her thighs with a knee then he was there, pushing inside her, making them one.

She kissed him harder, wrapping shaking arms around his neck as she met his first thrust with one of her own.

"Only God knows why, but I can't get enough of you, Nikki Harper," he whispered before covering her mouth with his again.

Nikki closed her eyes and kissed him back, banishing the L-word from her thoughts or it was likely to fall out of her mouth. Because God also knew the reason *she* couldn't get enough of *him.*

She got lost in the sensations of their bodies moving together, Pete's legs entwined with hers, the beat of his heart against hers. The way their breathing fell into sync, the way he anticipated her pleasure as much as she did his.

When he shouted his release and stilled above her, she tilted her hips. She let go, climax roaring over her as well.

She held on tight, wrapping herself around Pete. She didn't want to let him go...ever.

He laughed and she felt it rumble in his chest.

"You okay, sweetness?" He kissed her neck before pressing a tender one to her lips.

"I am." Nikki smiled and met his eyes in the dimness of his room.

"You're holding on pretty tight."

Nikki flushed and loosened her arms. Made her legs fall to the bed. "Sorry," she whispered.

Pete cupped her cheeks and smiled. "Don't be. I like it. I love how you lose control with me. You're gorgeous when you let go. When you come for me."

Heat rushed her limbs. Her body was sated, heavy from pleasure, but his words were like an on-switch. She bit her lip to keep from moaning.

"I'll get something to clean us up," Pete said. He slipped from her body and the bed before Nikki could say a word.

She closed her eyes and tucked her hands behind her head, trying to convince her heart to calm. When emotion rolled over her and tears leaked from behind her eyelids, she called herself every name in the book.

Foolish and *idiot* were headlining *coward*.

No matter that Andi thought Pete cared about her. He'd never said, and Nikki wasn't about to risk voicing her feelings first.

Every time he made a comment about their age difference and told her he didn't deserve her, it was like solidifying some sort of plan. Pete didn't need to tell her. She just knew.

When the case was over, *he* would be done with her. His jokes were as good as stating the fact.

His mother had said she'd have to fight for him.

How the hell was she supposed to do that?

* * * *

Luca paced the shitty motel room about five miles from Antioch. He'd moved on from the one closer to the small city's center. The place he'd spent the night with Prostitute Barbie had kept him too long.

Caselli's reinforcements would've found him there. Even if they'd assumed he'd run after the second fucking botched attempt on Berto and his whore.

They were both still alive.

A quick call to the hospital posing as law enforcement got the answer he didn't want to hear.

"Fuck me." He dragged his hand down his face, ignoring how the two-day stubble scratched his palm.

I don't want to die.

He looked around the room. This place wasn't a chain. A U-shaped building right off the highway. Some stupid mom-and-pop place that actually rented rooms by the hour.

So truckers could catch a nap. Suuuuuuuuure.

At least the deadbolt worked better here. Place was cleaner, too. No bugs in the bathroom. *Waterbugs, my ass. Them fuckers looked like roaches.*

Luca hated to admit it, but cockroaches made his skin crawl.

Sighing, he gave himself a pat-down, feeling better when he touched the two guns he had on him. His trusty Beretta and the backup SIG were both in their normal places on his body. There were a few more weapons in the bag on the bed. At least he could protect himself.

The glass of the single window facing the parking lot shattered and Luca rolled across the bed on instinct. Pieces of the doorframe went flying as someone kicked the door open.

Hit his knees and drew his Beretta.

Black boots came into view before another shot went off. His ears rang, but Luca pushed to his feet and pulled the trigger twice.

Pain exploded in his already injured shoulder, but he took another shot, cursing under his breath.

I will not die here.

The shooter grunted, falling to his knees and holding his belly.

Luca rounded the bed and kicked the asshole in the gut. The guy went down on all fours and dropped his gun. Luca grabbed it and tucked it into his waistband.

"Get up. Frankie, you fucking son of a bitch, get the fuck up."

Frankie grunted and complied when Luca stuck his forty in the man's face.

"Sorry, Luca, it was orders." He moaned, almost-black blood seeping through his fingers when he cradled his stomach again.

"Orders. Fuck orders. Who else came with you?"

The man shook his head and Luca punched him. Frankie toppled over and Luca cursed as both his bullet wounds—old and new—shouted a protest. He didn't dare rotate his shoulder. It'd burn like a bitch.

"Who. The. Fuck. Came with you?" Caselli never sent only one guy.

Unless he didn't see Luca as a challenge.

He growled. That pissed him off.

"Only me. Me." Frankie's bloody palms rose in submission as he lay on his back.

Luca kicked him in the balls.

Frankie screamed but didn't get up.

"Give Mickey my regards." Luca aimed his Beretta at Frankie's head and pulled the trigger.

Chapter Twenty-Four

"Can we meet up?"

He sat up straighter on the couch. Pete turned the TV down and shot a glance over his shoulder. Nikki was still in the kitchen. *Good.* "What's up?" He held his cell tighter to his ear.

"I'll tell you when we meet. I'm not alone." Raleigh's voice shook. More than normal.

It's something serious.

"Who's with you?"

"Someone who needs to talk to you."

"When?" Pete asked.

"Now would be good. My…friend is twitchy."

"I don't suppose you'd let me take you to the station?"

"No way. You know I won't go there. Neither will my friend."

"I need about an hour." Pete sighed. He couldn't bring Nikki. He needed to arrange for someone to protect her.

He'd track down Lee—Pete wouldn't walk into the meeting alone. No telling who was with Raleigh.

"Done."

They arranged a meeting place near the warehouse district. Ironically, it was the same spot where Raleigh had been supposed to meet him that night last year when he and Andi had run into Carlo Maldonado. Pete had been shot. Twice. The CI hadn't showed.

"You better not be pulling some shit on me, Raleigh."

"No way, boss. Seriously."

"I'll take your ass in if I have to."

"I know you would. But I'm trying to help you."

Pete arched a brow. "Help me?"

"Billy was my friend."

Shit. It was serious, all right. "Is this about Luciano Marchetti?"

"We'll talk when we meet."

The line went dead and Pete cursed under his breath. He had no choice but to wait for whatever Raleigh had. "This had better be good."

"What had better be good? The movie?"

His gaze collided with Nikki's gorgeous brown eyes. She was holding a bowl of popcorn. Standing in front of him in blue yoga pants and a too-tight white ribbed tank, he wanted to do a lot more to her than just wrap her in his arms and curl up with her on the couch.

"I have to grab Lee and go out, sweetness." He stood and took the bowl from her hand, setting it down on the coffee table. Pete tugged her close and kissed her.

He'd meant it to be fleeting, a goodbye for now, then it melted into something more.

Nikki slipped her arms around his neck and moved her mouth under his until they were panting against each other and his cock was pressing against his crotch.

"Do you have to?" she whispered.

Pete cupped her cheeks and caressed her soft flushed skin with both thumbs. "Yes. Unfortunately. I won't be gone long. I'll have someone come stay with you."

"I can't go?"

"No, darlin', I need you here, safe."

"You'll come home to me?"

His heart thundered. *Home. To Nikki.* Didn't that appeal? "Yes, sweetness. I'm going to meet a CI. Remember the guy from the trailer park?"

She nodded, but a tremor shook her frame.

Pete rubbed up and down her arms, careful to avoid her stitches. "He has some info for me. Lee's going to come, so I don't want you to worry, okay?"

"How does Andi deal?" Nikki whispered.

"What?"

Her brown eyes bored into his. "She watches Cole do what you do every day. But *she* does it, too."

"Hey, hey." Pete pressed a quick kiss to her mouth. "Andi has me at her back. Cole has Jared. We all have our eyes open. And we're talking about Antioch. It's not the big city."

"No, but you walk into danger anyway. Shootouts and drug deals."

"Nikki, this job is my life, and I know what I'm doing."

Something flashed across her expression, but it was gone so fast he couldn't read it. Her mouth slid into a hard line and she nodded. "Okay."

He kissed her again, but she was no longer supple in his arms. What had he said to upset her? "I'll be careful, I promise."

"Okay," she repeated.

Pete needed someone to cover for him while he was out. He called Jared Manning first, but he didn't answer his phone. He didn't blame him, though—the guy wasn't on-call. He struck out next with Sully, the detective who *was* on-call. Sully was chasing down something of his own. Sully apologized profusely, but he couldn't come.

"Shit."

"What's wrong?" Nikki asked. She watched him warily from the corner of his couch.

"I'll have to call dispatch. I don't want to bother Cole, and I can't get another detective. I'll see if Chloe can come."

"I'll be fine, Pete. I know how to use a gun. You have some around here, I'm sure. Or I could get mine. It's in my bag."

"No way. Sweetness, I'm not leaving you here without a badge to go with those guns."

Nikki looked as if she would argue, then only nodded.

Pete caressed her cheek and called for a patrol car. Chloe was working an accident, but said she'd send two of her guys. It would have to do. He waited until the cruiser parked across from his house and kissed Nikki one last time.

"I'll see you in a few, okay? Lock the door. Stay close to your cell. Crowley's across the street and Benton is in the area."

She nodded and squeezed his hand. "We'll both be fine."

He threw her a smile and jogged to tell Officer Shannon Crowley what was up. Satisfied the guy would tell him if Nikki so much as sneezed, he climbed into his pickup and found Lee's number in his contacts.

"I like you, Pete Crane, but this better be good," she said by way of greeting.

Pete laughed. "I'm on my way to pick you up."

"That good, huh?"

"Of course, if I'm bugging you past eight p.m. it's gotta be good."

Lee sighed.

Pete heard a familiar male voice in the background. And water running. Damn, he was interrupting them. "Tell my brother I said hi. And that I'm sorry for ruining y'all's evening."

"I suppose he'll just have to understand."

"Brief you when I get there."

"Roger."

He hung up and shook his head, throwing his phone in the cup holder. Pete was missing out on being home with Nikki and Lee was losing valuable time with Nate.

Should he feel better or worse he wasn't the only one suffering?

* * * *

Well, the ride wasn't so bad, even though it wasn't his Hummer.

Luca turned the wheel on the black BMW the stupid—dead—fucker Frankie Mancini had driven to the motel where he'd tried to kill him. Must have driven it all the way from New York, if the license plates were any indication. A big sedan, it was a smooth glide, and now it was his.

Fuck Caselli.

He should have called his *ex*-boss and told him how he'd enjoyed popping Frankie. How he'd gotten off on whacking his stupid fucking nephew. Luca would definitely do it over.

No going home now. He was on his own.

Sure as hell wouldn't make it easy for Caselli to take another swipe at him.

When he'd left the motel, Luca had stolen new plates for his new car and searched the crap out of the whole vehicle as soon as he'd risked stopping. Ended up back in Antioch, in the darkest corner of the lowest level in the small parking garage of the mall. No one even looked at him. He'd spotted a few cameras, but he'd parked as strategically as he could. Tried to be out of camera view, but it was hard to tell. Hopefully Big Brother wasn't watching him.

There was a couple of grand in a small suitcase in the trunk of the Beemer. Adding it to the ten thousand dollars he'd taken back from the drug addict driver, he had enough to get by for a few weeks — maybe.

Luca would get a new job. He knew people. Even had some family in California.

He'd head that way and pay them a visit. Maybe his cousins would be ticked off enough to go after Caselli.

But before he could go, he had some business left in Antioch.

Caselli had ordered him to leave the witness alone.

Fuck. That.

Besides, the bitches had seen him. He needed to take care of it now that his boss had abandoned him.

Luca was out of a home, a job. Caselli had a tendency to screw you over every way he could until he found your ass and had you killed. He'd have to be careful. Tie up all the loose ends. Lie low when he left Texas.

Hell, he'd have to lie low when he got settled at his uncle's place. His old boss knew way too much about him. If the man figured out he'd made it out of Texas alive, no state would be safe. Probably would be able to make a simple phone call to have him killed in

California. No telling if the man had friends on the West Coast.

Caselli might be afraid of a little bloodshed, but Luca wasn't.

Guess who doesn't get to pick anymore?

The bigger the body count, the more of a *fuck you* it would be to Tony Caselli, Jr.

Luca smiled.

The old woman was staying at the rehab center. Berto's whore had been her nurse. It wouldn't take a genius to find out who the redhead was and get her there. Then he could kill them both. Take out any cops who might be hanging around. Maybe even that blond guy who had been with her the day he'd killed Mickey. That fucker had shot at him.

"I love when I'm right."

It'd only taken about ten minutes to find out the redheaded chick's name was Nikki Harper and her grandmother, Molly Jenkins, was most indeed still at the rehab center.

He'd even found out her doctor's name was Michael Bishop, and the night-time doc currently working at Health Solutions was one Marcus Greene.

"Damn, I'm good." Luca rubbed his hands together.

It was gonna be almost as good as blowing something up.

Chapter Twenty-Five

Pete tilted the girl's chin up into the dim light of the old shed. Angry black and blue marks covered her throat. The bruises jumped when she swallowed. "Did he rape you?" he asked.

"He paid like anyone else. He was just rough about it." Her words were so matter-of-fact he had to bite back a cringe. Like getting choked was a part of her acceptable day-to-day.

"You want to press charges for the assault?" Pete asked. He knew what her answer would be, but it wouldn't hurt to put it out there. It was something substantial enough to slap on a warrant if they needed it.

The prostitute smirked and shook her head. Her pale blue eyes flashed, daring him to contradict her.

"You sure it was him?" Lee asked, leaning closer to examine her marred skin.

"He didn't sound like he was from around here," she said.

Pete released her and she took a step back. He glanced at Raleigh, who was standing to the side, arms crossed over his thin chest.

"Like an accent?" Lee asked.

"Yup. Up north or some shit."

"Tell him everything, Misty," Raleigh said.

"He paid me extra—a lot extra—to do a little surgery."

"Surgery?" Pete asked.

"He had a bullet in his right arm. I dug it out for him. Bought meds and stuff from CVS. Wrapped him up."

Lee shot him a look.

Definitely Marchetti.

"Where'd he take you?"

"Motel 6 on Main, but he's not there anymore. When my pim—friend—went to kick his ass for roughing me up, all his shit was gone. Someone else was in the room."

Pete smirked. *Friend. Right.* He wasn't bringing her in, but he didn't feel the need to call her out, either.

"I told him to leave off the guy anyway," Raleigh said. "I'd bet money he's the one who killed Billy."

"What did he look like, Misty?" Pete didn't doubt it, either. The girl had had a run-in with Luciano Marchetti. But he wanted to hear everything.

"Not as tall as you. Dark hair. Evil-as-fuck brown eyes. But he knows how to dress. His pants and shirt were designer. Had a couple of guns."

Yup, their guy. Pete had a screenshot of Marchetti from the grocery store surveillance footage on his cell. He dug his hand in his pocket. "Crap."

Lee glanced at him. "What?"

"I left my damn phone in the truck."

"Ah. No worries, I have him on mine, too." Lee pulled up the picture on her cell phone. Held it up for Misty. "This him?"

"Yes. That's the fucking bastard."

"Good deal," Lee said.

"Anything else you can think of?" Pete asked.

Misty shook her head. "Kick him in the balls when you find him."

Pete chuckled. "Gladly. Here's my card."

"I can't take that. If my pim—*friend*, my friend— finds out I talked to you, *he'll* kick my ass."

"All right. If you need me, Raleigh can find me." Pete looked at his CI. "You hear anything, you call me again, got it?"

"Yeah, boss, you know it."

Pete sighed as they headed out to the pickup. "Another fricking dead end."

"Nah, we found out where he *was*. Wanna go check out that motel?"

"Tonight?"

Lee shrugged. "We're already out."

"Woulda thought you'd rather call Nate back. It's not even ten."

She smiled. "I got all night for your little bro."

Laughing, Pete opened the driver side door. "More than I wanted to know."

The FBI agent winked.

His phone lighting up from the cup holder caught his attention and he grabbed it after climbing onto the bench seat of his Silverado.

Damn. Six missed calls from four different people. And a text from Nikki. Three voicemails, but he wasn't going to take time to listen right now. "Shit."

"What's wrong?"

Pete met Lee's dark eyes. "Sorry, but Nate'll have to wait. And we'll have to check out the motel in the morning."

The phone ringing made him jump and Lee shot him a look, but she said nothing as he put his cell to his ear.

"Crane."

"You been listening to the radio?" Jared Manning asked without preamble.

"No, dude, but you should answer your phone. I called you earlier," Pete said.

"Sorry. Been over at The Spring Inn."

"That the place off the highway, right outside of town?"

"Yup."

"That's not ours. No jurisdiction over there." Something had to be up.

"Nope, but I met my buddy over here, he gave me a heads-up. He's a detective with the Sheriff's Office. He knows what we're workin'," Jared said.

"What happened?"

"A guy with a New York driver license, said to have been driving a nice black Beemer, got himself shot."

"Marchetti."

"No. Name's Francis Mancini. Agent Dawson know him?"

Pete put Jared on speaker phone. "G'head and ask her. She's with me."

"Agent Dawson, the name Francis Mancini ring a bell?"

"Frankie the House, yeah. I know him." Lee nodded when Pete caught her eye.

"The House?" Jared asked.

"Because he's a big SOB. You got him in lockup or something?"

"Not exactly," Jared said.

"Shit. Luca got himself an expiration date," Lee said.

"Yeah, but look who expired first," Pete said. "We're headed over to the rehab center, but we'll keep our eye out for a black BMW. Did you put out a BOLO?"

"The deputy first on scene did when the owner of this place reported seeing it. Late model, one of the big sedans, the six or seven series."

"All right. You hear anything, keep us posted."

"You bet, thought you'd want to know," Jared said.

"Hey, Jar, thanks for all your help on this one."

"Anytime, bud."

"This is bad." Lee shook her head when Pete shoved his cell in his jeans. "If Luca killed The House, he knows Caselli's turned on him."

"Over Mickey Donati?"

"Blood is thicker than water, even if the guy's skull was just as thick. Caselli's sister's kid and all."

Pete's gut tightened. A feeling of dread settled over him and he tried to shake it off. He tightened his grip on the steering wheel and pulled out of the parking lot behind the warehouse.

The old shed they'd been in looked even more dilapidated when the headlights of his truck passed over it.

"What're you thinking?" he asked, turning the Silverado onto Commerce Street.

"Luca... He's going to do something stupid."

"Why do you say that?"

"He's smart, and cruel, like Cole Lucas said. But worse, he's desperate. We're in for it."

"Obviously he took the Beemer. You don't think he'd just get the hell out of Dodge? He killed the guy. Knows there're more where Frankie Mancini came from. Caselli doesn't stop until you're dead, if he wants you dead. I mean, didn't you guys have to put Maldonado and Gallo in protective custody right off the bat last year?"

"Yeah, we did. But him running? I think it's too much to hope for. Not just yet. I mean, he's stayed all this time. Two attempts on Maria. Failed to kill her *and* Alberto Carbone."

"Shit." Pete slammed his palm into the steering wheel. His heart pounded and sweat broke out on his brow that had nothing to do with the heat of the Texas summer evening.

Something's wrong, his gut shouted.

He told it to hush and focused on what his temporary partner was saying.

"Yeah." Lee sighed. "We better head out to both motels tonight, even if the body isn't in your jurisdiction. There might be some Luca evidence in either room."

"You're right, we probably should. But I can't until I know Nikki's back with me—us—safe. And I want to slap another cop on her grandmother at the rehab center."

"Not a bad idea. At least we don't have to worry about the Carbones—Matas—or whatever they're calling themselves. Madison and the marshals have their protection handled."

Yes, but that meant he had to worry about Nikki and her gram more.

"Shit, shit, shit. I want this bastard. Wanna know where he is *now*. I want to cuff his ass, or shoot his ass. Don't know which one appeals more."

Lee smiled, but it was grim. "C'mon, let's go get your girl."

Chapter Twenty-Six

"Ms Harper, please."

"This is she. Who's this?"

"Dr Greene from Health Solutions. I'm calling about your grandmother."

Nikki's heart sped up and she swallowed back a gulp. "What's wrong?"

"I need you to come down here right away. Can you do that for me?"

"What's going on?"

"We'll discuss it in detail when you get here. Don't worry, but hurry." The doctor's voice was firm and fear gripped her gut.

It's bad. So bad he won't tell me over the phone. "Why won't you tell me what happened?"

"Dr Bishop is on his way. We'll both meet you, Ms Harper."

She ended the call and rushed up the stairs to Pete's room, throwing on the closest pair of her jeans. Nikki didn't bother taking off her tank, just yanked a T-shirt over it. She needed to go. *Now.*

Dialing his cell number, she sucked in a breath and shouted at herself to calm down. "You've reached Detective Pete Crane, from Antioch Police..."

"Dammit. Voicemail." She tried again, only to get the same.

Nikki didn't leave a message.

She grabbed her purse and locked the house. After dashing across the street, she yanked the door handle of the cruiser as she reached it. Nikki slipped into the passenger seat as soon as Officer Shannon Crowley hit the unlock button.

"Take me to Health Solutions," Nikki demanded.

"Whoa, what's wrong?"

Meeting his amber eyes, she took another breath. "I need to get to the rehab center. My grandmother's doctor called."

"I'm calling Crane."

"I tried, twice. Voicemail."

But Shannon wasn't listening to her. He already had his cell to his ear. "You're right. Did you leave a message?"

"No. Shannon, please. Please take me. Something's wrong."

He hesitated. "I would feel better if we got a hold of Crane."

"I would, too. But I don't have time. The doctor called..." Fear squeezed her chest and her eyes smarted. She blinked tears away.

Do not cry right now.

Shannon sighed and dragged his hand through his dark hair. "I'm clearing it with Sarge before we go."

"Okay, I'll text Pete, I promise." Nikki sent a quick message to her detective as the officer called Sergeant Stein.

He started the cruiser after Chloe gave him the okay to take Nikki and assured them she'd try to get a hold of Pete, too.

"I don't like this," Shannon murmured as he headed down the street.

"I don't either." She clutched her phone, praying Pete was okay. He hadn't answered her message.

But then her grandmother took over her thoughts. The doctor's words kept rolling over and over in her head. *Don't worry, but hurry.*

What if it was Gram's heart again? She couldn't lose her grandmother.

As soon as he'd turned into the flat lot of the rehab center, Nikki jumped out of the cruiser before Shannon had even pulled to a full stop.

"Nikki, wait a second," he shouted.

Ignoring him, she rushed into Health Solutions. She heard the rattle of Shannon's keys and the leather of his gun belt creaking as he jogged to keep up with her. Nikki didn't slow or wait for him.

When she rounded the corner toward Gram's room, the cop outside the door shot to his feet as soon as she and Shannon were in sight.

"Where's the fire?" Officer Joe Benton asked, his palms up.

She sucked in a breath and made herself skid to a stop. "Is Gram all right?"

"Yes." Joe thumbed in the direction of the door, left ajar. "The nurse is in there now. Giving her night meds. But she's been watching TV and talking to me most of the evening."

Nikki pushed her way into the room. She had to see for herself her grandmother was okay.

Please be all right.

Both cops followed her.

"Dr Greene called me…"

She didn't miss the look Joe and Shannon exchanged, but she ignored them, heading straight for the nurse.

It was the tall black girl, Rebecca. One of the nurses who'd taken care of Gram the night Maria had gotten shot.

"Nikki-baby," Gram said, smiling as she set her empty water cup on Rebecca's tray.

"Rebecca, what's going on?" Nikki asked.

Wide dark eyes met hers. "What'd you mean?"

"Dr Greene called me."

"I don't like this," Shannon muttered. He grabbed his cell and started dialing, turning his back to them as he made the call.

Joe tensed, his hand hovering over his holstered gun.

"He did?" Rebecca asked, but her eyes darted from cop to cop.

The bedding rustled as Gram sat up straighter. "Nikki, is something wrong?"

Nikki moved to the bedside, taking her grandmother's hand. "I'm not sure."

"I'll go get Dr Greene. I'm sure he'll straighten things out." Rebecca spiked the paper water cup in the trashcan and tucked the tray under her arm.

Sighing, Nikki dragged a chair to Gram's side. She slipped into it, shaking her head.

"Shit." Shannon pocketed his phone, his eyes darting to her grandmother. "Sorry, ma'am."

Gram flashed a grin. "Please, boy. Heard and said worse."

"What's wrong?" Nikki asked.

"Still can't get Crane. But Sarge is starting over this way."

"Good," Joe said. He surveyed the room and Nikki's stomach jumped.

He was young—a few years younger than her. He'd only been off training for a few months.

Nikki wanted Pete.

"Where's your detective, Nikki-baby?" Gram asked, as if she'd read her mind.

"He had to interview someone."

Gram nodded, but Nikki didn't get a chance to comment before Rebecca stepped into the room with Dr Greene on her heels.

Tall and lanky, the young doctor had both hands in the wide pockets of his white coat. His fair brows were drawn tight as he came closer. "Ms Harper, I didn't call you."

"Son of a bitch," Joe and Shannon said at the same time.

Nikki leaned forward in the chair, dread rolling over her. "What?"

The doctor looked even more concerned. "I've been in my office, going over patient charts most of the evening." He glanced at both cops. "What's going on?"

"That's what we'd all like to know," Joe said.

"Nikki, give me your phone," Shannon barked. The officer immediately started scrolling through her call log when she'd complied. "Damn, it's a blocked number."

She winced. "I'm sorry. I should've paid more attention to the caller ID, but when the man said he was Dr Greene, I freaked. He wouldn't tell me what was wrong, just that I needed to get down here."

Sickeningly familiar popping sounds make them all freeze. Dread turned to fear and Nikki clutched Gram's hand. Her heart kicked into overdrive.

Rebecca whimpered.

Shannon cursed and drew his gun. Joe took one look at the more senior officer and did the same.

"Nikki, close the door. Lock it. Try to call Crane again."

"Patient rooms don't lock." Rebecca's voice shook.

Dr Greene put his arm around her.

"He's coming for us. Rebecca and Dr Greene should leave. Now." Nikki stood, refusing to let tears and fear take her over.

"No, you all need to stay here. Barricade the door. Nikki, get on the damn phone," Shannon ordered. At the same time, he reached for his shoulder mic and called out, "Shots fired!"

God, Pete where are you?

"Benton, let's go." Shannon gestured.

The younger officer gave a curt nod and they slipped into the hallway.

Gunfire came closer.

Pop. Pop. Bang. Bang.

Where the hell were the sirens?

People were screaming. Footsteps barreled up and down the hallway. Shots kept going off. Now it sounded like more than one gun.

God, please protect Joe and Shannon. And all the people out there.

Nikki glanced around the room. Unlike Gram's first room, this one had a small raised window about five feet off the ground and they were on the corner of the building.

No way of escape.

"We should barricade the door like the cops said." Dr Greene's Adam's apple bobbed.

Rebecca screamed as the door burst open.

Nikki threw herself over Gram.

Luciano Marchetti dragged a whimpering nurse into the room, gun to her head. "Hello, ladies." He pushed the weapon into the poor woman's temple.

She yelped.

"Kim, oh my God," Rebecca breathed, tears streamed down her cheeks.

Gram clutched at Nikki's shoulders, but she didn't move off the elderly woman.

The evil bastard laughed. Then he pulled the trigger. Kim's body slid to the ground in a sickening thud, blood everywhere, and Luciano Marchetti stepped over her body as her blood started to pool.

Like Kim is nothing.

"You must be the good doctor. Goodbye, Dr Greene." He shot the doctor in the head.

The poor man didn't have time to react as he fell.

It was like watching a horror movie. Nikki's heart galloped, threatening to exit her chest. Her stomach roiled, bile rose. She swallowed over and over to keep from throwing up. Blinking didn't make the scene before her go away. Her nails bit into her palms as helplessness rolled over her.

We're going to die.

Everything seemed to slip into slow motion. Gram held Nikki tight around the waist.

Rebecca kept screaming. Until Luciano Marchetti shot her, too. She collapsed to the floor like a heavy sack of sand.

Tears wet Nikki's cheeks but she didn't move as he turned toward the bed.

Luciano Marchetti raised the gun.

Nikki screamed.

Chapter Twenty-Seven

Sirens greeted them when they turned onto Main Street.

"Hmmm, wonder what's up," Lee said.

"I dunno. I didn't grab the portable I keep at home. It was dead, so I slapped it on the charger after work," Pete said.

Lee didn't answer as a cruiser flew by them, lights and sirens. Going the same direction they were. Toward the rehab center.

Shit.

Pete shot his temporary partner a look. She said nothing, but his heart landed in his stomach. *Something's wrong.*

He didn't bother grabbing his cell and calling Dispatch. They were right around the corner from Health Solutions.

"Son of a bitch." Lee made a fist as they pulled into the lot.

His heart hit overdrive from its new residence in his gut. Bile rose and Pete had to swallow to keep from chucking his dinner. He knew—just knew—what was going on.

Marchetti.

"Cole's car is here," the FBI agent said.

Pete's head spun.

Nikki.

He'd left her. Again.

They got out of the truck and shut the doors at the same time. Lee and Pete exchanged another look and she drew her weapon. His partner was ready. For anything.

Chloe and her whole shift—five cops—stood not far from Cole's blue Dodge Challenger. His buddy walked up to him, racking a semi-automatic twelve-gauge, and pressed it into Pete's hand without a word.

"What do we have?" Pete croaked.

"Active shooter. Crowley called it out. But now neither he nor Joe Benton is answering the radio." Cole wore an over-the-shirt bulletproof vest. He popped the trunk of the Challenger and threw one at Pete, then another at the FBI agent.

Reflex made his free hand rise to catch it.

"Marchetti," Lee said. She let out a string of curses and holstered her Glock. "Gimme something better than this."

Cole smirked as Sergeant Stein handed Lee an AR-15 assault rifle.

"Chief and Lieutenant Wells are on the way. Lieutenant Davis will mobilize SWAT, too," Chloe said. Her guys surrounded them all, some with shotguns or an AR-15, some with handguns. All twitchy. All ready to storm Health Solutions.

Pete's stomach flipped.

He'd let his guard down. Again. Assumed she'd be safe. And now she could be dead inside the rehab center. "No." The whisper was anguished, even to his own ears.

Cole shot him a look, one dark eyebrow up, visible in the rotating red and blues of one of the cruisers. "Dude, suit up so we can go."

Visions of Nikki and her grandmother lying in pools of blood danced into his head. He swallowed hard. Pete couldn't shake the image. He shivered—honest to God shivered. Maybe he was going to throw up, after all. His pulse pounded in his ears.

The voices of his co-workers faded in and out as Chloe briefed everyone on the layout of the building. She barked position orders and answered questions.

"Pete." Cole—all six feet four inches of him—got right up in Pete's face, bumped him chest to chest.

He blinked, meeting Cole's steel eyes. Struggled for coherent thought. Words. *Anything.*

"Dude. Get it together. *Now.*"

"I'm fine." But his voice cracked.

"Right. Sure. Gimme the damn gun and put the vest on. Or you're not going in."

Anger boiled up from Pete's gut. "The fuck I'm not going in there."

Cole gave a curt nod, a ghost of a smile playing at his lips. "That's what I'm talkin' about. Get it done so we can go kill this bastard."

Lee stepped up to him as Cole backed off. Put her hand on his forearm. "You okay, partner?"

Shit. She hadn't missed their little exchange.

He forced a nod.

"We got this." Lee raised her voice, so all the cops could hear. "We got this," she repeated.

The guys nodded or grunted, their faces hard and determined.

"How we doing this?" Sergeant Stein asked.

"I'll lead," Cole said.

Pete nodded. He was okay with that. After all, Cole and Lee had done this more than the guys and gals of Antioch PD.

"One condition," Pete barked.

"Yeah?" Lee asked. The smirk on her face said she knew what he was going to say.

"*I* kill the bastard."

Cole grinned. "Wouldn't have it any other way, buddy." He slapped Pete's back.

Shots sounded as they approached the building in formation, but the frosted glass prevented them from making out anyone or anything on the other side. Light glowed through, but that was about it.

Cole led, with Lee next, in front of Pete. Chloe and her guys fanned out behind him, two of them watching their asses.

People's screams greeted his ears with the whoosh of the automatic doors, and a few employees in scrubs fled the building. The cop whom Chloe had left outside gestured for them. Fire trucks and ambulances should be there any second. Probably SWAT, too.

Doctors, nurses, patient techs were injured, clutching shoulders, arms or limping, walking arm in arm. Bleeding, looking anguished.

Pete sucked in a breath and flexed his fingers on the shotgun. *Head. In. Game. Now.*

Their unit moved forward, breaching the building.

Even before they'd reached the front desk, bodies— three, no, four—were everywhere. Pools of blood, spatter and smears on the wall. A nurse rocking and moaning, red staining the front of her scrubs, leaning against the wall of the nurses' station.

No pausing, stopping, checking for signs of life. Not yet. They were on a search and destroy mission. Stop the threat, then assess. Prevent more loss of life.

They stepped over a body of a patient tech who looked younger than Nikki. Shot in the head, lying on her side.

Pete didn't let it affect him. He couldn't.

He needed to get to her.

Save her.

Please, God, don't let us be too late.

They turned as one down the hallway leading to Mrs Jenkins' room.

Black boots were visible first, then uniform pants. Young Officer Joe Benton was down in front of the first room on the left, partially obscured by the open door to a patient room. Pete couldn't see where he was hit.

Officer Shannon Crowley was next, right outside of the second patient room on the right. A small pool of blood under his shoulder. His left leg was hit, too.

Neither cop moved.

Please let them be alive.

There was no one else in the corridor.

The bang of a big gun went off. Then a pause, and another shot. A male voice spoke. Pete couldn't make out the words. A woman screamed, but it was cut off with another gunshot.

Cole gestured for them to split on either side of the doorway to Nikki's gram's room. The door was open.

"Police!" the shout went up collectively.

Luciano Marchetti had his gun trained on Nikki and Gram. The guy was hit, bleeding. *Good.*

Nikki was lying on the bed, obscuring as much of her grandmother's thin small form as she could.

Without missing a beat, or acknowledging the half a dozen cops that had just poured into the room, Luciano Marchetti pulled the trigger.

Nikki screamed.

Pete acted on instinct, aiming and firing the shotgun. He wasn't the only one. Cole and Lee—hell, maybe all of them—opened fire on the bastard until he fell in a heap at the end of the hospital bed. A mess of black clothing and red blood.

As soon as he was down, Cole and Lee rushed forward. One of them kicked Luca's gun away.

He left them to handle it as Cole knelt and announced the asshole was dead.

Chloe started barking orders for her guys to fan out, assess injured and tally dead. Radio chatter echoed from multiple portables. Sirens wailed from outside.

Pete didn't give a shit.

He tossed the shotgun to one of the officers and rushed to her.

Nikki sobbed on the edge of the bed, her grandmother in her arms.

His gaze darted up, down, all over both their forms. No blood. *Thank God.*

She took one look at him and Pete's heart stuttered. Tears stained her beautiful face, her brown eyes were puffy and red-rimmed. It didn't matter. She was alive. She was safe.

Nikki rushed into his arms.

"You're okay, you're okay." He repeated the words over and over, squeezing her against his chest but he was shaking as much as she was.

He told himself it was just the adrenaline dump. But it was more. He loved her.

Love? Him?

But the sentiment held firmly. Made him shake even more.

Fine time for a revelation.

"Nikki!"

Pete winced at Chief's shout and released her.

The man crossed the room in two strides, medics on his heels. Their boss grabbed her by the shoulders, despite Nikki's immediate protest that she was fine. As soon as Paul Martin seemed to realize she was indeed unhurt, he pulled Nikki into his arms and held her tight.

Her grandmother muttered something under her breath, and Pete glanced her way. *Guess Chief was right when he'd said she didn't like him.* Mrs Jenkins had her thin arms crossed over her chest, glaring at Chief Martin.

Seeing his boss holding the woman he loved was a slap in the face. *'If you touch her inappropriately, or one hair on her head is harmed by anyone or anything, your ass – your badge – is mine.'*

Pete shoved his hand through his hair. He was fucked.

Cole sidled up to him when he backed up so the paramedics could check out Mrs Jenkins and Nikki, despite their loud objections.

Pete smirked. *Like grandmother, like granddaughter.*

"You good?" Cole asked.

He forced a nod. "Yeah. You call Andi?"

"Yup. Didn't want her to worry."

"Good."

His buddy stared him down. "You sure you're okay?"

Not in the slightest. "Of course." Pete squeezed Cole's shoulder.

Cole scrutinized him until he wanted to squirm, but finally nodded. Pete released a breath he'd not realized he'd been holding.

"We got a lot of cleanup before we'll be able to hit the sack tonight."

"Not like you're sleeping much anyway, with Micah," Pete said.

"You said it. But who needs sleep anyway? I'll sleep when I'm dead." Cole grinned, flashing dimples.

Lee joined them, but her voice didn't signify as he caught one of the medics sitting Nikki down on the end of the bed, pulse monitor to her finger. His love was being compliant, but her expression shouted she wasn't happy about it.

Pete stared, his own heart skipping as Chief and Gram hovered.

Look at me. But she didn't. He told himself it was for the better.

Luciano Marchetti was dead.

She could move out of his place, settle back into her apartment. Get back to normal. That was what they both needed. Wanted?

"Pete?" Lee's voice made him jump.

"What?"

"Did you hear what I said?" Her brow furrowed.

"I'm sorry, what?"

Amusement rippled across Cole's face, but he said nothing. No doubt the guy had followed Pete's gaze.

Pete squirmed like he'd been caught watching porn.

"The body count is high. Six dead, more than a dozen injured," Lee said.

"Bastard," Cole muttered.

"Crowley and Benton?"

"They'll both live," Lee said. "Crowley's hit three times, nothing vital. Benton's vest stopped two to the chest. When he fell, he hit his head. Nasty gash, maybe a concussion."

"Could have been way worse," Pete said.

Lee murmured agreement and Cole nodded.

"Crane, a word please." Chief joined their group, but Cole and Lee made themselves scarce in about two seconds flat. *Traitors.*

"What's up, boss?"

"Nikki's coming home with me tonight."

From the end of the bed, Nikki looked up. She must have heard her name. Their eyes met then Pete looked back at his boss. His instinct was to shout *Hell no,* but it really was for the better. She could come get her things from his place in the morning. There was no reason for them to remain under the same roof, really. "All right."

From the corner of his eye, he saw her brown eyes widen. Hurt flashed as she locked her jaw and looked away.

Pete fought the urge to close his eyes. He squared his shoulders and breathed through the pressure in his chest, ignoring the pain that threatened to creep up on him.

Chief nodded and threw his hand out. "Good job tonight."

He shifted on his feet, taken aback by rare praise from his boss. "Uh...you got this here? I'm gonna help Lee and Cole get statements and head to the station to write this up."

"You don't have to do that tonight." The Chief studied him, hazel eyes intense.

"I want to."

"Okay." His boss backed off, returning to Nikki's side.

He watched Mrs Jenkins begrudgingly shake Chief's hand.

Nikki wouldn't look Pete's way.

It's for the best.

Chapter Twenty-Eight

He hadn't fought for her.

Tears streamed down Nikki's cheeks and she twisted her hands into tight fists, ignoring the sting when her nails bit her palms.

All right. Two words reverberated in her mind. Pete hadn't batted an eye when their boss had made yet another decision for her. Without asking her.

So instead of snuggling into the warmth of the man she loved, she was curled on a bed at her boss's house. Alone.

She closed her eyes and swallowed the sob that inched up her throat, threatening to burst out. Chief's room was across from the guest bedroom. With her luck, the man was the world's lightest sleeper. Nikki had no desire to explain her tears.

It's over.

Marchetti was dead. Her reason for being at Pete's house. At his side.

Relief should be flooding her, especially after tonight. Gram was okay. More than okay. In yet another new room, but she'd be back home soon.

Despite the heart issues, and stress from the Marchetti situation, she was recovering from the stroke nicely. Dr Bishop had come to Health Solutions to examine her and help the others in any way he could. His prognosis for Gram was the only good news she'd had all night.

The poor people who had died tonight... Nikki bit her fist and called herself every name in the book for being selfish. Not thinking about them, despite the prayers she'd said.

She couldn't focus on the tragedy, the loss. What she'd witnessed tonight. Dr Greene had died instantly, as had the nurse Luciano Marchetti had dragged into Gram's room.

Rebecca was going to make it, but others had died. Many more had been injured.

The scene swirled in her head. She didn't want to think about it. The other alternative was therapy for the rest of her life. How much could a person's mind take?

Then again, Pete's rejection was probably enough to land her there anyway. It was too much. Salty icing on a big crap cake.

He's done with you.

He doesn't love you.

"What did you expect?" The whisper felt like a shout.

They'd fallen into the situation together. They'd fallen into bed together. Nikki shouldn't have fallen in love.

She needed him. Needed his arms around her, his lips against hers to banish everything. The screams, the gunshots... The blood. People...had died. In front of her. Because of her.

257

The bed spun and Nikki rolled onto her back. Clutched the sheets with both hands. Her heart pounded. Every breath was like a dagger piercing her lungs. "No."

Sweat broke out on her top lip and brow as everything centrifuged together in her mind, amplifying. Watching a movie on fast-forward with full volume.

Bile rose and her stomach lurched. *No!* The shout wouldn't breach her lips.

The bedroom door burst open and Chief Martin was at her side in seconds. "Nikki." When he sat and tried to gather her to him, she thrashed.

No...no...

Nikki couldn't be encased. Enclosed. *Don't touch me!*

"Nikki." His voice was firm as he helped her sit up, resting his hands on her shoulders. "I think you're having a panic attack. Take a deep breath."

She shook her head and tried to push him away. Chief held her firmly, without hurting her.

"Look at me. *Look at me* and take a deep breath. Breathe through it. C'mon, we'll count it out. One..."

Nikki sucked in air, cursing the hot tears on her cheeks.

"Two...three... That's it... Four..."

Her chest rose and fell in rhythm with his calm tone.

"One more... Good job." He paused, looked deep into her eyes. "Better?"

Nikki rushed forward and hugged him. Closed her eyes against his thick shoulder and prayed her tears would cease.

Chief held her until her heart calmed.

She pulled back and nodded. Cleared her throat. "I'm good. Thank you. Never had a panic attack before..."

"It's only natural after what you've been through."

"Please don't remind me. I...need to move on..."
From this, and from Pete.

"I know." Chief nodded. "I'll help you any way you need. I want you to take some time off."

"No," Nikki said quickly. "No. Please don't make me. I...need...to work. I need to get back to normal."

"Honey, you can't pretend it didn't happen."

"I know. But...please..."

The man who'd been like her second father, despite the blame Gram had for him, frowned. Bushy salt and pepper brows drew tight. "Nikki—"

"Please. If you want to help me, you'll let me come to work."

After a long moment of appraising her, Chief nodded. He reached for her hand and squeezed. "I want you to talk to someone. Soon. Call tomorrow and set up an appointment." He didn't have to use the words *psychologist* or *psychiatrist.*

"I actually think I will."

"Good."

They sat on the bed in his guest room in silence. It was companionable. Didn't fix the hole in her chest, but it helped. A little.

"Nikki, I wanted to talk to you about something. Not sure now's the right time, though."

"I'm okay. Go ahead."

He met her eyes, taking a deep breath, as if this was difficult for him. That could only mean one thing—or person, as it were. Nikki swallowed back a gulp.

"What was wrong with Crane tonight?"

Her stomach flipped. *Here goes.* "What'd you mean?"

Chief stared her down, hazel gaze intense, shrewd. "Did you have a fight?"

Nikki smirked. "Not tonight."

"He wasn't normal tonight, kiddo." Her boss looked away for a moment, expression thoughtful. "I've known the man a long time. Seen him in many a stressful situation. He knows how to handle himself, and his business. Something was wrong tonight. Something happened. Something involving you."

She couldn't play stupid. Chief had known her a long time, too. And he wasn't referring to the shooting. "He did handle things tonight," Nikki said, even though it wasn't going to get her out of the third degree.

"Right. But that's not what I'm talking about." *We both know that* went unsaid.

She looked down. "It's complicated."

Chief gently tilted her chin up, forcing her gaze to his. "Uncomplicate it for me."

Closing her eyes, Nikki took a breath. Words wouldn't come.

"Do you have feelings for him?" Chief asked.

"Yes."

He didn't say anything for a long time. Then her boss nodded.

"Don't try to tell me it's like Stockholm Syndrome or that crap." Nikki winced at her defensive tone.

Chief's mustache twitched as he fought a smile. "I didn't say a word."

"So, you're okay with it?" she whispered. "I know there're rules...but Andi and Cole—"

"Are not you and Pete Crane."

Nikki narrowed her eyes. "Is this really about Pete or is it about me?"

The man sighed. "Both."

"I don't need to ask your permission." *Besides, he doesn't want me. So why am I telling you all this?*

"Detective Crane is a good man," Chief Martin said finally, as if she hadn't snapped.

"Most of the time." *Except for tonight when he pushed me away.* Nikki forced a nod, trying to ignore the ache in her chest. Being a good man hadn't kept him from crushing her tonight.

She stared at her boss who was so much more than just the man she worked for. It wasn't like him to back off. So why wasn't he laying into her about Pete? He couldn't possibly be *okay* with it. He'd never liked a single one of the few boyfriends she'd had.

"Try to clear your head before you make any decisions. You've been through too much. Nothing I ever wanted for you. It'll be bad for a while. But eventually the nightmares will stop." His voice cracked and he cleared his throat.

Shock and pain mixed with old loss hit her. Not the subject change she would have wanted, but Paul Martin was talking about his own nightmares. About her parents—something he never voiced. At least not to her.

"You know I don't blame you, right? I never have. I read all the articles, watched news clips, read police reports. It wasn't your fault he killed them. Gram is wrong for the way she feels. And I'm grateful you've always been there for me, despite how she treats you. You never stopped coming to see me. Never missed a birthday. Gave me a job I love."

He made a choked noise and looked away.

Nikki pulled back, studying his profile. This man was proud and stubborn. And about to break down. She'd never seen that her whole life. If she acknowledged it in any way, Paul Martin would be gruff with her. She didn't want a wall between them. She loved him.

Squeezing his hand, she smiled when he looked back at her, ignoring his misty eyes. "I think I can sleep now. Thank you."

Chief gave a curt nod.

She pressed a kiss to his cheek.

He stood, one corner of his mouth up. "So, work in the morning?"

"Yes, sir. You have a meeting with the mayor."

Chief groaned. "What time?"

"Noon, it's a lunch meeting."

"Good."

"Good?"

He smiled. "Yup. We're going in late."

Nikki managed a small laugh. "I won't mind sleeping in. It's been a long night."

When he retreated from the room, pain and sadness came back full force and she tried not to think about Pete.

* * * *

Pete looked at the beer and sighed. "Pretty sad you're drinking at four p.m. on a Tuesday." First time he'd heard a voice all day. Too bad it was his own. And besides, what the hell else did he have to do?

Grounded. Benched.

Administrative leave. Kurt Jamison, his friend and fellow detective, was heading the internal investigation. Expect to hear from him soon, and take it easy. Like a paid vacation, Kurt had joked.

Yeah. Right.

Jamison had said it was pretty straightforward, a formality—it'd only take a week or two to wrap things up. The guy would have to get with all the officers who'd been a part of the Health Solutions raid the night Luciano Marchetti had died.

Their action in the incident wasn't being pulled into question. But none of them were allowed to work. It meant a crapload of overtime for the rest of the department.

Without work, a new case to keep Pete busy, Nikki haunted him. The look on her face when he'd let her go with Chief without a word. The hurt in her eyes.

He hadn't slept worth shit last night—this morning, since he'd not gotten home until after three. All he could see was Marchetti pointing a Beretta at her. Pulling the trigger. Pete panicking that they'd been too late.

The feel of her in his arms afterward, remembering what it was like to hold her, kiss her, make love to her. Loss rolled over him in waves.

You let her go.

Pete might have only sent her home with someone else, but it felt final. Like breaking off a relationship they'd never actually defined. Besides, whenever he let Nikki out of his sight he put her in danger. It wasn't logical to worry about her with his boss. Paul Martin had been a cop for over twenty years. He was far from stupid. Fully capable of protecting the woman Pete loved.

Was he jealous?

Nikki was in *Pete's* bed, after all.

Was, idiot. Was.

"Fuck." He dragged his hand down his face, ignoring the stubble on his cheeks. Why shave if he couldn't go back to work?

Dropping Lee off at DFW Airport a few hours ago had made things worse. Like a double hit to his gut. The case was over. He'd said goodbye to his temporary partner. No telling when he'd see her again. The bad guys were dead—no trial to come back and testify for like last time. When he'd asked if she had to leave so quickly, she'd just said if Antioch PD didn't need her, her unit—her partner—did. She'd been the first one Kurt had interviewed.

Nate hadn't come to see her off. When Pete had called him, his brother had been moody and standoffish. He wouldn't answer any questions about the lovely FBI agent.

Lee had been normal, teasing and laughing with Pete all the way to Security when they'd had to part ways. She'd smiled and hugged him. So if she'd been affected by something that'd happened with Nate, she'd hidden it well.

It'd really suck if *both* of the Crane boys had had total strikeouts with the women they cared about.

No way, dude. Your sitch is on you.

His eyes swept the living room. Nice furniture. Awesome TV. Pictures on the wall. Fireplace in the corner. But somehow, Pete's heart was empty in the silence. *Stuff* didn't fulfill him.

He loved her. He missed her, no matter he'd seen her just the night before.

Pete sighed. How could he have fallen for her so quickly? He'd vowed after Cara that love would never happen for him again. And it hadn't—for ten long years.

He hadn't been a cloistered born-again virgin or anything. When internal shit had built up, he'd taken a lover from time to time, but the four months Liz had been around had been his longest tryst. Pete had known her for years, run into her at court, testified in cases she'd been on a few times.

Attraction had turned into having drinks, which had wound its way into meaningless sex. It'd been good. But couldn't hold a candle to the way Nikki made him feel.

Sex with Nikki had turned into making love probably before time number two. The girl had him twisted up.

Girl. Twenty-four for another two weeks.

He was old, incapable of loving her the way she deserved. Besides, their boss would never condone it. Badge or ass, right?

Was he a coward? Afraid, at thirty-five, that Nikki would crush him like Cara had? She'd wake up in his bed one morning and agree with him... He was too old for her, and she deserved better. Someone with a more positive outlook on life.

He wasn't a naïve kid anymore. *She* was, wasn't she?

The doorbell rang and he jumped, then swore at himself. He put the frosty bottle on the end table after a fortifying gulp. Yanking his white ribbed tank straight as soon as he hit his socked feet, he slunk to the door.

So what if he wasn't dressed for public consumption. At least he'd managed a pair of basketball shorts instead of just boxers.

If it was Jamison to get Pete's take on what'd happened, the guy would have to deal.

His cell had rung a few times, but he'd not answered. Didn't really want to talk to anyone.

His heart hit overdrive when he opened the door, even though she greeted him with a glare, hands on her lovely hips. "Nikki, what—"

Nikki rushed into his foyer after kicking front door shut. Her supple body slammed into his and she threw her arms around his neck.

Kissing her was natural, without thought, and made him hard as a rock in about two seconds, despite the four beers. She pressed closer, forcing the kiss deeper, and Pete groaned into her mouth. Their tongues dueled and collided.

She tasted as sweet as always. Addictive. He need more.

He needed Nikki.

Damn, they shouldn't do this. What they'd had was over. He wasn't good for her. But he wanted her. And hell, she'd started it.

He pushed her against the closed door and she wrapped her legs around his waist, pulling him closer. Her knee-length gray skirt bunched around her hips. His cock throbbed as she shoved her pelvis up, hitting him just right.

"I want you," Nikki breathed, rubbing her full breasts into his chest. Her nipples were hard buds and he hadn't even touched her yet.

Why? I hurt you. But the words wouldn't form. He wouldn't tell her that having her once more wouldn't change his mind. They couldn't be together. He ignored the voice that reminded him he'd never told *her* what he'd decided.

Pete kissed her in answer, shoving into her mouth. She kissed him back, nibbling his bottom lip and sucking on his tongue as she yanked his thin shirt up. Her hands scorched his bare skin. His cock pounded. If he didn't get inside her now, he was going to lose it in his pants.

Her caress traveled down the small of his back and inside the waistband of his navy shorts. He shivered as she squeezed his ass.

"No boxers?" Nikki asked, pulling away from their kiss. Her dark gaze was a mix of desire and amusement and Pete's heart skipped.

She was gorgeous, her high cheekbones flushed with color, her red locks loose and mussed as they played around her shoulders.

He groaned as her hand came around front, fingertips brushing his cock. He tried to shrug. "I'm benched. Why not?"

Smirking, she tilted her head and he didn't miss the invitation. Pete spread hot kisses down her neck. Working the buttons of her white blouse, he exposed more of her creamy skin, the curve of her breasts in the barely there red lacy bra. He sucked a hard bud into his mouth through the fabric.

She whispered his name, leaning into him as he found her mouth again.

His previous thoughts about why he couldn't have her melted away. He shut his brain down and just felt. Nikki in his arms, her hot skin beneath his lips, floral perfume tickling his nose. Her breasts rubbing the cotton of his tank, her thinly covered sex against the fabric of his shorts.

Not nearly enough.

Nikki shoved his shorts off his hips. His cock was in her hand even before the material hit the hardwood floor. Air greeted his balls and a tremor racked him. Pete let her touch him, stroke him, biting back a moan. His blood sang.

"Sweetness, you're gonna make me—"

She nipped his bottom lip and pulled her hand away. "No. Not like that."

He couldn't agree more. He wanted inside her. *Now.* Pete reached for her panties, and Nikki wiggled, helping him divest her of the scrap of red lace. He kicked his shorts away so he wouldn't trip.

Chuckling, he held up the red thong. "Why bother?"

Nikki grinned and his stomach flipped. "I like pretty panties. The skimpier, the better."

"I can't complain." He kissed her, cutting off her laugh.

Moaning, she rocked her hips forward. Her stilettos hit the floor with echoing thuds. Then her bare heels dug into his ass.

Pete thrust into her, sliding home on a grunt of his own. He intended to give her a moment to adjust, but Nikki moved with him immediately, burying her face against his neck.

"I just want to feel," she whispered, her breath teasing his overheated skin. She tightened her hold around him and shoved her pelvis up, making them both moan.

The sex took over then and Pete drove into her over and over, until they were both covered in sweat and clutching at each other to stay upright against the door.

When she whimpered and writhed, he grabbed her hips hard, propelling forward one last time. Nikki screamed and buried her hands in his damp hair, arching her back.

Her core contracted and he bit his lip as his cock jolted inside her. She continued to rock in his arms, her body milking every ounce of his orgasm. He suppressed the shiver that threatened to shoot down his spine and locked his knees so he wouldn't fall — or, worse, drop Nikki.

When her legs slid to the floor, Pete held her tight. Harsh breathing from them both was the only thing that greeted his ears.

Say something. Tell her how hot that was. Tell her what she does to you. How beautiful she is. Anything. Everything.

Tell her you love her.

But he couldn't. It wasn't fair to Nikki. So he pulled her closer, ignoring how her breasts felt against him. Ignored how her hips felt against his softening, sensitive cock when he slipped from her core. Ignored how her scent teased his nose, and how her hair tickled his cheek.

Her clothing was mussed, her shirt open, skirt still hiked. If he looked at her, he'd carry her upstairs. Pete closed his eyes and sucked in a breath.

They spoke at the same time. "We can't do this again."

"I love you, Pete."

Chapter Twenty-Nine

Nikki's head spun as Pete recoiled, pushing her away so fast she almost fell on her half-naked ass.

"What?" they asked at the same time. Neither of them really needed a repeat of their last statements.

She stared into his green eyes. His face was flushed, his hair mussed from her hands. The fair stubble on his cheeks just made him more appealing. Roughness against her neck and her breasts had caused her to combust for him. Beer on his lips had made his kiss taste even better.

Pete studied her, his eyes raking up and down. His expression was unreadable.

Panic was the word that came to mind. Her detective was freaked the hell out by her confession.

Idiot. You knew better than to say it, Nikki Harper.

Hurt threatened to close in on her. Breathing was a struggle for reasons other than hot sex against his front door. Her chest ached as much as her heart. Eyes smarted with tears though he had yet to say a word.

Instinct told Nikki all her worries about rejection were about to come true.

"Nikki…" His voice was a croak and he messed his blond locks up even more as he shoved his hand into them.

She squared her shoulders and yanked her skirt straight. He cleared his throat when she started buttoning her shirt, but she didn't look at him, even when she tucked it in, smoothing the front of the silk over her breasts.

"Will you listen to me?" Pete whispered.

"What's to listen to? You said it all."

"I don't want to hurt you."

"Too damn late for that." She made tight fists at her sides. Locked her jaw to keep the threatening sob at bay. *Do not cry right now.* Maybe chanting it would help.

He said nothing, but his socked feet were suddenly damn interesting. Pete wouldn't look at her.

"What's your problem?" Nikki snapped. "We were fine yesterday. Before you left to talk to your informant. *Yesterday,* Pete. Then you let Chief take me home, take me away from you. Without a fucking word."

His green gaze met hers with the harsh word she hardly ever uttered. But at least it'd gotten his attention. "I knew he'd keep you safe."

Nikki's heart tripped at the look on his face. "Thought that was *your* job."

Pete blanched and took a step back. Said nothing, but his eyes bored into hers.

What the hell had she said?

"Not anymore." The whisper was anguished and her vision blurred as she lost the battle with her tears. Pete winced.

"Why?" She took a step toward him, but her detective stepped back again. Nikki's heart sank. "Don't you care about me?"

"Not the way you need me to."

Gasping, she covered her mouth with a hand as Pete retreated even more — now he was almost in his living room.

It was as good as coming out and saying *I don't love you.* Pain threatened to cave her chest. Panting, she fought to stay upright.

You can't make him love you.

She could accept that his feelings weren't the same, right? She'd been the one to open her big mouth. He wanted her physically, but that had never been in question. Wasn't Pete's fault Nikki wanted more.

"Nikki, I'm not right for you."

Frowning, she focused on his words and yelled at herself to get it together. "What?"

"I told you from the start."

"Told me what?"

"I'm too old for you. Besides, Chief wouldn't condone us being together."

Straightening, Nikki glared as anger boiled up from her gut. Anger was good. Better than hurt. "That's a barrel of bullshit."

When he shook his head and failed to speak, heat rose in her neck. But she wasn't embarrassed. Nikki was *pissed.*

"So I mean nothing to you? An easy lay? You think everything is going to just readjust and go back to normal at work, Pete Crane? It won't go that way."

"Which is why I don't do this," he muttered.

Hurt hit her again. Nikki trembled and swallowed back a sob. "Does it matter at all what I think?"

"It won't change anything." He squared his shoulders and broke eye contact again.

"*You're* making the decision that you're no good for me. Yet another thing I have no say in. A decision made *for* me. You're going to throw this—us—all away because you're trying to think for me?"

Pete said nothing. He wouldn't meet her eyes again, either.

A sob escaped and tears cascaded. Nikki stood there for a moment, her arms wrapped around her middle. *Hold me,* her heart cried out. But he was frozen ten feet from her, looking anywhere but at her. Despite the fact he could hear her crying.

She cursed her stupid heart and foolishness. Retrieved her shoes, glared at her red lace thong.

Then Nikki fled Pete's house, slamming the front door on the way out. She cried so hard she had to run to her car so she wouldn't collapse.

I love you, Pete.

His head reeled. He told himself it was the alcohol. Put his hand to his forehead. Pete's whole body shook. His teeth even rattled. "And what did you do? Lied. Crushed her. Made her cry. Ass. Hole."

The lump in his throat grew until he almost choked. His vision blurred. *Shit.* He was going to cry, too. *What a pansy.*

After ripping his basketball shorts off the wood floor, he yanked them on, and cursed himself to hell and back. Her scent was all over his clothes. Rapid movements kicked it up, teasing his nose.

It made him feel even worse.

He whipped the beer off the end table by his recliner and downed the whole thing. Threw the empty bottle across the room. It hit the wall and shattered, but Pete didn't give a shit. Clean-up would be later. Tomorrow. Maybe never.

His cell phone blared but he ignored it and went into the kitchen for another beer, which he gulped down the same as the last. So fast his head spun. He put his hand to the wall to steady himself. Grabbed another one and hit the living room.

Just as he sank into the recliner, his landline rang. He ignored it. The old-school answering machine with its generic robotic voice kicked on. Pete waited for the inevitable dial tone, but Andi's voice greeted his ears instead.

"Hey, partner, just checking on you. Heard about the admin suspension. Been calling you all day. Are you okay?" Micah's wail was audible in the background. "Gotta go, but call me. I'm starting to worry."

The dial tone after she'd disconnected rang in his ears.

Pete stared across the room. The dark broken glass littering his otherwise clean floor. Beer splatter on the wall.

His cell alerted him to a text message, but he didn't even glance at the device lighting up on the coffee table.

I love you, Pete.

I love you, Pete.

I love you, Pete.

Her voice wouldn't leave his mind.

"Stop!" Pete cradled his head as guilt and pain made him double over in the chair.

He shouldn't have taken her against the door. He'd let his dick do the thinking. He loved her. Had to have her. Like always.

Closing his eyes did nothing except play it all over in his head. Flashes of her body, her smile, her laugh, her gorgeous hair and eyes glazed with passion. Her mouth rising to meet his. Not just today, but all the times they'd made love in his bed, in his shower.

Pete forced a breath then another as his chest constricted. He felt like he'd been shot in the lungs again. Planting his hands on his thighs, he panted.

He'd lied to her. Told her he didn't love her.

Nikki had walked — no, *fled* — out of his front door.

Left her lacy red panties, too. As if to remind him what an asshole he was. Who had sex — made love — to the love of their life *before* crushing her? Lying to her. Tears and the look on her face, in those dark eyes, topped it all off.

The barely there underwear glared from across the foyer.

Pete chugged his latest beer and flipped on the radio that sat on one of the built-in shelves next to his fireplace.

Big. Mistake.

Bryan Adams' gravelly voice sang *Everything I Do, I Do It For You.* Nikki had told him just the other day that she loved that song.

"Fuck me." He dragged his hand down his face and slapped the radio so hard it wobbled on its perch. "No more classic rock for you."

Beer was better. Beer...and a ball game or something. One of the million nothing-but-sports channels had to have the latest Rangers game, right?

If not, he'd just drink until he passed the fuck out.

Chapter Thirty

Something echoed. Pounding?

Pete winced and moaned, pushing his face into the couch. Covered his ears when the noise wouldn't go away. Had to be the TV.

Rattling was next, right when he was about to drift off. *Keys? Really?*

Only two other people had a key to his house. He didn't want to see either of them.

The door creaked when it opened and closed. Loud enough to wake the dead. Shit, he should get that looked at.

Footsteps on hardwood were like shouts. Pete's temples throbbed. "Go away."

"What the hell are you doing?"

He froze. *Not Nate.*

"Andi, leave me alone."

"No." She shuffled around the room. He heard the TV switch off. Heard the rustling of Styrofoam and glass bottles clinking together.

"Stop cleaning up after me." Squeezing his eyes shut, he hugged the couch. Wished his partner gone. It didn't work.

"Get your ass up and do it yourself then."

Pete rolled toward her and glared. "Go home. Leave me be."

His partner's blue eyes flashed. "No."

Ignoring him, Andi disappeared into the kitchen. When she returned, she had a broom and dustpan in hand. She started sweeping up the broken glass from the beer bottle he'd played *splat* with.

Pete sat up. Damn good thing the couch was beneath him, but it didn't keep the living room from spinning. He clutched the plush arm with clawed hands and crushed his eyes shut. Sucked in a breath. "Andi."

She continued to clean, dumping the glass into a trashcan she must have dragged into the room.

"Andi."

Pausing, his partner glanced over her shoulder. "What?"

He sighed. "You don't have to do that."

"I do. You've done the same for me." Andi finished the job then took the supplies back into the kitchen.

"God, you're such an ass," Pete whispered to himself, hunching his back and cradling his throbbing head

"You got that right." She stood in front him.

Pete didn't know what to say, so he remained silent, staring at Andi's teal flip-flops. Her toenails were painted a pale iridescent blue. He would've smiled if he didn't feel like death. Polished nails were about as girly-girl as his partner got.

"So *this* is what it looks like," she mused. "Can't say I ever thought I'd live to see the day, to tell you the truth."

"What are you talking about?" Pete snapped, glaring up at her.

"Detective Pete Crane. Wallowing."

"I am not *wallowing*."

One dark eyebrow arched and Andi crossed her arms over her chest. She wasn't going to call him on his bullshit. Then again, she didn't have to. "No one has heard from you for three days. Three. Days. You're not answering either phone, emails, hell, not even a text. Chief thought you'd killed yourself or something."

He snorted, but her expression was serious.

"You've scared him, partner. Seriously. You're looking at Shrinkville at best before he'll let you come back. Thinks the stress of this case made you lose it. So even when Kurt's done with the investigation, you're screwed until a doc clears you. Which, by the way, you're delaying for everyone. Kurt's made his way through Chloe and the rest of the guys. You're it. Nobody can come back to work until he's talked to you. He told me this morning you're ignoring him, too."

"Shit."

"Yup, partner. You screwed the pooch your first round out. And in case you were wondering, your victims are fine. Some US Marshals showed up and got them into witness protection. Alberto Carbone even agreed to testify when Lee and her team get that ass Caselli."

"Well that's good," Pete said. Part of him had still assumed the Carbones — Matas or whatever — wouldn't agree to WitSec.

Andi took a seat next to him on the couch, then made a face.

"What?" Pete asked.

"When's the last time you showered?"

He was torn between a smirk and a cringe. "Why?"

"Old beer and gross man. Not exactly what you usually smell like."

Pete laughed. He couldn't help himself.

"When's the last time you ate something?" She looked him up and down.

"I don't remember."

Sighing, Andi shook her head. "C'mon, let's get you showered and over to my place. Cole's barbecuing."

"What am I, a kid?"

"You're acting like one." Andi gave him a long look that made him shift on the edge of the couch. She hadn't mentioned Nikki, but he should've recognized it was a *yet.*

"I don't want to talk about it." His words were rushed.

Andi cocked her head to one side. "No shit. Didn't think you'd volunteer. Get your ass in the shower. Ethan's anxious to see you. You won't disappoint *my* kid. And shave that crap off your face, or I'm gonna start calling you Blondbeard the Pirate."

Fighting for a straight face, he shook his head. "I think that was Blackbeard."

"Well, you do look like you've barely survived a sea monster."

Pete stood, stretching his back and yawning. He headed to the stairs without another word. If he opened his mouth, he'd spill something stupid about Nikki. He paused with one hand on the banister. "Hey, Andi."

She was already off his couch, continuing her clean-up job. "Yeah?"

"Thanks, partner."

Andi's blue eyes said, *What for?* But she nodded and tossed a takeout container in the trashcan.

Her head swung back around so fast she could have ended up with whiplash. His partner pointed to something and Pete followed her gaze.

"Totally not touching *those*," she said. Eyes wide, Andi looked torn between amusement and horror.

Heat crept up Pete's neck and he wished the floor would open up to swallow him whole. Nikki's lacy red panties. He'd never bothered to grab them off the floor by the front door.

"Uh...yeah. About that shower." Pete climbed one step, then another.

"They'll still be there when you get back," Andi called after him.

* * * *

Pete entered the house in front of his partner. The baby was caterwauling. Andi scooted around him, but he still beat her to Cole. Her husband was pacing in their living room, trying to comfort their son.

"Give me that baby before you break him," Pete said.

Relief washed over his buddy's face. "I don't know what his deal is. He's clean, fed, burped, the works."

Andi hovered, but allowed Pete to gather Micah close.

Pete rocked the little guy and held him higher on his shoulder when Micah finally went from bawling to whimpering. "There ya go, buddy." He inhaled the sweet clean baby scent and was able to smile genuinely for the first time all day. He rubbed Micah's onesie-covered back.

Cole muttered something that sounded like *Little traitor* and Andi laughed.

Pete flashed back to a tiny Ethan in his arms, rocking him the same way, feeding and holding him when Andi had needed him.

"Unca' Pete, Unca' Pete!" As if the little boy had heard his thoughts, Ethan rushed into the room from the hallway like a whirlwind.

Cole swept their older son up into his arms and brought him close to Pete and Micah.

"Hey, squirt!" Pete returned the kid's high-five, flashing a smile.

"My broder's loud," Ethan said, causing them all to laugh. He made a face, scrunching his little nose up.

"Sometimes he sure is, buddy," Cole said. "Now that y'all are back, I'm gonna start dinner. Been smoking the brisket all day."

"Y'all? Looks like we're turning you into a Texan after all," Pete said.

Andi grinned and leaned up to press a kiss to her husband's cheek.

Cole chuckled and set Ethan to his feet. "Don't have a choice. You know I hate not fitting in, Petey."

Pete paused, not sure he'd heard correctly. When Andi laughed, he mock-glared at her man. "I'm going to kill Lee."

Cole turned on his heel and whistled as he headed toward the sliding glass doors that led to their covered patio.

Andi looked as if she was trying not to grin when he met her gaze. She shrugged.

"Thanks for coming to get me."

Expression sobering, she nodded. "You needed it."

"Still, I love you for it," he said.

She slipped her arm around his waist and squeezed. "Love you, too. You're family, partner."

Pete made himself relax and smile when his heart galloped. *Family.*

Do not think of her. Do not say her name, even in your head.

"Don't get all serious on me, Pete. Relax for now. We're gonna eat some BBQ and chill."

"Unca' Pete," Ethan said at the same time. "Can we play?"

Andi smiled and ruffled her older son's red curls. "I'm sure Uncle Pete would love that, baby."

Pete looked down into Micah's little face. He pressed a kiss to the infant's dark, downy hair before gently transferring him to his mother's arms. Then he hauled the four-year-old to his hip. His arm gave a sudden unwanted protest, but he ignored it and grinned at the kid. "Let's go see what we can get into."

"Yeah!"

Playing with Ethan made him feel better than he had in days. He didn't even think about Nikki—much. The little boy was a redhead like his biological father, and Pete couldn't help thinking about *his* redhead.

He contemplated sitting on the floor playing Legos with a different little boy. Nikki's brown eyes and red locks. His child.

Pete shook himself. Since when did he think about kids—as in having some of his own? Since when was spending time with Ethan not enough?

Slamming the door on that train of thought only melted into a picture of the tears in her eyes before she'd fled his house. He'd pretended not to notice.

Don't you care about me?

Not the way you need me to.

Could he have been a bigger asshole?

Your fault. It was all on him. No question about it. No going back. Right?

Ethan sensed his mood change and asked if he was all right.

Perfect. A four-year-old had noticed his pain. Maybe he was going nuts.

Andi saved him from answering her son by shouting for them—food was ready.

Dinner was great, like always. But watching Andi and Cole affected him in a way it never had before. Their interaction, teasing, touches and especially the light kisses they shared just about killed Pete.

Envy sat in his stomach like a boulder. Threatened to ruin the taste of the kickass brisket Cole had smoked. His personal sauce recipe could rival some of the best Texas barbecue Pete had ever eaten, but he couldn't even manage to tease his friend about it.

Pete couldn't stop watching them.

He wanted what his partner had with her husband. And he wanted it with Nikki. So badly his whole body ached from it.

The wife, the kids to fill his huge empty house…the works. It was all back in his picture again. Too bad the woman he loved pretty much hated him.

You broke her heart. It's too late.

"Pete, you all right, dude?" Cole asked, his arm around Andi.

She was nestled against his side on the bench of the breakfast nook, their baby asleep in her arms.

Ethan sat next to his parents in his booster seat, licking a red popsicle. Making a sticky mess, but he was adorable, like always.

"I'm good."

"Right," Andi said.

Pete groaned.

Cole cleared his throat, his eyes darting to Ethan. "I think it's about bedtime for E-man."

"Nooooooo," Ethan whined.

"How about a story?" Cole asked, not fazed by the four-year-old.

Ethan's bottom lip pushed out in a first-class pout.

"How about two stories?" Andi asked.

Cocking his head to one side, the little boy considered both his parents. "I pick?"

Pete bit back a smile.

"Of course," his dad answered.

Ethan grinned and clapped his little hands. "Okay!"

Andi laughed.

Cole planted a loud kiss on her cheek and pulled Ethan out of his booster seat. "Say goodnight to your Uncle Pete."

"Night, Unca' Pete!"

Andi winced. "Ethan, not so loud."

Pete chuckled and ruffled his hair, giving the little boy one of their signature high-fives. "See ya soon, squirt. Be good for your dad."

"You want help?" Andi asked, wiping Ethan's sticky mouth before planting a kiss on him.

He giggled and kissed her back. Noisy and innocent.

Pete grinned.

"I got it, babe. Get your partner straight." Cole threw a wink his way and disappeared around the corner with their son on his hip.

"Nice," Pete muttered.

"What? You knew it was coming," Andi said, totally unrepentant. She stared until he shifted in his chair at the table. "I'm going to put Micah down. You move one toe and I'll kick your ass."

Sighing, he waited for her to return, squirming like he was waiting for detention to be over.

Instead of starting to clean up like she normally did after they had dinner together, his partner returned to her seat at the table, flipping on a white and blue baby monitor before setting it down between them.

"Want help with the kitchen?" Pete asked. He cursed his voice when it cracked.

"The dishes can wait."

"Dammit, Andi. I don't want to talk about it. I told you that."

"You never let me get away with that crap, so I'm not about to let *you* off the hook."

Pete didn't say anything as misery threatened to crush him.

"Hmmm, don't like your words being flung back at you, huh?" Andi said. Her blue eyes bored into him.

"Hell, no." *Quit looking at me like that.*

"Then I'll just sit here with my mouth shut. Wait for you to come 'round. You're not stupid, partner."

I am stupid. A freaking idiot. "What're you waiting for?"

"You've yet to get over your damn self."

"Could I try 'It's none of your business'? Would that work?"

She snorted and crossed her arms over her chest.

"Didn't think so," Pete whispered. "Look, I really don't want to talk about this."

"No shit." His partner arched an eyebrow. "Rather talk to Cole?"

"No."

"Being in the hot seat's no fun, huh?" Amusement ripped across her beautiful face. Her signature ponytail danced around her shoulders.

Pete growled and looked away from her.

"Pete." Andi put her hand on his forearm and made him meet her gaze again. "I love her, too."

He closed his eyes and sucked in a breath. His chest was killing him. Words wouldn't come.

"I just want you to fix this. You're hurting, she's hurting and it's ridiculous."

"Ridiculous?" he croaked.

"Absolutely." Her firm tone jolted him.

"God, she called you, didn't she?"

"Yes. But it doesn't matter. I would've still taken one look at you and told you to get your head out of your ass."

One corner of his mouth lifted. "Gee, thanks, darlin'."

Andi smirked and cocked her head to one side, staring him down. "Last year, when Cole left and I found out Micah was on the way, what did you tell me?"

"Shit, Andi. Really?"

"Yes, really, Pete."

He didn't need a reminder. Pete remembered the conversation like it was yesterday. Remembered his partner's tears, too. He'd held her, reminded her he'd always be there for her. Told her to go after the man she loved.

Heartache sucks ass, but regret is even worse. His words. God, he'd kill her if she said it out loud right now.

"Pete?" Andi prompted.

Dragging his hand down his face, Pete shook his head. "It's different."

"How?"

"It...just is."

"Bullshit."

"How's it going in here?" Cole slid into the kitchen sans Ethan and crossed his arms over his broad chest. He leaned on the counter instead of joining them at the table.

"He's asleep already?" Andi asked glancing over her shoulder.

"Yup. Cleaned him up, got him into PJs and he was out before we were done with book number one." Cole nodded, his steel gaze landing on Pete.

"No way." Pete straightened in the chair. "You guys aren't going to double-team me. Is this some kind of intervention?"

"Does it need to be?" his partner's husband asked without missing a beat.

"Fuck. Me."

"No thanks," Cole said much too brightly.

Andi looked amused when Pete's gaze swept over her. She scooted closer, grabbing his hand. "You love her, she loves you. It's as simple as that, partner, so fix it. Apologize for being the colossal ass you were and get her back."

"What'd you tell me when I came back to Antioch?" Cole asked.

Pete groaned. "Not you, too. Whipping my words back in my face."

"Hey, not my fault you give great advice and can't listen to it. Sooooo what did you say to me?"

"That it was about damn time you showed up."

"Right. I wasted months. *Months* away from Andi and Ethan, and missed the beginning of her pregnancy because I was too stubborn to realize where I belonged. If it wasn't for you, she'd have been totally alone. I'll always be grateful for that, dude. But don't do what I did. It's only been a few days. Go get your woman. Tell her how you feel."

Andi and Cole locked gazes as if he wasn't in the room. Love was palpable between them.

Envy and fear hit him in the chest. "What if she won't give me another shot?" The words were out of his mouth before he could censor them.

Had he really just admitted he was afraid?

His partner swung her head back around and met his eyes. "Oh, Pete. She loves you."

"What if that's not enough to forgive me?"

Andi was out of the chair and wrapping her arms around him in seconds. "I've never seen you like this," she whispered.

Pete flashed a wry smile. "Yeah...I've...never felt like this before. So you couldn't have seen it."

She pulled back, smiling gently. Her eyes were misty and his stomach fluttered. "I like it. I want you to be happy so badly. I want you to have what I have."

Cole pushed off the counter and tugged his wife into his arms. The guy probably couldn't take Andi's tears any more than Pete could take Nikki's. Especially when they were his fault.

He swallowed back a wince and watched his friends embrace.

Cole kissed Andi then met Pete's eyes. "I wouldn't trade her or those two little boys for the world."

With a lump in his throat, all Pete could do was nod, but his partner's husband didn't look away.

"Whatcha gonna do, Crane?"

Chapter Thirty-One

The paper airplane sailed in, landing on the carpet right in front of her desk.

Nikki stared. Swallowed hard.

Tremors started in her arms and shook her whole body by the time she made it around her desk and bent to pick up the folded paper. She braced herself on the wood side so she wouldn't topple over.

Plane in hand, she headed straight to the doorway. Peeked her head out and looked up and down the hallway.

Totally quiet. No one around. Not even voices coming from the lieutenants' offices across the hall.

Chief still wasn't back, either. His meeting at City Hall must've run over. Or maybe he'd gone to grab lunch at Dixie's.

Shaking her head, Nikki wandered back to her desk and slipped into her chair. She set the folded contraption in front of her.

The last four days had been hell. She couldn't sleep. Couldn't stop crying, and no amount of makeup could cover the bags under her eyes.

It was a wonder she'd held it together for work, but she'd managed. She'd had to. Hadn't wanted Chief to catch on that something was wrong. Wasn't fond of the idea of another third degree about Pete, among other things.

At least she didn't have to see him. The internal investigation was taking care of that. He wasn't supposed to be at work.

Obviously the mandate didn't apply today.

No one else would have flown the paper airplane into Chief's executive suite. It had to be Pete.

Nikki ached to see him. Kiss him, touch his hand, wrap her arms around him, even just talk to him. Her stupid, traitorous heart wouldn't let go.

She'd confessed her feelings to her grandmother, unable to do so without sobbing. Gram had held her and told her time would heal all wounds.

Not this time.

Four days, or forty—hell, forty *years* wouldn't change the way she felt about him. Nikki would love Pete for the rest of her life.

Damn lotta good it'd do.

He was it. The one. Or he was supposed to have been.

Pain threatened to cave her chest all over again. *Not at work. Not. At. Work.*

When she'd called Andi, she'd felt like a child tattling on a classmate, but her friend had listened to her cry and consoled her as best she could.

Andi had asked if Nikki wanted her to talk to Pete. She'd shut the detective down quickly, but doubted her outspoken friend would actually hold her tongue to the stupid man. They were best friends, as Andi had so aptly pointed out. She probably told him everything.

Nikki's heart skipped. Would it hurt or help?

She made a fist, narrowly missing crunching the paper airplane. Should just throw it in the garbage. It didn't matter.

Do it.

But as soon as it hit the rim of her black plastic trashcan, Nikki snatched it out.

Was he somewhere watching? Could he see her? They worked in a police department, after all. Cameras everywhere.

Sucking in a breath and steeling herself, she studied the airplane. Shaped carefully, its every fold lent to superior aerodynamic abilities. A prize winning piece of origami, right?

When she flipped it over, she noticed a slight imprint.

Handwriting.

Pete had written something inside the plane?

The paper rustled as she unfolded it slowly. Like unwrapping a present.

Nikki's breath caught at the first sight of the familiar handwriting.

I'm sorry. I love you.

In blue ink, each letter formed with a neat stroke.

It was silly to think she could *feel* love from the two short sentences, but she did.

Vision blurring, tears cascaded. "Oh, Pete." Nikki's whisper was shaky to her ears. Her hand shot to her mouth.

He loved her?

She shoved her chair back so fast she almost fell over. Ignoring her wobbly legs, she rushed to the doorway.

Where she smacked full force into the solid wall of Pete's chest. He caught her up and held her close.

Kept her from falling. "I'm sorry, sweetness. I was trying to be respectful and stay back. Wait...until you...read it. But I...just couldn't hide anymore."

Hide anymore.

Did he mean more than staying out of sight right now? Nikki's heart sped up. "I was coming to find you."

When she met his beautiful green eyes and saw the emotion there—love, tenderness, heat—she had to bite her bottom lip to keep the sob in. She buried her face against the cotton of his green tee and wrapped her arms around him. Nikki couldn't win, though—tears wouldn't be held at bay. She cried until she shook against him.

"Oh, darlin'. Don't cry. Not anymore. Not because of me. Nikki—"

"I love you," she whispered. The words tumbled out of her mouth. They wouldn't be kept inside. It didn't matter that she'd told him before. Didn't matter that he'd hurt her, because he loved her, too.

Pete froze. His heart thundered against hers, she felt it all the way to her core.

He cupped her face, forcing her to meet his gaze. When he thumbed her tears away, a tremor shot down her spine. "I love you, too." He kissed her. Lightly, teasingly.

Not nearly enough.

Nikki tried to lean up and press her lips to his, but he held her still.

"I want you to look at me when I tell you. I love you, Nicole Grace Harper."

Sniffling, she could only stare. Words dissolved on her tongue. His expression was open, his eyes honest. Love. All she could see was love. And it made her whole body weak.

"I was… Well, a colossal ass, as Andi put it. And I can't tell you how sorry I am that I hurt you."

"It's okay." How could it not be when he was looking at her like that? She swallowed against the lump in her throat.

Holding both her hands, Pete guided her to the waiting chairs. He sat Nikki down and pulled a chair next to hers. Caressed her cheek. "No. It's not. Not at all. I lied to you."

"Lied to me?"

"I lied when I told you I couldn't love you like you needed me to. Because I already do. I love you so damn much, Nikki."

Her breath caught and she wrapped her arms around him. Pete hauled her onto his lap and took her mouth.

She kissed him back with all her might, forcing the kiss deeper. Showing him what she'd told him. Feeling what he'd told her.

Even with her eyes closed, as he kissed her until her toes curled, tears slid down her face. Tears of hope and relief. The love of her life loved her back.

Desire unfurled low in her belly and she squeezed her arms around his neck. Pete held her just as tight, his erection pressing into her hip. Her sex throbbed for him, it'd been too long.

Now wasn't the time. This wasn't the place. They needed to stop. Before they couldn't.

Nikki pulled back, struggling through breaths as he panted against her. "We're at work."

Pete cupped her face and kissed her tears away. One corner of his mouth shot up. "That's not a problem for me anymore."

Her stomach fluttered. "What'd you mean?"

"I met the love of my life at work."

Grinning, she kissed him hard and fast. "Ditto. But I meant we can't do what I want to right now. Besides, *our* boss might saunter in at any moment."

Pete chuckled. "Not likely. I begged him to disappear this afternoon."

She cocked her head to one side. "Oh yeah?"

His expression became sheepish. "Explained I might have to grovel."

"Oh?" Nikki arched a brow.

It was a wonder Paul Martin hadn't spilled the beans. He wasn't very good at hiding his emotions where she was concerned. And as far as she knew, their boss hadn't caught on that all was not well with her and Pete.

"I told him I love you, sweetness. I told him I screwed up." His green eyes bored into hers and she stilled on his lap. "So he agreed to give me one shot to fix it."

"Really?"

Pete nodded, flashing a lopsided grin that made her insides melt. "He said if you wished it, no one would ever find my body."

Nikki giggled. "He didn't say that."

"He did. Told me a quick death is the best I could hope for if I ever hurt you again." His expression sobered. "I won't hurt you again, I promise."

She smiled softly, cupping his cheeks. "I want a normal relationship with you, Pete."

"I want that, too."

"Meaning, hurt might come with the territory. We'll argue, but then we can make up. It's what love's all about." Nikki kissed him. It slipped into something long and deep, leaving her quivering in his arms.

"Hmmm, is this making up?" he breathed against her mouth.

"It's a start." She kissed him again until this time he parted their lips.

"I love you, Nikki Harper. But I don't like your last name."

Nikki pulled back, studying his eyes. Her stomach flipped.

He looked as if he was fighting a smile. "Stand up, sweetness," Pete whispered between soft kisses he pressed all over her mouth.

She locked her wobbly knees as the love of her life got down on one of his. He dug in his pocket and presented her with a little black box.

Nikki's heart pounded so hard her head spun. Her vision blurred and she covered her mouth with a hand to hold back the sob.

Pete opened the box, revealing a one-karat marquis solitaire—her favorite cut. "Will you ditch the Harper and be my Nikki Crane?"

A giddy laugh bubbled up. Leave it to her man to be unique in his proposal. Nikki nodded, because words wouldn't cooperate.

He exhaled and kissed her knuckles before sliding the ring onto her left ring finger. It fit like a glove.

"It's gorgeous," Nikki whispered, turning her hand until the diamond caught the light.

"You're gorgeous," Pete said. His eyes were misty and she gasped.

"I can't wait to marry you."

"I promise I'll make you happy. I love you so much." His jaw clenched in an effort to contain his emotion and her heart melted for him even more, if that was possible.

She caressed his cheek. "I love you, Petey!"

Pete growled, shooting to his feet and pinning her to his chest. When their eyes met, Nikki flashed a grin. Then he proceeded to kiss her into oblivion.

Epilogue

Five months later…

"Pete, you good to go?" Andi's voice made him jump. She paused just inside the doorway. Her chestnut hair was piled on top of her head in an attractive mess of curls, and the royal blue sheath hugged her body. It was sexy yet understated, with a split up the side.

He did a double-take. "Damn, you look hot, partner."

Andi blushed and touched her cheek.

Nikki had picked the style out for the bridesmaids and Andi — maiden of honor — swearing they'd be able to wear them again. Not that his anti-feminine partner would.

Seeing her all dolled up reminded him what a beautiful woman she was.

"Hey now, that's my wife," Cole said, coming from the other side of the room, a grin on his face that belied his stern tone. His dimples flashed, then he locked eyes on Andi. "Hmmm, babe. Never mind this wedding nonsense. Maybe we could just get out of here?"

Pete laughed.

She mock-glared, her face an even brighter shade of red.

Cole crossed the room and kissed her. His partner loosened up and snuggled into her husband for a moment.

"Mama, you look pretty!" Ethan announced. He held onto the small ring bearer pillow he was to carry down the aisle.

Andi reached for his hand. "Thank you, baby."

Pete grinned. The kid had saved her further embarrassment. He looked adorable in his little tux with a royal blue cummerbund like Cole, Nate, Pete and the rest of the groomsmen. His red hair was tame, his curls trimmed.

"You look so handsome."

Ethan beamed.

"Actually, you all look awesome." Andi's blue eyes swept over the three of them before returning to her son. "You remember what you're supposed to do? Just like we practiced?"

The little boy nodded, his blue eyes solemn as he recited his task.

"Good job, squirt," Pete said, slapping his little hand with a loud high-five.

"Nikki's gonna be my aunt!"

Cole chuckled.

Pete's head spun. This was it. She was about to become his wife. His pulse thundered in his ears and his stomach flipped.

"Dude, you all right?" Cole hit his shoulder.

He met his friend's steel eyes. "I'm great. About to be someone's husband."

"It's not that bad," Cole said, making a face in his wife's direction.

Andi punched his arm and Pete laughed.

"There's my partner under all that girl getup."

She laughed and nodded. "Yup. They're ready for you. Ethan, Cole and I need to go." Andi took her son by the hand.

Cole patted Pete's chest. "Take a deep breath. It's all good. You're about to begin your life, not end it." His buddy winked and led his family out of the room.

Pete took two deep breaths.

Nerves flipped his stomach until it was a giant knot as he stood in his childhood church and waited for the love of his life to come to him.

The more people who weren't Nikki who walked down the aisle, the antsier Pete got, even though their bridal party was made up of family and friends. All grinning as they took their spots. Everyone couldn't be happier for them.

He couldn't look at his mother as his father seated her in the front row. She was already misty-eyed. Pete couldn't lose it before he even saw his bride.

When his gaze swept her family's side, Gram grinned at him.

Nate winked as he came to stand beside Pete. It did nothing to calm him.

Everyone laughed and awwwed when Cole had to grab an over-excited Ethan and make the kid stand still at the altar next to them.

When *The Bridal March* started, his heart was in his throat.

Then she was coming to him, on Chief's arm.

The most radiant thing he'd ever seen. Family, friends, the whole crowd melted away and Pete couldn't tear his eyes from Nikki.

It wasn't the intricately beaded princess dress. It wasn't her long shimmery veil. It wasn't even her beautiful red locks that were done up in a complicated, curly style.

It was her big brown eyes that shone just for him.

Nikki was his. She always would be.

Chief gave her away when prompted.

Then she was at the altar with him, holding his hands. Looking deeply into his eyes. Pete could feel the love radiate all over.

She cried when she pledged herself to him.

His voice was heavy and scratchy when he said his vows.

When the preacher told him to kiss his girl—his wife—Pete almost lost it. He wasn't going to cry in a church full of people, so he gathered her to him and covered her mouth with his.

Coherent thought quickly dissolved as Nikki opened for him like she always did. She pressed closer and he got lost in her.

Until a catcall, then a whistle had him reluctantly pulling away. He might have been embarrassed he was in a church, but when his wife grinned, Pete laughed and kissed her again.

"Hey, hey, save that for later," Nate called.

Cole stood next to his younger brother, flashing two thumbs up.

Nikki's cheeks were adorably pink when Pete met her eyes. He cupped her face.

People cheered as the reverend introduced Mr and Mrs Peter and Nicole Crane for the first time, but he couldn't look away from her. His heart jumped and he was convinced that wherever Nikki was concerned, it always would. "Thanks for taking a chance on me," he whispered.

"Sometimes even a paper collision is a sure thing," Nikki said.

Pete laughed and put his arm out to her. "Shall we go, Mrs Crane? We have a party to get to, I hear."

"They won't start without us, Mr Crane." She winked.

With one last much-too-quick kiss, Pete led his wife toward the beginning of their forever.

About the Author

C.A. is originally from Ohio, but got to Texas as soon as she could. She is married and has a bachelor's degree in Criminal Justice.

She works with kids when she's not writing.

She's always wanted to be a writer and is overjoyed to share her stories with the world.

C.A. Szarek loves to hear from readers. You can find her contact information, website details and author profile page at http://www.totallybound.com.

Totally Bound Publishing